PRAISE FOR CATHE

"Prolific author Hyde raises thorny issues around domestic violence, examines the power of misplaced guilt, and illustrates the bonds of shared experience in her take on a ripped-from-the-headlines story. Her characteristic empathy is on full display . . ."
                                    —*Booklist* on *A Different Kind of Gone*

"Beautifully conceived and executed and incredibly touching."
                                    —Bookreporter on *Just a Regular Boy*

"Readers who want tales of love, family, and emotional strength in the face of hardship will cheer on Anton, Edith, and their efforts to create a family in the midst of pain. A great choice for fans of Hyde."
                                    —*Library Journal* on *My Name is Anton*

"*So Long, Chester Wheeler* will change you in ways that you can't imagine a book could . . . Once you read this story, there is no chance that you will ever forget it. It is a rare treasure that doesn't come along often."
                                    —Bookreporter

"A tender tale of new families born of chance and the determination to bring light into darkness."
                                    —*Kirkus Reviews* on *Have You Seen Luis Velez?*

"Fans of Catherine Ryan Hyde will adore her new novel . . . No one in this story is perfect. But despite our flaws, we are all worthy of love and able to share our love, just as Stewie so beautifully demonstrates."
                                    —Bookreporter on *Dreaming of Flight*

"Multilayered and heartwarming."

—*Booklist* on *Seven Perfect Things*

"A story about good people doing their best to survive, combined with a message that will cause readers to close the book feeling a bit more hopeful about humanity."

—*Kirkus Reviews* on *Take Me with You*

Rolling
Toward
Clear Skies

Also by Catherine Ryan Hyde

Rolling Toward Clear Skies

A Novel

Catherine Ryan Hyde

LAKE UNION

PUBLISHING

Published by Lake Union Publishing, Seattle

www.apub.com

Amazon, the Amazon logo, and Lake Union Publishing are trademarks of Amazon.com, Inc., or its affiliates.

ISBN-13: 9781662504457 (hardcover)
ISBN-13: 9781662504464 (paperback)
ISBN-13: 9781662504440 (digital)

Cover design by Shasti O'Leary Soudant
Cover image: ©Sterling Lorence Photo / Getty Images

Printed in the United States of America

First edition

Rolling Toward Clear Skies

PART ONE

TWO GIRLS

Chapter One

Interviews with Elephants

Maggie stuck her head into the kitchen to see her two daughters sitting at the island-style table, glued to their phones.

"They're not here?" she asked. The girls barely looked up, if at all. "They were supposed to be here ten minutes ago."

Her older girl, Willa, spoke without looking away from the phone's screen. Her thumbs never paused in their tapping.

"They're waiting for you in the living room," she said.

"And you didn't *tell* me?"

It wanted to come out as a shriek, a blast of irritation, but Maggie didn't want to be overheard from the living room.

"We thought you heard. They rang the bell."

I must have had the hair dryer on, she thought. But she didn't say it to the girls, because they clearly were not listening—at least, not if they could help it—and did not care.

"Where's Alex?"

"Some man is interviewing him in the den."

"Alone? I thought we were doing the interview together."

"Don't know what to tell you," Willa said.

Maggie stood with her feet planted a moment, regulating her breathing. On the one hand she had kept them waiting long enough.

But she could feel her mind hover just at the edge of losing her temper, and needed to compose herself.

She took three long breaths, holding them for a few seconds and then letting each of them out as a sigh.

She walked to the living room.

The woman host who would interview her, Eleanor Price, was checking her own makeup in a small compact mirror. A cameraman was setting up round white fabric reflectors to enhance the lighting.

"I'm so sorry to keep you waiting," Maggie said.

"Oh, don't be silly," Eleanor said, quickly closing the compact and dropping it into her purse. "We needed to set up anyway."

She was younger than Maggie. Younger even than she looked on TV. More Alex's age. Her blond hair was stylishly short and she wore a light-lavender skirt suit—and too much makeup, Maggie thought, even for television.

"My girls were supposed to come tell me when you arrived, but they fell down on the job. I don't know what I'm going to do with them sometimes."

"Oh, you have teenagers and they don't always do what you wish they'd do? What an utterly unique situation." She put just the right ironic inflection on the statement to convey support for Maggie's parenting.

"Good point," Maggie said, reaching out a hand. "Margaret Blount."

The woman shook it.

"Eleanor Price."

"Yes, of course. I know. I watch your show. Good thing it's on Sunday morning or I'd never get the chance. And even then it's only if I'm not on call, and barring emergencies. Is my makeup okay? I don't tend to wear much, and your producer promised me I could show up as myself."

"You're fine. You look fine. We're using mostly natural lighting anyway."

"I might be dressed too casually."

"Not at all. We're interviewing you in your home. You're supposed to look the way you look at home. Just because jewel-tone suits are my destiny doesn't mean they have to be yours. We'll just have Dave mic you up and we'll get started."

The cameraman handed her a tiny lapel mic, and Maggie unbuttoned her blazer to thread its wire underneath.

"We can clip this to the back of your belt," he said, still holding the small box receiver. "Or you can slip it in your pocket."

"Either is fine," she said. "Why is Alex being interviewed separately? I just assumed he'd be together with me in one interview."

"We just feel that . . . ," Eleanor began, "sometimes doctors come off too weighty over nurses and administrators. I'm not saying *you* would be. But we just want an equal perspective."

"Alex thought I'd overwhelm him in the interview?"

"Not at all. He said it would be fine. But this is just how we like to do things. I hope you won't mind."

"Well, it's your show."

"Okay then. Have a seat on the couch here and we'll get started. Talk to me, not the camera. That can be awkward if you seem too aware of the camera. Start by telling us your name, please, so we have just the right pronunciation. Not that your name is hard to pronounce. It's just what we always do."

"Dr. Margaret Blount."

"And then go on to tell us a little bit about yourself."

"Okay. I'm forty-one years old. Divorced. Two children, both girls. Gemma is fourteen and Willa is sixteen. I have a practice here in Vista del Mar with three other doctors. None of us are specialists of any kind. Internal medicine. We're people's primary care physicians."

"And when there's a disaster anywhere, like the one headed for the Gulf Coast now . . ."

"Well, not anywhere. We're limited by the fact that our clinic is on wheels. We don't go overseas, and if a disaster is all the way on the other side of the country we have to base our response on whether or not there would still be any good left to do once we got there."

"Right. Makes sense. And of course now we're talking about Doctors on Wheels. And don't worry, because we'll edit this. We can just chat about it, and you can stop and go in a different direction, or . . . whatever. Because we're not live, or even live to tape, say as much as you want and we'll take what we need."

"Wouldn't it be better to talk to Alex about Doctors on Wheels? He founded it."

"We will. We are. But we want to hear it from your point of view as well. You're the doctor."

"Ah. Now I'm beginning to see how doctors overwhelm interviews. With the interviewer's help."

Maggie tossed it out as a light joke, but it masked a slight nagging irritation. She glanced out the window into the backyard and saw the pool man setting up, which irritated her further. She had specifically told him to skip his visit that week because of the interview and the worry that he might make too much noise.

"Point taken," Eleanor said. "But you *are* the doctor. That's just a fact."

"One of the doctors. We also have a husband-and-wife team, two retired doctors. John and Lacey Bishop. And a driver and general helper named Brad—not a medical professional of any sort. He's the only one who gets a small salary. All the medical staff is volunteer. And of course Alex is a registered nurse. We have one of those huge forty-foot motor coaches—that's our clinic—and we also have two smaller RVs, one for Alex and me and one for the Bishops. Well . . . the nonprofit has one RV. The Bishops use their own. And Brad sleeps in the coach. Once the patients are gone for the day, there's plenty of room."

"Tell us in your own words what you do."

"We roll into a disaster area. Usually in the wake of a hurricane, but sometimes an earthquake or a wildfire. The hospitals are overwhelmed, of course, and they're usually having to resort to triaging patients in the parking lot. Sometimes they have patients in tents. But the weather is usually bad, since the weather was most often the disaster in the first place. Sometimes the hospital has a van of some sort, and when they hear we're in town they drive patients over to us. It's nice for them to have an option for anyone they have to turn away. We usually set up in a campground nearby so we have hookups. Sometimes they just tell the injured where we are and they have to get to us on their own. There's no one set protocol for all this. It's a disaster. People are doing the best they can with what they have, at a time when what they have is not enough."

"Why not just set up in the hospital parking lot?"

"They don't like us to do that. They never straight out say why, but I think it's a liability issue. You know. Treating patients on their property when we're not affiliated with the hospital."

"But . . . wait. Another thing. Don't you have to be licensed to practice medicine in that state?"

"There are some exceptions for emergencies, but just to be on the safe side we have a multistate license."

"And we're told you never bill these people the way the hospital would."

"We don't charge, no. We mostly see the uninsured and the lowest-income patients. Most of them have no home to send a bill to anyway. Usually it's been reduced to rubble or blown away."

"Everybody you see isn't low income, though, right? I mean . . . disaster is no respecter of financial status. It hits rich and poor alike."

Maggie felt her eyebrows jump up. For a moment she almost thought the interviewer was sharing some kind of odd joke. But she watched the woman's face, and she seemed comfortable in what she was saying.

"No, it does *not* hit rich and poor alike." Maggie paused, afraid her interviewer would take offense. Eleanor only tilted her head curiously, so Maggie kept going. "Not alike at all. It may take down both fancy homes and modest ones, but the owners of the fancy ones have someplace else to go. Earthquakes come with no warning, but when hurricanes or fires are headed for a residential area, there's an order to evacuate. The people who can afford to go *go*. By the time the disaster hits, almost the only people left in the area are the ones with no other options. Those are the people we go out to serve. We don't do it for the money."

"Which leads me to a key question. Why *do* you do it?"

Maggie shifted in her seat and did not immediately answer. She felt slightly off balance, owing to her own lack of preparation. She had assumed she would answer questions relating to who, what, when, and where. Somehow it had not occurred to her that she would be asked why, though she now felt it should have.

"Is that really a question that needs to be answered? Wouldn't we be more inclined to ask a person who *doesn't* care why he *doesn't*? I mean . . . isn't wanting to help a normal part of human nature?"

"*You* tell *me*," Eleanor said.

Maggie realized she had asked her interviewer to let her off the hook, and her interviewer had declined. It would not be a "let Maggie off the hook" type of interview. Another thing she felt she should have considered.

She didn't answer quickly enough, so Eleanor said more.

"You live in this lovely area," she said. "You have a successful medical practice. You have two daughters and patients who depend on you."

Maggie could feel something in her gut begin to twist as the sentence progressed. It felt wrong. Like a challenge to justify herself.

"There are three other doctors in the office, and I'm only gone a handful of weeks out of the year in an average year. If I have to cancel non-urgent appointments, or my patients have to see one of the other physicians, they tend to be understanding about it. It's not like I'm flying off to a spa or taking lavish vacations. The girls go to their father's. It causes a lot of rearranging for everybody here at home, but we manage."

"Because . . ."

That sat on the coffee table between them for a moment, causing Eleanor to feel slightly ruffled again. *Explain to us why you're a decent human being.* It seemed to have a pessimistic slant.

"Empathy?" Maggie said. But it came out more like a question. "Caring?"

She expected Eleanor to press the point, but her interviewer surprised her.

"Okay. I'll accept that. Now. A little bit of the elephant in the room in this next question, and I hope you won't mind. You and Alex are romantically involved. Have been for . . ."

She paused to let Maggie fill in the detail.

"About four years. But look. Before we go any further . . . I hope this is not about the difference between our ages. Because I'm afraid I'm not going to have very much patience for that. So many times we see a man with a woman twenty-five, even thirty years younger, and nobody bats an eyelash. But a woman with a man nine or ten years younger is shocking to everybody, and I don't understand why, and I think it points to something very wrong in our society."

"Oh, I couldn't agree more," Eleanor said. "I'm completely with you on that. No, I wasn't going to bring that up."

"Oh. Sorry."

"Not a problem."

"Then what's the elephant in the room?"

"This is Alex's brainchild, the whole Doctors on Wheels nonprofit. Right? His idea. He raised the funds for the vehicles and to convert the bus to a clinic."

"Yes, and he continually fundraises to keep us going."

"Fundraises . . . how?"

"The way any nonprofit would. He encourages individual donations from medical professionals in our orbit. And from medical corporations in our orbit. And a lot of the contributions are our own."

"Okay. He's key to the project. Now let's say it was someone else's project. Would your empathy still get you on that bus?"

Maggie realized, with a slight sense of disappointment, that it was a good question. One that she could not—should not—easily dismiss.

"I think if it was someone else's idea I'd be less likely to know about it. There's that simple logistic element to the thing. I think we gravitate toward the same opportunities as our loved ones. If I'd heard about it but didn't know anyone involved, I might be less enthusiastic because I might know less about their vision, or their protocols, or their sense of responsibility. I knew from the inside out that this was a good project. You can't really keep the two things separate. But I could easily have found Alex a couple of volunteers. They didn't have to be me. I wanted to be out there where people need a doctor because that's where I think doctors are supposed to be."

"Okay," she said. "Good answer. You can unclip that mic and Dave will take it back."

"Wait, that's it?"

"Should be plenty, yes."

"You don't want to know about the people we treat, or the experiences we have out in the field?"

"The piece is going to be a lot more than just this one interview. There'll be four interviews altogether, and of course we'll give some background on the organization. And a lot of the segment will be spent reporting on this Category Four hurricane bearing down on Texas. The piece about Doctors on Wheels is more of an adjunct to that."

Dave stepped up and unclipped her mic, and she unthreaded its cord from under her blazer and handed him back the receiver.

All the while she nursed an odd feeling that she had been right on the cusp of explaining what she really did out there, and why it was important, when her interviewer called time and pulled the plug on everything.

———

"What was your interview like?" she asked Alex in bed that night.

Maggie had just gotten off a FaceTime call with her mother, who had also wanted details on how it had gone.

They were on their sides, facing each other, up on one elbow. They'd both had to run to their respective offices after the interviews, and this was the first moment they'd had to talk. Well, except for over dinner, but somehow it wasn't a conversation Maggie wanted to have in front of the girls.

"It was . . . a little surface-y, but not too bad. Why? Was yours bad?"

"It left me with a weird feeling, but I can't quite put my finger on why. She seemed . . . I don't know. She wanted to talk about our relationship, which is fine on the surface of the thing. But also she made some reference to me going off into the field when I have daughters depending on me. And you didn't get that, right?"

"No, but I have no daughters."

"I guess I just felt like she had a little bit of a patriarchal slant, but I might be reading too much in. But another thing. I thought she was somebody who understood the world a little better. She thought there were a bunch of wealthy people out there in the cold waiting for us to treat them. And she used that phrase 'the elephant in the room.' It seemed strange. I guess I can see someone using it for a big thing like a family trying to have a normal life while one of the parents is alcoholic or abusive. But this was just a very small, kind of nuanced little thing. And I'm left feeling like, really? This is going to crush you if it sits on you? You honestly can't see to interview me around this three-ton gray thing?"

"I think it's their job to make things sound as dramatic as possible," Alex said.

While he spoke, he clicked around a little on his phone with his thumb. His head was down, looking at its screen, and masses of his curly dark hair fell over his face in a way Maggie found appealing. She reached out and brushed it away to better see his face, and he smiled.

"I suppose," she said.

"I'm *not* ignoring you."

"No," Maggie said. "I know you're not. I know what you're doing. You're following the path of that hurricane."

"Exactly," he said.

"Anything new to know about it?"

"Unfortunately yes. It just jumped the line into a Cat Five, and it's tracking farther east than predicted. Now landfall likely won't be Galveston. Now they're saying Lake Charles, Louisiana. Also it's speeded up a bit. We should probably get our houses in order tomorrow and leave early the day after."

"The girls will be thrilled," she said.

She didn't tell him she was being sarcastic. She didn't need to.

Chapter Two

Have You Met the Greater Good?

In the morning, while Alex was showering and shaving, Maggie called her ex-husband from the kitchen as her bagel was toasting.

"Dan," she said, the phone gripped tenuously between her ear and shoulder.

"Don't tell me. Let me guess. Her name is Mina and she just turned Category Five and aimed her sights on Louisiana, much to the relief of everybody in Texas."

"That's about the size of it."

"When do you want to bring the girls?"

"Anytime today is fine. We're leaving early tomorrow morning."

"Won't that get you there too late?"

"No, it'll get us there at the perfect time."

"It's at least a two-day drive."

Her bagel popped up, and she burned her fingers slightly transferring it to a plate. The combination of that mild pain and her ex trying to school her on the length of the drive added up to a slight irritation. But nothing more than she was used to.

"I know how long a drive it is, Dan. I know the timing of these ventures quite well. Almost like someone who does it all the time. When you're in vehicles that lift off the ground and fly away in hundred-twenty-five-mile-per-hour winds, the trick is to arrive after the wind leaves."

"Oh, right," he said. "I wasn't thinking of that. Well. That's why they pay you the big bucks."

Maggie assumed it was a mild dig at the fact that no one paid her to do this at all. She let it go by.

"I'll bring them around dinnertime."

"Fine with me," he said, and clicked off the call.

She slid the phone into her pocket and turned to see her younger girl, Gemma, staring at her in abject horror, her mouth gaping wide. She looked to Maggie like a caricature of a person theatrically broadcasting to the world that she was not okay with the current developments.

"I don't believe it," Gemma said.

"What don't you believe?" Maggie asked, sighing inwardly and gearing up for the storm.

"You promised me."

"I never promised you I wouldn't go to this one."

"You promised me you'd think about not going."

"I did think about it."

"And you're going."

"Yes."

"Because you care more about total strangers than you care about us."

Gemma turned and stomped dramatically to the stairs. Maggie followed, projecting her answer across the distance between them.

"I do not care more about strangers than I care about you. Want to know how you can tell? Because I feed you and house you and drive you all over town and buy you nice things and send you to private school and save for your college education. And for them I just provide enough care to keep them from dying. See the difference?"

Gemma ignored her whole line of reasoning.

"Willa!" she shouted up the stairs. "She's *going*!"

"I told you she would," Willa called back.

Gemma stomped up the stairs and Maggie followed.

The girls each had their own room, but Gemma stormed down the hall to Willa's room and stood with her arms crossed in the open doorway.

"You want to tell her, Willa?" Gemma asked over her shoulder. "Or should I?"

Willa joined her sister in the doorway.

"Tell me what?" Maggie asked, trying to ignore the twisted ball of dread forming in her gut.

"We hate it at Dad's," Willa said, "and we're not going. Now what are you going to do about it?"

"Yeah!" Gemma chimed in. "You can't force us. What're you going to do, call the police? Handcuff us? Hog-tie us and put us in the car?"

"Besides," Willa said, "even if you could force us to go to Dad's, we have keys. We could come back. You'll be away, so how can you stop us?"

Maggie allowed a brief silence while she gathered her internal forces. She ached to lose her temper, but she knew it would be more effective to say what she needed to say as calmly as possible.

"No, I guess if I'm away, I can't stop you."

Both girls broke into self-satisfied smiles.

Maggie wiped them away with her next sentence.

"I just don't think you'll be all that happy here with no cable TV, no internet, and no cell service."

"You would turn off the internet and the cable?" Willa asked. "Just to hurt us?"

"Just to make sure you don't think you can blackmail me into getting what you want. Because that's a precedent I know better than to set with you two."

"You can't take our phones!" Gemma shrieked. "We'll hide them and you won't even know where they are!"

"I don't have to take your phones. I pay for your cell-phone plans. I pay for those phones to have service. I pay for every minute you talk, text, and surf. One phone call to your cell-phone provider and those phones will be useful for paperweights, but not much else. Not that you have a sheet of paper in your lives. See, you don't even know this, because you never think about it. You think you pick up a phone and it just works. You think you turn on a TV and automatically get two hundred channels, like they're built into the TV. I pay for this stuff. If you want to go into a defiant mode, you're right—I can't physically force you to do something. But there will be consequences for your decisions. Which is always the case in life, so you might as well get used to it."

A long silence fell. Maggie stared at the girls and they stared back. She watched their faces change as they realized they had lost the battle. She watched their anger flit around behind their eyes, desperately wanting to lash out in some direction or another.

"Why did you think about it and decide to go?" Willa asked, her voice spitting with contempt, even for Willa. "Why don't you care more about what *we* want?"

"Because it seems like the more I give you what you want, the more you want. It doesn't make you happy. Just insatiable. Look. Bottom line, you're not as bad off as you think you are. Your only dilemma is where you prefer to be. Which comfortable house you like best. I'm on my way to see people whose houses just blew down on top of them and who can't afford a doctor to set their broken bones. It's not that I care about them more than you; it's that their needs are greater. I decided going was more in line with the greater good."

"I don't even know what that last thing means," Willa said.

"Well, you should, and I blame myself for the fact that you don't." Another long silence.

Willa turned away from the doorway and pulled her suitcase out of her closet. She threw it dramatically on the bed. Maggie watched her daughter's eyes fall on the framed picture of the three of them at Disney World seven years earlier. Willa marched over to it and pulled it roughly off the wall, sending the nail flying. She looked directly into Maggie's eyes and then shattered it against the dresser. Glass flew everywhere.

"You'll need to clean that up yourself," Maggie said. "If you break something accidentally, I have no problem getting the maid to do it. But that was not an accident, and I'd like you to take responsibility for it."

"I hate you," Willa said, holding Maggie's eyes with an iron gaze.

Maggie stood frozen for a beat or two, nursing an unusual and unsettling feeling. The sting of her daughter's proclamation seemed to have passed her by. She didn't even feel it. Instead she viewed the scene with something more like curiosity. It felt like seeing her life with new eyes, or from a different and more distant vantage point. And not in a good way. But at the moment she couldn't pin it down any more precisely than that. It was there to be felt, but not to be summed up in words.

"Well, I love *you*," Maggie said.

She turned away and walked back downstairs.

"But you sure don't make it easy to like you," she mumbled under her breath as she headed for the kitchen.

Alex was sitting at the table, staring at his phone and eating a carton of yogurt.

"Your bagel is completely cold," he said. "Want me to toast you a new one?"

"No, I'll eat it anyway. I don't want it to go to waste."

He looked up at her face, and she watched the alarm register in his eyes.

"Oh, this could not have been good," he said.

"I had a fight with the girls."

"You have fights with the girls all the time. I've never seen you look like *this* before."

"I don't know," Maggie said. But she did know. She set her face in her hands for a few seconds, then dropped her hands and picked up half of the cold, hard bagel. "I think some realizations are breaking through. Not in a happy way."

He waited for a time, probably to see if she'd say more.

"Well, I'm not going to ask you what they are," he said. "Because I know you. You'll tell me you're not ready to talk about it yet. And then later, when you *are* ready to talk about it, you will, without me having to drag anything out of you."

"Yeah, that sounds like me," she said.

They ate in silence for a minute or so. Alex scraped the last of his yogurt out of the carton and made a three-point shot into the kitchen trash with the empty container.

"I guess it just takes me a while to process things," she said.

"Take all the time you need," he said, and kissed her on the temple. "See you tonight."

Then he left her alone with her own thoughts.

Chapter Three

Maybe Take Them to India

Maggie rattled up out of sleep when the RV hit some kind of bump.

"Sorry," Alex said.

She opened her eyes. Stretched. Her cheek was cold from being pressed against the passenger window. It was dark outside, and other than the occasional streetlight along the highway, she could see only headlights. Theirs, and those of the other travelers.

It was raining hard, and the windshield wipers were swinging wildly, trying to keep up. She watched and listened to their steady rhythm and realized she was having trouble pulling her head out of sleep. It felt muddy and thick.

"Where are we?" she asked Alex.

"Texas. Mile after mile of Texas."

"Are you tired? Would you like me to drink some coffee and then drive?"

"I'm fine for now."

She watched the side of his face in the dim light. When oncoming headlights illuminated him, the mottled rain of the windshield was projected onto his skin. It struck Maggie as eerily beautiful.

"Here's the thing with the girls," she said.

"The thing you weren't ready to talk about on the day before we left."

"Right."

"I knew you'd tell me when you were ready."

"I realize I don't talk to you too much about the girls, and there's a reason for that. I know you're not their biggest fan."

"I never said that."

"I know you didn't. I know you have trouble with them, and I know it takes a lot of self-restraint not to complain about them out loud. And I guess I felt like talking about them to you wasn't really fair, because it's too much like inviting you to say what you're thinking about them. Sometimes your opinion of them comes through, even though you don't say it, and I know I've been a little defensive and short with you about that. And now I feel like I owe you an apology."

"I don't think you owe me any apologies. You're their mother. You're supposed to defend them."

"But I think I've been passing off your feelings about them as some kind of stepparent syndrome. Like the fact that they're a big part of my life, and not your children, is why you don't like them. And then when we were having that fight the other day I looked at them. Really looked at them. Like I stood back out of myself and looked at the situation with more perspective. And I guess I thought . . . How could anybody like them? I don't even like them myself. I love them. Of course. I'd do anything for them. But like them? How can I? They're spoiled and entitled and selfish. I'm not saying it's the first time I've noticed, of course. I just saw the thing differently. In the past I'd see them being awful and I'd think, 'Gemma is acting selfish' or 'Willa is acting spoiled and entitled.' And then the other day I looked at them and it hit me. They're not acting. This really is who they've become."

She paused, and Alex allowed the silence. Probably to be sure she was done.

"They're teenagers," he said, his voice soft. "Aren't most teenagers difficult?"

20

"Some more than others," she said.

"Maybe it's something they'll outgrow."

"I doubt it," Maggie said. "I mean . . . people can always change. I'm not saying the situation will never get better. But I don't think I can solve it by sitting back and assuming they'll morph out of the stage on their own. And I can't completely remove myself from the equation, because I'm the parent. I raised them. Now I have to look at what I did wrong. Not to suggest my liability is limited to this, but . . . I wanted to give them everything, but now they have everything and they just act like kids who have everything. They don't appreciate anything because nothing they have is anything they've ever had to live without. They just keep wanting more, and getting more never seems to make them happy. I feel like . . . if we just keep going like this, doing exactly what we're doing, we'll just keep getting these same results. Like my mother always says, 'If nothing changes, nothing changes.'"

"How do you propose to solve a problem like that?"

"No idea," she said.

She stared through the windshield for a few minutes, into the driving rain. If anything, it was coming down harder. It seemed to be raining in sheets instead of drops.

"Maybe I should take them to India," she said. She had told him quite a bit about how shocked she was by the poverty she'd seen there. But not everything. "The whole time I was there I kept thinking about the people I knew at home who complained about money. Because they had to take the bus to work instead of having their own car or because they lived in a small rented apartment instead of owning a house. I'm not dismissing or minimizing actual poor people in this country. Just . . . there I was in India, looking at people who were sleeping on the concrete banks of the Ganges River with nothing but one thin blanket. Monsoon season, forty degrees at night, with the wind howling down the river from the Himalayas. In the daytime they'd get up and beg, and if someone gave them a rupee then they'd buy a chapati from a street vendor and that would be their day's food. If nobody gave them anything, they wouldn't eat. We have so much. So much stuff that we take as a given and don't even think about, much less appreciate."

"Think they'd go there with you?"

"Probably not," she said.

They drove in silence for a few more rainy miles. In the side-view mirror Maggie saw the motor-coach-turned-clinic following behind them, its massive windshield wipers flashing back and forth.

"I always thought the private school was a mistake," Alex said.

"You've mentioned that before, but I never really knew why you thought so. I thought maybe you objected to my spending the money."

"I don't tell you how to spend your money."

"Okay, what then?"

"Did I ever tell you about when I was a kid and I was into riding?"

"Weirdly . . . not that much." He had told her he was crazy for horses but didn't have one, because his parents couldn't afford it—but that they got him riding lessons because they knew how important it was to him. "But you grew up in the city. You never really told me where you ride horses in the city. And back East . . . what kind of riding was this? Like something English?"

"Yeah, hunter-jumper stuff. And yes, the riding club was in a strangely urban area. It was decades old, and the city had just kind of built up around it. Anyway, my parents couldn't really afford to send me there for lessons, but they stretched themselves and did it anyway. Everybody there had rich parents except me. And they never let me forget it. When I was home in my own neighborhood I just felt like my family was normal, because we had pretty much the same means as everybody around us. But at the riding club I felt poor."

"The girls aren't the poorest kids at their school."

"No, but they're below the median."

"Interesting," she said. "I'll have to think about that. Now I want to see pictures of you riding horses when you were a kid."

"I'm not sure I still have any. I know my mother does. She still has my ribbons, from when I did show jumping. Junior class. You had to have a black show coat, and they were expensive, and so she *made* one for me. It was such an amazing thing for her to do. She had a sewing machine, and she made it to look like the show coats the other kids' parents bought them. But there were a few tiny differences, and the kids kept pointing them out. It was heartbreaking. I mean . . . it wasn't really. It was nothing. But to me it felt heartbreaking."

"Ouch," Maggie said out loud, nursing a feeling like a sword cutting down through her chest. "No, that's not nothing, Alex. That's real. That hurts."

"Sorry," Alex said. "I forgot you would feel that too. While we're on the subject of the way you pick up on these things . . . I mean . . . what do you feel when you're around the girls?"

"I'm not very tuned in to anger. I see it and hear it but I don't really take it on."

"But of everything that's going on when you're around them . . . what do you feel?"

"Nothing," Maggie said. "That's part of what worries me. When I'm around them I get nothing at all."

———

In the morning they had breakfast with John and Lacey Bishop in their RV while Brad slept in.

Lacey puttered at the tiny propane stove, cooking actual food, and John was outside in full rain gear, working on getting the TV hooked up to satellite.

They had stopped for the night in an RV park, because they were on track to arrive in Louisiana dangerously early.

Lacey Bishop set omelets in front of Maggie and Alex and then knocked on the window to signal her husband to come in.

Maggie took a bite, closing her eyes briefly and sighing.

"This is . . . amazing," she said. "Lacey, I don't know how you do it. When Alex and I are on the road we consider trail mix and ramen

23

noodles in the microwave to be fancy eating. How do you manage to actually cook in this little space?"

Lacey laughed.

She was back at the stove, cooking two more omelets for her husband and herself. She was an older woman, midseventies, with stylishly short, thinning gray hair, tanned skin, and a no-nonsense attitude toward the world.

"Honey," she said, "this's not my first rodeo."

"You and John have been hitting the national parks a lot?" Alex asked between bites.

"We're up to three weeks out of an average month. You try eating trail mix and ramen for that long."

"Whoa," Maggie said. "That's an uptick. You weren't going out that much last time we talked to you. I thought you wanted to travel less."

"And John wants to travel more. That's marriage for you. A series of compromises. Oh, speak of the devil."

The door of the RV opened and John stepped in, stomping his wet boots and shaking water off his rain slicker in the recessed-stair entrance.

"I got the TV going," he said.

He peeled off his wet slicker and hung it on a hook on the wall. Every time Maggie saw him he seemed thinner than the time before. He was over eighty, and she worried slightly about his health.

"We can get the weather on our phones, though," Alex said.

"Yeah, but this way we can all watch that Sunday-morning show. You know. That segment with Eleanor Price."

"You could have bet me a hundred dollars to tell you what day of the week it was," Maggie said. "And I just would have ended up a hundred dollars poorer."

———

"Oh, Alex looks great," Maggie said when he came on-screen. "Oh, honey. You look so handsome!"

"Well, you got yourself a catch," Lacey said, "and you must know it. Don't tell me you just now figured out he's good-looking."

Meanwhile they were missing parts of his interview, but it wasn't anything they didn't already know—details about the founding of Doctors on Wheels.

"I know Alex is handsome. But not everybody looks as good on TV as in real life."

Just as she finished the sentence the program cut to her interview.

"Ugh!" Maggie said. "Case in point."

They listened as she finished her first sentence.

"I wanted to be out there where people need a doctor because that's where I think doctors are supposed to be," her image said on the small screen.

It turned out to be her *last* sentence as well.

They cut to the administrator of a hospital in a small California town they'd visited a year earlier, when it had been ravaged by wildfire.

"That's *it*?" Maggie shouted.

"They gave me so much more time," Alex said.

"Yeah, but they should. The whole project was your idea. But why even make me sit for that? I put on makeup for that sentence. There's an hour of my life I'll never get back. They could have just said 'Give us one short quote from you.' Oh well. I didn't want to be rich and famous anyway. But I looked like some creature that just rose up out of a lagoon somewhere. That's what I mind."

"You looked gorgeous and you know it," Lacey said. "You're a beautiful woman. Why, look at all that thick auburn hair. That head of hair's what makes me so jealous. Oh, honey, I miss the days when I had hair. On my head, I mean. Not on my chin and upper lip."

"Wait," John said. "They're doing an update on the hurricane."

They stared at the screen as aerial footage played.

"This must be the first flyover," John said. "Now I feel like we're late."

"We can be there in three hours," Alex said.

They fell silent again and watched the screen. A plane—or helicopter, but more likely a plane since the storm was still so close—was flying over street after street of houses submerged except for their roofs. Here and there people on those roofs waved desperately at the plane as they filmed. Then the scene cut to a flight over a neighborhood with no roofs at all—except for a handful of fragments floating upside down in the floodwater—and a solid wall of cars washed up against a bridge abutment.

"Lord have mercy," Lacey said. "This is even worse than what we were thinking. Lord have mercy on those poor people left alive down there. John, go wake up Brad and tell him to call the local hospitals and get one to find us a campground and then call us back with it. And if they want to be waiting there with patients when we drive in, that's fine. Then drive this RV, John. We've got to get to those people as fast as we can."

Chapter Four

The Day We Were Angels

The first patient to come through the door was a young boy—maybe seven, Maggie thought—in his father's arms. His mother hurried nervously behind.

They all three were soaked to the skin and blinked miserably into the bright lights of the clinic.

There were others behind them, all adults, and they would go to John and Lacey, but Maggie had taught herself to look only at the ones headed for her station.

"Where do we go?" the mother asked. "Which one of you is the doctor?"

"We're all three doctors," Maggie said, indicating the Bishops with a sweep of her arm. Alex was still rushing back and forth in the bus, setting up with some help from Brad, and she pointed to him as he flew about. "And Alex is a registered nurse."

She looked back at the mother, whose eyes had grown wide.

"Three doctors and a nurse? Oh my gosh! I almost can't believe it! At the hospital they told us there was no available doctor hardly anywhere in the state of Louisiana and probably not in most of East Texas to boot. You hear what she said, Darren? Three doctors and a nurse."

"Put your son down here on the examining table."

The father set the boy down. He was wrapped in a new, stiff-looking gray blanket of the type emergency personnel might hand out. The father unwrapped the blanket and Maggie saw three daggers of splintered wood embedded in the boy's flesh. The biggest was between his shoulder and collarbone and looked to be about seven inches long and two or three inches wide. The ones in his upper arm were smaller. Each was surrounded by a circle of blood about the size of a silver dollar, staining his Captain America T-shirt.

The boy looked up into Maggie's eyes. He did not look panicky. He seemed resigned to the moment. He told her with his eyes that he trusted her, even though they'd never met. What choice did he have?

She never took her eyes off the boy's eyes as she spoke.

"What's your name?" she asked him.

He remained silent.

"This is Stevie," his mother said.

"Hi Stevie," she said, still holding his gaze.

"The hurricane sent a tree flying right at our house," the father said, his voice quiet. Almost reverent. "We saw it coming and we tried to run. We don't have a storm cellar, so we just had to make a run for it. The tree smashed a shed to smithereens and all the pieces went flying. You just couldn't believe how fast they were flying."

"They told us at the hospital that the life-and-death people had to come first," the mom said. "We wanted them to just give him a little sedative and pull them out. Or give him some sedative and we would. But they said no. We shouldn't. We should come here."

"It's not quite as easy as just pulling them out," Maggie said, still holding the boy's eyes in an act of solidarity and trust. "You see how little blood we have now. That's because the shards are holding back the bleeding. When they come out we'll need to be sure no splinters are left behind, and that there's no damage to the muscles underneath. And then we'll need to put in a few stitches."

"Well, we trust you," the mom said. "We never met you before in our whole lives, but we trust you. I mean, what choice have we got?"

Maggie wanted to tell her that her son had said the exact same thing with his eyes. She chose to say nothing on the subject instead.

"Hurts," she said, "doesn't it, Stevie? I can feel how that hurts."

He nodded ever so slightly. She was almost left wondering if it was her imagination.

"Okay, Stevie," she said. "Here's what I'd like to do if it's okay with you. If you'll open your mouth for it, I want to put a little bit of medicine on your tongue. It won't taste very good, but it'll make you feel more relaxed all over. You'll still be awake and all, and you'll know what I'm doing. But the whole thing will seem kind of far away."

Stevie only stared into her eyes in silence. Then he opened his mouth and let his tongue extend slightly.

"Alex," she said, and he appeared at her side instantly. "Midazolam. Point five. Please."

She extended her gloved hand back over her shoulder. Just seconds later an oral syringe was set down on her palm.

"Thank you, Alex," she said.

She squirted its contents onto Stevie's tongue, and he grimaced at the bitterness of it.

"Yeah, sorry about that," she said. "I know that's nasty. Now here's what I'm going to do. I'm going to take a very thin little needle and put it in right beside where those hurtful pieces of wood stabbed you, and after I do, those parts of you won't feel anything for a while. That way when I take these daggers out and stitch up the wounds, it won't hurt you at all. Are you okay with needles, Stevie?"

"He's real good about his shots," the mother said. "Never makes no fuss at all. He's a real stoic boy."

"Yeah, I'm getting that," Maggie said, still not taking her eyes away from Stevie's eyes, which were beginning to soften and lose focus.

"We don't tell him he's got to be, though," the mother added. "It's just how he's always been."

Maggie looked away from the boy, whose eyes had drifted closed, and located Alex. She opened her mouth to tell him what local anesthetic she wanted, but he already had it in his hand.

"Is this right, Doctor?"

He held it out for her examination.

"Perfect," she said.

She filled a syringe and injected a small amount near each wound.

"Okay, let's get the worst one over with first. Alex, have some hemostatic gauze nearby just in case."

"Will do," he said.

"I'm going to have to cut off this T-shirt," Maggie said to the parents. Because the boy's eyes were still intermittently drifting closed. "You wouldn't happen to have a spare?"

"I'll get the shirt," Alex said, and began to work over the boy.

"We didn't think of that," the mom said. "Or anything else. We just ran."

"That's okay. You can wrap him in the blanket until you get him something else to wear."

Alex stepped back, the shirt hanging in shreds from his gloved hand.

Maggie looked down at the boy's bare torso, and it broke her heart. Almost literally, from the feel of it. He was so thin. So vulnerable. His skin was milky white. He looked so fragile. He had not deserved this violent assault from nature. Or from anyone or anything.

She carefully cleaned the skin around the wound. Then she grasped the wood shard as close to the skin as possible and gently retracted it. It didn't bleed nearly as much as she had feared. She examined the wound carefully with her penlight, dabbing away blood as needed.

"This is good," she said to the parents without looking at them. "This is actually very good. No splinters left behind. It didn't rupture any major blood vessels. All in all, there just wasn't as much of it under the skin as I'd feared. But it'll need four or five stitches."

She pulled out a drawer in the rolling tray beside her examination table, knowing she would find all her suturing equipment there.

"You're an angel," the mother said. "You're all angels, all four of you."

"No, we're just people," Maggie said.

"I'm not saying you're not regular human people. But you're our angels today, and I'm not backing down on that."

"Well, we're glad we could be here. We're going to send you home with antibiotics. Make sure to give them without fail, every eight hours—and give the whole course, every pill, even if he tells you he feels fine." She carefully placed and tied off the first suture. "Do you have someplace to go, or are you in a shelter?"

"We're gonna go to my sister's in Lafayette. We would've gone there before Mina hit but we were so sure it would miss us, and then by the time it made that turn it was too late. We figured by then the highways would be even more dangerous than the house. Not sure now if we were right, but that's what we thought."

"In situations like this I think you just take your best shot," Maggie said.

"I'll tell you one thing, though," the father said. "Next time we hear there's a hurricane anywhere near—even if it's like two hundred miles away—we're going a thousand miles in the opposite direction."

"Probably wise. Promise me you'll have him rechecked by a doctor in Lafayette as soon as you can. I want to know someone is making sure these are healing properly."

"Of course we will," the mother said. "We'd do anything for our boy." And with that second sentence she dissolved into tears. "What do we owe you for this?" she asked, the sobs twisting her voice around.

"We don't charge," Maggie said, tying off another stitch.

"They told us that. The van driver from the hospital told us that, but we couldn't hardly believe it. I told Darren he must've got that wrong. Didn't I, Darren? I told him he must've meant to say you don't charge as much as the hospital. The other thing just seemed too good to be true. We're not absolutely broke. We're not rich but we could give you *something*."

"Did your house survive?"

For some reason this caused the mother to clam up and say nothing.

"Not too likely it's salvageable," the father said.

"Then you should put your money into *that*."

"You're angels," the mother said. "I swear, you're absolute angels, all of you. Just angels is what you are."

———

The girls came in at about two in the afternoon. They did not seem to be accompanied by anyone.

They clung very close together, bumping shoulders as they moved across the clinic toward her. They appeared to be about the same age as her own daughters. Sixteen and fourteen, she guessed. Their clothes and hair were soaking wet and muddy, but Maggie could see no obvious injuries.

But their eyes . . .

Maggie looked into their eyes and felt as though she were falling down a deep well. Their pain stabbed through her midsection and left her shaky. Something had happened to these girls. Something had happened to all the patients she'd seen that day. They had all survived a devastating Category 5 hurricane. But somehow what had happened to these girls was worse. She could feel it.

"Have a seat on my table," she said, as gently as possible.

They sat side by side, their shoulders still pressed together. Maggie could hear them breathing. It was the terrible, raspy sound of lungs filling up with fluid.

"I'm Maggie," she said. "What are your names?"

The older girl spoke for both of them.

"I'm Jean," she said. "And this is Rose." Through a charming Louisiana accent, her voice sounded hoarse and rattly with phlegm.

"Sisters?"

Maggie was really making small talk. It was obvious they were sisters. They both had the same thin, straight, sandy-blond hair. Their eyes were an identical color of pale blue.

"Yes ma'am."

"What can I help you with? I can tell there's something wrong in your lower respiratory systems, but is there anything else I don't know about?"

The older girl opened her mouth to speak but fell into a spasm of coughing instead. She shook her head.

"I see," Maggie said.

She put the earpieces of her stethoscope into her ears and listened carefully at each girl's chest and back, asking for deep breaths as needed. They were both clearly suffering from a lower respiratory illness that had turned into pneumonia. But the hurricane had moved through only hours before, and these girls had been sick for days, if not weeks.

"How long have you and your sister been sick?" she asked the older girl.

"Couple of weeks," Jean said, her eyes cast down to the clinic floor in shame.

"Did your parents take you to a doctor before the hurricane hit?"

"No ma'am."

A pause fell. And stayed. Maggie wanted to know why not, but did not want to force the girls to defend their own parents. Meanwhile she nursed the deep feeling of dread in her gut that poured like water off these two sick, lost children.

Jean seemed to read her question from the silence.

"Our dad lost his job," she said. "And when he lost his job we lost our insurance. My mom wanted to take us to the emergency room but he said it would run its course."

"And where are your parents now?"

No answer came back to Maggie. Just a wave of pain and panic that felt like it might knock her off her feet.

"Did you get separated from them in the storm?"

Both girls nodded weakly.

"Is anybody with you?"

They shook their heads the tiniest bit.

"Okay. We'll deal with this. We'll start you on antibiotics. We'll ask the state emergency-services people to match you up with whoever's out there looking for you. What's your last name?"

"Bradshaw," the older girl said.

"Have you eaten?"

Both heads shook weakly.

"Okay, just stay here a minute. We'll get you all sorted out. You can relax now. It's going to be okay."

But it was clear on a feeling level that they did not believe it would be okay.

Maggie found Brad in the driver's seat of the motor coach, reading a paperback book. He was the youngest member of the team, only in his late twenties, with wild blond hair and a relaxed attitude.

"I have a job for you," she said quietly. "These girls have pneumonia, and nobody's looking after them. I'd like you to please tell the van driver they're not going back with him. They'll just end up in some huge, overcrowded shelter with thousands of other people while they look for their parents. They need antibiotics and they need medical supervision. They could die in a matter of days without any intervention at all. We're going to keep them here until I know they have somebody. Do me a favor and put it out to emergency services that we're looking to match them with their parents. Jean and Rose Bradshaw are the girls' names. In the meantime we'll put them in our little RV and Alex and I will sleep in the clinic with you tonight."

Brad nodded and pulled out his phone.

Maggie moved back to the girls, who still sat shoulder to shoulder on her table, looking terrified and lost.

"Okay, we're on it," she said. "Brad's going to figure out who's out there looking for you. I'm going to give you an antibiotic injection to get you started, and then it'll be pills after that. Let me show you where you'll be staying until somebody comes to claim you."

"That's kind of you, ma'am," the older girl said.

In that moment Maggie was overwhelmed with a strange sensation. As though this were some kind of science-fiction movie and these two girls were her own two girls, but in a parallel universe. Like the world had divided up the fates of two pairs of girls, and now she had seen both extremes of what life could shape a pair of sisters to become.

Chapter Five

Who We Were When We Arrived in This Place

It was after six in the afternoon, the clinic door was closed and locked—barring emergencies—and all the patients had gone home except the two girls in Alex and Maggie's RV.

The five grownups were sitting on plastic chairs in the clinic, eating ice cream out of individual cartons.

"You know we ought to have a real dinner," John Bishop said, scratching his bare scalp.

"Fine, honey," Lacey said. "Then *you* get up and make it. Because I'm not moving. I have had a *day.*"

"I guess ice cream is good," John said. "All things considered."

Lacey turned her laser-sharp attention onto Maggie.

"Here's where I can't seem to put two and two together about those two girls," she said. "You told us they have pneumonia, but that storm's not twenty-four hours past."

"Obviously they were sick before the storm came through," Maggie said.

"Did you ask if they'd had any previous medical care?" John asked.

"The older girl said her father lost his job and their health insurance went with it."

"You still have to get your children care," Lacey said. "One way or another."

"Mother wanted to take them to the ER. Father said it would run its course without intervention."

"Father was wrong."

"Catastrophically wrong," Maggie said.

"Maybe they shouldn't be getting those girls back when they're found."

"I don't know," Maggie said. "I hate to have a couple's kids taken away over financial insecurity."

"It's not about their finances," Lacey said. "It's about that father's judgment. Why, those girls could've died."

"Still could," Maggie said. "But I hate to play God."

"Ohhh," Alex said suddenly. He had been silent up until then, as he tended to be when tired. "*That's* why. I wondered what was going on when Brad told you emergency services needed their parents' names and their home address and you said you'd get it from the girls in the morning. That seemed so unlike you."

"You don't want the parents found?" Lacey asked.

Maggie didn't answer straightaway, so Alex said it for her.

"She's buying herself more time to treat them first."

"Well, good for you, girl," Lacey said, "for doing what you've got to do. But think about what I said. I'm not talking about playing God, because we don't get to decide anyway. I'm just talking about tipping social services and letting them take a deeper look."

"Maybe," Maggie said. "I mean, yes to thinking about it. Of course, I'll definitely think about it."

They scraped their ice-cream cartons without talking until the knock came at the motor coach's door.

"Oh, lordy," Lacey said under her breath. "We're still not done."

Maggie got up to answer it.

Standing outside the bus in the pouring rain was Stevie's mother. It filled Maggie with a sudden jolt of panic.

"What happened? Is he okay?"

"Oh, yeah, Stevie's fine. Thanks for asking. He's asleep at my sister's house."

Only then, with the worst possibilities put to rest, did Maggie notice that the woman was carrying a large covered pot, like a soup pot.

"I made you homemade chicken soup at my sister's house. Even the noodles are from scratch. I brought enough for everybody. That man nurse and those nice older doctors and that young fella who drives the bus. I brought a lot. You can just keep the pot. We can always get another pot, but we only got the one boy, and they don't sell more Stevies at the store."

"You drove all the way from Lafayette to bring us this?"

"Doesn't seem like much compared to what you did."

"That's so kind. Would you like to come in?"

"No, no. I'll be getting back. And you all must be exhausted. No, I'll just hand it to you and go."

And that was exactly what she did.

———

"Do we have something like a tray?" she asked Alex.

Maggie was preparing to try to carry two bowls of soup to the girls at the same time, with a piece of Lacey's bread on the side of each.

"We have an equipment tray," Alex said.

"That'll do. We can always sterilize it afterward."

"Want me to hold an umbrella over you so it doesn't rain into the soup?"

"Actually, I think it finally let up for a minute. Just keep my soup warm. I'll be right back."

Maggie carried the tray to the door of her and Alex's RV, set it down briefly on the steps, and knocked.

"Who is it?" Jean's hoarse, phlegmy voice called out. "I mean . . . we'll be right there. I mean . . . will we? I don't know if we're supposed to open this door for anybody."

"It's just me, Jean," Maggie said. "Doctor Blount."

"Oh thank goodness," Jean said.

She opened the door, and Maggie stepped inside.

Maggie was pleased to see that the girls had used the shower, as Maggie had encouraged them to do. They looked clean and dry now. They had put on Alex's T-shirts that Maggie had left out for them. As expected, they fit the girls like nightshirts. Rose was still tucked into the camper's main bed, sitting up. Looking shy.

"I brought you some homemade soup," Maggie said.

"That was very nice of you, ma'am," Jean said.

"You don't have to call me ma'am. You can call me Maggie."

"No ma'am," Jean said, averting her eyes.

"No you can't call me Maggie?"

"Yes ma'am."

"But I'm saying you can."

"But I can't, ma'am. I just can't. I couldn't bring myself to do that. It's just not how we were brought up."

"Okay. Suit yourself, I guess. Go ahead and take a seat at that little table and you can have something hot to eat."

Both girls sat with their hands folded politely in front of them while Maggie served the soup. She took two soup spoons out of the drawer beside the sink and two paper napkins from the drawer below.

"This looks really good, ma'am," Jean said. "I don't know how you managed this, being as we're out in the middle of a campground and all, but we sure do thank you."

"It was a gift from the parents of a boy I treated today."

"Oh, that was nice of them. Wish there was something *we* could do."

"Just get better," Maggie said. "And we'll be even. Now don't mind me, but I'm just going to listen to your lungs again. See if that injection of antibiotics I gave you is helping yet."

"It is, ma'am. We can feel it."

"Good. But I'd still like to listen." She pulled her stethoscope out of her pocket. "Deep breaths, Jean," she said, listening at the girl's chest and then back. She moved over to the younger sister, who flinched ever so slightly. "Deep breaths, Rose." She pulled the stethoscope out of her ears and folded it back into her pocket. "That seems like a slight improvement," she said to the girls. "I'm encouraged."

She sat down on the couch across from them and tried to look straight into their faces, but they insisted on staring down into their soup.

"Go ahead and dig in," she said. "I just want to ask you one quick question. I know you told me earlier that your dad stopped your mom from taking you to the emergency room. And—I know. He was worried about money, and I get that. But just . . . other than that . . . how are things for you girls at home?"

Jean's eyes came up to hers and held them for a moment. And Maggie knew in that moment that the girls were not being abused at home. Because Jean didn't look away. Also Maggie could see a mild confusion in the girl's eyes, as if she couldn't imagine what kind of information Maggie was looking for.

"I think . . . normal?"

It struck Maggie in that moment that most kids probably think their home life is normal, however it actually is. She remembered Alex saying, "When I was home in my own neighborhood I just felt like my family was normal, because we had pretty much the same means as everybody around us." Still, Maggie was not getting a sense that the girls were being abused.

But something had upset them deeply. That feeling was still there.

"Well, I'll leave you two to eat and then sleep. Remember you're on bed rest, so just stay down unless you have to go to the bathroom or something. And I might come around two or three times in the night to check on you, so if you hear that door lock pop open, don't be alarmed. And the other doctors will come check on you during the day when I'm tied up."

"Yes ma'am," Jean said.

Maggie still had not heard the younger girl's voice.

"Ma'am?" Jean said as Maggie headed for the door.

Maggie stopped, and waited.

"I just wanted to say it's awful nice of you to let us stay here. We heard stories about that shelter. A couple in the van from the hospital was telling us about that place. I guess there are, like, thousands of people all stuffed in there, and the cots are just inches apart so you can barely walk between them, and nobody ever turns off the lights. It sounded pretty scary."

"We'll take good care of you until your parents can be found."

The girls stared at their soup and said nothing.

Maggie walked back outside, struggling with how to interpret that silence.

It struck her as she left that she had still not asked them for their street address, or their parents' first names. She wondered if her subconscious had done that on purpose to buy more time, as Alex had surmised.

The rain let loose again, just a sheet of it all at once, and by the time she had walked from one campsite to the next she was soaked to the skin.

She stepped inside the bus, peeling off her jacket and stomping her feet on the mat to shake water off her boots. Alex handed her a towel.

"Thank you," she said, and used it to dry her hair.

It was dawning on her that, while they could certainly sleep in the clinic, they couldn't shower there, or do much to get comfortable.

"Just once," she said, "I'd like to be out in the field in nice weather."

"Then what exactly would the emergency be?" Lacey asked. "Too much warm sunshine?"

"A nice dry earthquake, maybe," Maggie said.

Alex handed her a bowl of the hot soup and a spoon from the Bishops' camper, and she balanced it on her knees and ate, and really did feel better for it.

"We're heading back for the night," Lacey said. "But you can come over and shower if you want."

"Thanks," Maggie said. "But maybe in the morning. I've had enough of this day. I just want to eat and go to sleep."

———

Maggie lay awake next to Alex on two examination tables they had pushed together to form a makeshift bed. There was only one small blanket, but the clinic had a propane furnace, and the temperature was comfortable.

"I think I'm too tired to sleep," she said.

"I hear you."

They kept their voices low so as not to disturb Brad, who had bedded down in a loft bed over the cab area of the bus.

"Those girls . . ." she began.

And then she stalled, unsure what she wanted to say.

As was Alex's way, he only waited to see if she cared to finish the thought.

"They're so . . . this sounds like a terrible thing for a parent to say, so you may never quote me on it, but they're everything I wish Willa and Gemma could be. They're sincere and polite and appreciative and kind. Humble. Maybe too humble, but I guess I'm feeling like . . . better that than the other way around. And their father almost got them killed, so I'm not thinking it's a result of absolutely perfect parenting."

"Especially since I'm pretty sure there is no such thing."

"I'm having trouble wrapping my head around the whole situation," she said.

Alex seemed to think for a while before answering.

"Who really knows why people turn out the way they do, though?" he asked after a time. "I mean, there's the whole nature-or-nurture debate, but nobody can really say for a fact why two kids with the same nurture tend to turn out so differently. Maybe we come into the world as exactly who and what we are."

"Oh, I don't even want to *think* that," Maggie said. "If I believe that, then I'm saying there's no hope for change."

"Life can always change people," Alex said.

They lay in silence for a few minutes.

Then Alex said, "Here's a question about the Bradshaw girls. Have they asked about their parents?"

"Asked about them?"

"Have they asked how the search for them is going?"

"No. Not once."

That just sat still between them for a moment.

"What do you make of that?" he asked.

"I'm not sure what to make of it. What do *you* make of it?"

"I was just curious," he said. "I'm not ready to make any guesses about it either."

Chapter Six

What You Get for Tempting Fate

"I need you to write down your street address," Maggie said to the girls, but mostly to Jean. So far Rose still had not spoken to her. "And your parents' first names. Otherwise you'll tell me and I'll forget by the time I get back to the clinic. Especially the address. I'm not all that good at holding numbers in my head. My mind is too busy."

"Yes ma'am," Jean said.

Maggie handed her a prescription pad and a pen, because she had nothing else available in the way of paper. It struck her as oddly symbolic, though. As though the correct prescription for these girls would be parents, which unfortunately were not available in any pharmacies.

"I'm going to listen to your lungs again, and then I'll be gone all day, so I'm trusting you to come over to the clinic if there's anything you need. John Bishop will check in on you. Oh, and Brad's going to come by for your clothes this morning. He'll knock on the door and you just gather up what you were wearing when you came in and hand them to him. He's getting a ride into the nearest operational town to try to find a laundromat today."

"Yes ma'am," Jean said.

She handed Maggie back the pad, and Maggie slid it into the pocket of her sweater.

She pulled out her stethoscope and listened at the girls' backs. She did not have to tell them to take deep breaths. They knew.

"That sounds good," she said. It did not sound good, except in relation to how it had sounded the previous day, which was really all she'd meant. "That's good progress for not even one whole day. I'm starting you on oral antibiotics today. I'm leaving these prescription bottles on the table with a couple of bottles of water and I want you to take them exactly as it says on the label. I wrote your names on the bottles. Make sure you get the right one, because you don't both weigh the same. I'll give this information about your parents to Brad, and he'll pass it on to emergency services. So far nobody's called looking for you, but this way they can start hunting down your parents and see where they ended up."

She paused, hoping for some reaction besides total silence.

She was confronted with total silence.

"Okay," she said, "I'll leave you on your own for now."

"Ma'am?" Jean said as Maggie's hand rested on the door handle.

It was a tentative, scared little thing, that word.

"Yes, hon?"

Another long silence.

"Nothing," Jean said. "Never mind."

Maggie sighed as quietly as possible and stepped out into the cool morning.

The rain had blown through, leaving the sky a brilliant blue between heavy white cumulous clouds.

"Sure," Maggie said to the sky. "Act as if nothing ever happened."

She lowered her eyes again, and saw the hospital van pull up to the clinic bus.

She took a long, deep breath and steeled herself to do it all over again, all day.

———

She was splinting a woman's wrist when Brad tapped her on the shoulder. It was maybe four hours later, but Maggie found time hard to judge on such days.

"Take a quick break and find me between patients," he said quietly.

"Okay."

Then she returned her attention to the woman in front of her.

She was maybe twenty years older than Maggie, which was not especially old, but she carried herself like an old person. Her white hair had been pulled back into a barrette, but most of it had come trailing down again.

"Just put a cast on it," the woman said. "Can't you do that here?"

"We can, but it's not going to help you much. I can show you the x-ray." Alex had been quite proud of his ability to raise funds for a compact portable x-ray machine the previous year. "It's not like a greenstick fracture in a long bone. This wrist is shattered. It's going to require surgery."

"I can't afford surgery. I don't qualify for Medicare for another three years."

"I think you'll need to look into what help the state can provide. I'm sorry. I know it's a problem. But I also know you want to have full use of this hand for the rest of your life. I'm going to secure it in this splint, and in a couple of days when the crowds thin out at the hospitals, I want you to go in and see what you can arrange."

The woman clucked her tongue dismissively. Almost judgmentally.

The moment Maggie had finished securing the elastic bandage around the splint, the woman got up and flounced out of the clinic. She did not say thank you, or goodbye.

Maggie held up one finger as a *Just a minute* signal to the man waiting to be seen next. She joined Brad in the cab of the bus, taking a seat on the passenger side.

He looked grim.

"You're not going to like this," he said.

"Go ahead and tell me anyway."

"It's bad news about the girls."

"They can't find the parents?"

"Worse. They found bodies at the address you gave me."

"Oh," Maggie said. It was just a quiet breath of air with a small word inside.

They both sat quietly for a moment as Maggie let that news settle in and find a place to rest inside her.

"Apparently a ceiling came down at their house," Brad said. "They found the parents trapped underneath it. I guess they couldn't get out. And then the floodwaters came up. Somebody has to tell Jean and Rose."

"I think they might already know," Maggie said.

She was wordlessly poking around inside the feeling she'd been picking up from the girls. It felt like a good fit for watching your parents drown and being unable to do anything to save them.

It also explained their silence on the subject, and the lack of questions.

"They still need official word," Brad said. "If you want, they'll have a social worker come tell the girls, and see if they have any other family. Or somebody from the state police will come talk to them. But they're kind of hoping you'll do it. Partly because nobody wants that job, but mostly because the girls know you a little. And they don't know any of the other people who would come."

Maggie spent a moment strangely aware of her breathing. As if it were no longer automatic. As if it might stop entirely without the correct attention from her.

"It should be me," she said.

"That's what everybody's hoping you'll say."

"But I'm not going to tell them and then leave them alone. It'll have to be after clinic hours today."

"If we'd taken the social-worker route it would be tomorrow."

"Okay then," Maggie said. "That's how it's going to be."

She walked through the clinic and nodded her head to the man who was waiting.

Then she went back to work. For the rest of the day she concentrated on the tasks in front of her. She did not allow her mind to drift—to turn to the unthinkable task that lurked there, waiting for her when the work was over. Still, it was always there. She could feel the weight of it. It never once left her alone.

———

They'd barely had time to lock the clinic door at the end of the day when the pizzas arrived.

Alex answered the door.

Maggie couldn't see around him, and didn't try. She was dreading the idea of one more patient and hoping someone else would volunteer.

Instead she heard Alex say a loud and cheerful thank-you. When he turned around, he was holding a stack of four pizza boxes.

"Did we order pizza?" she asked.

"We did not," Alex said. "It was volunteer pizza. It showed up without our having to ask."

The Bishops came in closer, their noses working the air.

"Now that's my kind of volunteerism," Lacey said.

"Local pizzeria took pity on us?" John asked.

"Exactly," Alex said.

"I'm going to bring some to the girls," Maggie said. "And I'm not going to tell them until after they've eaten. They need to eat, and you just know the minute I tell them they'll lose their appetites."

"Or they'll eat," Lacey said, "and you'll tell them, and they'll throw it right back up again."

"Then I'll give them time to digest it," Maggie said.

"I hope you're not having trouble ripping the bandage off this wound," Lacey said.

"Of course I am. But I'd also like to get it behind me. I just really want them to have a good meal first."

"I'll bring paper plates from our rig," Lacey said.

As soon as she got back with them, Maggie pulled two slices onto each of two plates and walked them over to the RV.

Jean saw her coming and opened the door.

"Ooh, *pizza!*" she said in that magical accent.

It was the first time she had sounded like a child to Maggie.

"I brought you two slices each, but there's more in the bus if you want it."

"Oh no ma'am. Two slices each should be just fine."

"Okay. Good then. I'll give you some time to eat, and then I'll come back later, and we'll talk a bit."

Maggie quickly regretted tipping her hand. She could feel ice form in the air between them immediately.

"Talk about what, ma'am?"

"This and that. Our next moves."

She turned away, probably too abruptly, and walked back to the motor coach, through the dusky late afternoon. She looked once over her shoulder. Jean was still there in the doorway, watching her go.

———

"This thing with the girls is absolutely, without a doubt, the most heart-breaking situation I've ever come across out here in the field," Lacey said.

They were sitting around the clinic in their plastic chairs, surrounded by empty pizza boxes, watching the sky darken outside. It had begun to spatter rain again, and Maggie was thinking how tired she was of the sound of it hitting the bus. Everyone had finished eating except Brad, who was on his fourth slice.

Alex had turned his chair to face one of the windows and was caught up in studying something outside, but Maggie didn't know what.

"Those poor, poor girls," Lacey continued. "I mean, it just could not tug at your heartstrings more."

"Here's a lesson about tempting fate," Alex said to her.

"Not following, hon."

"I'm saying it just got more heartbreaking. How about two girls whose parents drowned in a hurricane, and they don't know it yet but they're about to find out . . . and one of them is sitting outside in the rain feeding her pizza to the skinniest, most pathetic-looking stray puppy you've ever seen in your life."

"No," Maggie said, feeling her brain try to reject the information. "That's got to be the made-for-TV-movie version of the thing. That can't be our real lives."

"Take a look for yourself," Alex said.

Maggie got up and stood at one of the big windows.

Rose was sitting on the folded-down outside stairs of the RV, her hair and freshly laundered clothes dripping with rain. One by one she pulled little bits of the crust off her pieces of pizza and held them out to the pup.

He was emaciated, and obviously shy and scared. Maggie could see his hesitance to approach anyone, but the food won out. He was maybe five or six months old from the look of him, and of indeterminate breeding. Big for a pup. Maybe thirty pounds already. His legs were skinny and long, and his tail seemed permanently curled between his back two. He had a short, brownish coat and almost comically huge, floppy ears. Maggie could see every one of his ribs, even from the next campsite.

"I'm going," she said.

She stepped out into the rain.

Both the girl and the pup saw her immediately. Both reacted as if they'd been caught robbing a bank.

Rose skittered back into the RV, and the puppy ran underneath it.

As Maggie walked closer, she could see him huddled under there, big ears flopping onto oversize paws. Scared eyes wide. She could see his tail tapping submissively.

She tried the door of the RV, hoping it would be unlocked. She had not thought to bring the keys.

It opened easily.

Both girls were under the covers in bed, though of course Rose was dripping wet.

"I'm sorry, I'm sorry, I'm sorry," Rose said.

It was the first time Maggie had heard her voice. She had the same charming Louisiana accent as her sister, but her voice was higher and thinner. Less sure of itself, if such a thing were even possible.

"You don't have to be sorry," Maggie said.

"I know you brought the pizza for *us*, ma'am. I know you didn't say to give it to any dog, but he was so hungry. He told me so. Oh, I know. That sounds crazy."

"No, it doesn't sound crazy."

"It's not like he told me in any English words."

"I understand what you mean," Maggie said.

"You do?"

"Yeah. I do. I've had animals communicate things to me. Now come on out from under the covers so we can dry you off. Oh, but . . . you know what? Never mind. Those sheets are probably already as wet as they can possibly get. Let me just bring you a towel for your hair."

Maggie reached into the bathroom and pulled out a hand towel. She sat down on the bed next to Rose, who scooted over to give her room. The girl took the towel and began drying off her hair.

"It's not that I'm mad because you wanted to share your pizza with the dog," Maggie said. "But you have pneumonia, and we want you inside warm and dry, not sitting outside in the rain catching a chill."

"So, can he come in?"

"The dog?"

"Right," Rose said. "The dog."

"I suppose. If that's the only way to keep you warm and dry inside. Wipe the mud off him as best you can, and tomorrow we'll try to see if anybody's looking for him."

"Thank you, ma'am," Rose said. "You're really, really, *really* nice."

Maggie took down another of Alex's T-shirts from an overhead cabinet and handed it to the wet girl.

"Run into the bathroom and change," she said.

Just seconds later Rose was out of the bathroom and back under the covers.

Maggie had brought her head around to the task before her, and the girls seemed to sense the change in mood.

"You said you wanted to talk to us, ma'am," Jean said, as if reading Maggie's thoughts.

"I wanted to ask you girls if you already know anything about what happened to your parents during the hurricane."

Rose immediately burst into tears, while Jean held on to her perfect stoicism and Maggie tried to pretend she couldn't feel all that pain right along with them.

"Yes ma'am," Jean said, her voice barely a whisper. "We saw the whole thing. Well, we didn't see them. We couldn't see under that great big piece of ceiling. But we heard them calling out for somebody to help them. And then . . . not. I'm awful sorry, ma'am."

Maggie felt her mouth fall open.

"Sorry? Why would you be sorry?"

"I should've told you, so they didn't have to have people out there looking for them. But I just couldn't bring myself to say it."

"Scoot over," Maggie said. "I'm getting right in the middle between you two."

There really wasn't room for three people in that little RV bed, even if two were small and slight. But Maggie squeezed in anyway.

Meanwhile Rose continued to cry quietly.

"Jean," Maggie said, "have you let any of what you've been through in the last few days catch up with you in any way? I haven't seen so much as a tear from you."

"No ma'am."

"Can you tell me what that feels like it's about?"

"I needed to be strong for Rose."

Maggie turned her head toward the younger girl.

"Rose, do you need your sister not to cry?"

Rose shook her head. "No ma'am. I kinda wish she would."

"You heard her, Jean."

"I'm used to holding stuff in."

"Try just not holding for a while."

They lay together in silence for a time. If Jean ever cried, it was a thing too quiet for Maggie to hear.

———

Next thing Maggie knew it was morning, with the light through the window blinds shining into her eyes. Her back was stiff from the cramped position, and the sleeping girls had her in a death grip. They had their arms and legs wrapped around hers as though they were drowning and Maggie were the only life raft left on the planet.

But at least the dreaded task was behind her.

A movement caught her eye and she turned her head to see the puppy staring at her, wide-eyed, from under the dining table, thumping his tail nervously against the linoleum floor. Apparently Rose had been the last one to fall asleep.

Chapter Seven

Who Has Time to Chew?

"We have grandparents," Jean said.

It felt like the first good news Maggie had heard in days.

They were squeezed in together at the little breakfast table, Rose and Maggie on one side, Jean on the other. They were eating cereal for breakfast. The puppy was still hiding underneath. Maggie could feel him sniffing her ankle.

"Well, that's good to hear. Where do they live?"

"Mobile, Alabama, ma'am. But they're . . ."

Maggie braced for a deal-breaker. They were in a nursing home, or had already been deemed abusive.

"What?" Maggie asked. "They're what?"

"Just kind of . . . old."

"That's not so bad, right? How old are they?"

"My dad was a lot older than my mom. So they're like ninety-something."

"Do they live in a nursing home or some kind of retirement community?"

"No ma'am," Jean said. "They just live in a regular house."

"Write down their address," she said, sliding her prescription pad and a pen across the table.

"I don't think we should go there," Rose said while her sister was writing.

"It's not like we have a lot of choices, genius," Jean said.

"Why don't you think you should go there?" Maggie asked, feeling it was her job to poke around looking for signs of trouble.

"It's not like they love us so much or anything. And I don't think they'd let us bring Sunny."

"Who's Sunny?"

Rose pointed straight down through the table.

"Oh. Him. Well, honey . . . we don't even know yet whether someone owns him. Maybe somebody's looking for him."

"If anybody is," Rose said, "they don't deserve to have him back again, because they don't feed him. Look at him. Dogs don't get that skinny in just a couple days, right?"

"No, that's true. They don't. But maybe he ran off and got lost weeks ago and his owner has been looking for him ever since."

"He told me nobody cared about him," Rose said, staring down into her cereal.

"We have to check, though."

Maggie stuffed the last two bites of her cereal into her mouth at once. Then she pulled her phone out of her pocket, leaned down to nearly floor level, and snapped a photo of the puppy looking terrified.

She stood up, picked up her prescription pad, and texted the photo to Brad with the note: "Please see if anybody is looking for this dog. There must be some kind of database."

"Give me a day or so to work on all this," she told the girls.

As she stepped out into the bright morning, she pretended not to notice Rose slipping her half-full cereal bowl onto the floor under the table.

The sky was a perfect, cloudless blue, and the air felt warm and still. It was almost enough to help Maggie believe the worst of everything was over.

———

"Here," she said to Brad, and handed him the prescription pad. "Good news. They have grandparents."

She had just stepped into the clinic bus. He seemed to be on his way out. He was shrugging on his jacket as he spoke.

"Oh. That works. Anywhere near here?"

"Mobile, Alabama."

"That's not so bad. I'll call social services right now."

"Don't go for a minute. Two things. Before you talk to them . . . one, ask them to see if the grandparents will take the dog."

"What dog?" Brad said.

"The one who's in the RV with them as we speak."

"The one you just told me to put in a database to look for its owner."

"That's the one, and by the time the girls leave we'll know if anybody is looking for him. Highly unlikely though. Just ask if the grandparents can take their dog. Don't make it clear that he wasn't their dog twenty-four hours ago. That doesn't help their case."

"Okay. Not a problem. I'm taking the Bishops' RV into town. Need anything?"

"Let me think," she said.

Through the window she saw the hospital van pull up, and it filled her with dread. And pain. She could already feel the pain of the people who were about to walk into the clinic. And they hadn't even gotten off the bus. The bus hadn't even stopped yet.

"Dog food!" she said suddenly.

She seemed to think of it and say it at exactly the same time.

"What kind of dog food?"

"I . . . don't know. I have no idea. I don't have a dog. He's a puppy, though. I guess get some food that's good for puppies."

"Canned? Or dry kibble?"

"Dry kibble, I would think. It's a hundred times better than what he's been eating, which appears to be nothing."

"Will do," Brad said. "I'll call social services on the way."

He stepped out the door before Maggie could put together an answer. She was watching the van driver help an obviously injured older woman to the door.

Brad stuck his head back in again.

"Wait, what was the other thing?"

"What other thing?"

"You said before I call social services, two things."

"Oh. Right. Tell them I'd prefer it if they didn't take the girls to Alabama for three or four days. However long we're here. I'd like them to remain under medical supervision for the time being."

She looked up to see Alex step into the clinic. From where, she wasn't sure. Maybe breakfast at the Bishops'. John and Lacey were right behind him. In any case, they had all stepped inside just in time to hear that she'd opted to hold the girls longer.

She said—more to Brad, but it was really for Alex's benefit: "Jean said the grandparents are in their nineties. They might be fine at keeping an eye on the girls, or the girls might be fine monitoring their own meds. But I don't really know. I can't see what kind of supervision I'd be releasing them into. If social services wants to come and do a welfare check, that's fine by me. But I'd like them to stay a few more days if I have any say in the situation at all."

"Got it," Brad said.

He stepped out the door just as the older woman patient stepped in. Alex rushed to take her arm and help her up the steps. He and Maggie carefully avoided each other's eyes. Or maybe that was Maggie's imagination. But they knew each other pretty well, so probably not.

———

They took a break for lunch. It was the first day they had done that.

While patients waited in the hospital van, they ate sandwiches that Brad had picked up in town. John had been nice enough to walk out there, check for emergencies, and explain that they were falling behind on eating and sleeping and it was beginning to take a toll.

Maggie sensed that Alex wanted to talk, but she knew he wouldn't draw her out in front of others.

It was Lacey who called her out. Lacey didn't have a lot of internal rules. Either that or she was a rule breaker at heart.

"Why are you really holding on to those girls?"

"For the reasons I stated . . ." Maggie said. But she trailed off a bit at the end, rather than adding a solid period to the sentence.

"And . . . ?"

"And nothing. I'm not sure what kind of care they're going to get when they leave here."

"And isn't that true to some degree with every patient you treat?" Lacey asked.

"Yeah. Maybe. But I don't know those people as well."

Lacey's husband poked her in the ribs with his elbow to get her to stop talking. She did not stop talking.

"That's the part I'm questioning. You sure that's wise? Getting emotionally attached? It's kind of breaking the first rule of medicine."

I thought the first rule of medicine was to care, Maggie thought. *Not to make sure you don't.* But she didn't say it, because she knew what Lacey meant, and it was not an entirely unreasonable point.

"Actually, I think it's something about doing no harm. But let's just say, for the sake of conversation, that it's about keeping my emotional distance. How long have I been breaking the first rule of medicine, Lacey?"

"Well," Lacey said, her mouth full of pastrami sandwich, "I've known you twelve years. But my guess would be . . . from the get-go."

"Right," Maggie said. "From the get-go."

They ate in silence for a few minutes. Maggie was hoping that would be the end of it.

That was not the end of it.

"I just think it might be better not to get too attached."

"Better for me, you mean."

"Maybe better for everyone. I don't know. They just lost their parents. Now they will've had you acting like a mother hen for a week, and then they'll split from you."

"I would think having a mother figure in the interim would be a net plus."

"I think so too," Alex said.

Maggie shot him a grateful glance.

"Look," Maggie said, setting down her sandwich. "Rose is already attached to the puppy. And that's the crucial second loss I don't want the girls to have to bear. If they stay a few days, we can be sure he's really a stray, and then hopefully we can pass him off as having been their dog all along and he can go to Mobile with them. Which doesn't negate the other things I said. But if you're looking for a slight ulterior motive, there you have it."

"Okay," Lacey said. "I figure you know what you're doing."

The statement didn't entirely track, because if Lacey had really felt that way, she likely would never have brought it up. Also, the doubts were not unfounded. Maggie was getting attached to the girls and she knew it. And it might turn out to be a mistake.

———

She walked over to check on them before the patients were invited back into the clinic. She carried the twenty-five-pound sack of puppy kibble on her shoulder.

She had the key to the RV with her, but she knocked on the door to be polite.

"Come in," Jean called.

Maggie stepped inside.

The puppy was up on the bed with the girls, but when he saw her he slithered onto the floor and hid under the table.

"Is that *dog food?*" Rose asked, her voice thick with wonder.

"This is puppy kibble, yes."

She wasn't looking at the girls when Rose bear-hugged her—she was getting a plastic bowl down out of the cupboard—so it surprised her.

"I love you I love you I love you," Rose fairly shouted, holding tightly to Maggie's waist.

So there it was. Just what she'd been warned to avoid. Also just the opposite of what she got at home.

"You're very sweet," she said to Rose, "but I'm just making sure everybody eats." She took a knife out of the drawer and used it to cut the top of the bag. The puppy groveled closer, his nose working the air. "Here's the thing about the dog. We're going to at least take a shot at getting your grandparents to let you bring him. But I want you to act like he's been your dog since he was old enough to wean. If they think you've had time to get attached to him, they might not want to ask you to absorb another loss. I'm figuring let's hurry and fatten him up."

Rose stepped back and looked up into Maggie's face.

"You're the nicest person we ever met," she said.

Maggie felt herself shrink away from the compliment.

She poured kibble into the plastic bowl and set it on the floor. The puppy scrambled in and ate so fast that his motions seemed like all one blur. He ate as though he would be assaulted and relieved of the food in a matter of seconds. He did not appear to chew. He scattered kibble everywhere in his panic, then dashed back and forth catching the spilled pieces with almost comical speed.

"I'm sure your parents were nice people," Maggie said quietly.

"Not like you, ma'am," Rose said.

They fell silent until the pup had finished his food and retreated to his insufficient hiding place under the table.

"Our mom was pretty nice," Jean said. "Most of the time. She was never mean exactly. But when she got scared she just sort of . . .

disappeared. I mean, not really. You could look and see her standing right there. But in another way she was gone. It was like she had a room inside her that she could go into and shut the door. I don't know how to explain it any better than that."

"I get it," Maggie said.

"But I know she loved us. Our dad wasn't really mean or violent or anything, but he just wasn't a very nice person to be around. I'm not sure if he loved us or not."

"I'm sure he did," Maggie said.

"But you never met him," Jean said. "I'm not sure how you'd know."

"I just know it's rare for a parent to have no love for their children at all. It's much more common for them not to know how to show it. In fact, I'd say that last thing is pretty much an epidemic."

"Thank you, ma'am," Jean said. "That's nice to think anyway."

"Can we give him more dog food?" Rose asked, still from a place close to Maggie's side.

"Yes, but give him a chance to digest what he just ate first. We don't want him to get sick. And don't forget to let him out to go to the bathroom."

"Yes ma'am. Thank you so, so much for getting dog food. But . . ."

Several beats passed, and Maggie felt she'd better push a little.

"But what?"

"What if they say they won't take him?"

"Then I'll take him."

That just sat on the RV floor in silence for a while. Maybe a full minute. Everyone seemed surprised—even Maggie, who hadn't known she was about to say it.

"Rose is right, ma'am," Jean said. "You're the nicest person."

———

"I wasn't about to say it in front of the Bishops," Alex said to her in their makeshift beds that night, "but there *is* the one other factor."

"That being . . . ?"

"The fact that those girls are like Willa and Gemma but in Bizarro Backward World."

"Oh. Did I tell you I felt that way? I didn't think I did."

"Not in so many words, but yeah."

"You think I'm making a mistake?"

"I think, unlike Lacey Bishop, I trust you to live your own life, mistakes or not."

"Which doesn't really answer the question."

"Only time will tell, right?"

She lifted up onto one elbow and looked into his face in the dim light.

"I told them I'd take the dog if they don't get to bring him. And I should have asked you first."

"You don't need my permission to get a dog. It's not like we live together."

"Close enough. You're at my house more than you're home."

"I'm just surprised you didn't offer to take all three."

It was a joke, and also it wasn't. Maggie could tell it wasn't because nobody touched the subject beyond that. They just rolled over and tried to get some sleep.

Chapter Eight

Water Stains on the World

In the morning she sat with the girls in the camper, watching them eat. Coaxing the puppy to trust her and come closer. She knew better than to reach out to him so soon.

He was just close enough to sniff her hand when she looked into his eyes and he looked into hers. A shock wave of troubled feelings ran through Maggie, starting as a tingling in her forehead and quickly traveling down to her gut.

"You were right, Rose," she said.

Rose's head came up. She had been staring down into her cereal bowl, shoving spoonful after spoonful into her mouth.

"About what, ma'am?"

"He's never had anybody to care about him."

"Oh, did he tell you that, too?"

"I suppose you could say that."

"It's nice of you to want to make friends with him."

"Well, I figured since there's a chance I might be about to take him home . . ."

The sentence trailed off into silence. The puppy slunk back under the table. Maggie watched the girls exchanging terse, weighted glances, communicating something with their faces and eyes.

When that seemed to fail, they began to chatter at a volume just under a stage whisper. But the RV was not a big enough place to talk without being overheard. Maggie wondered if they knew she could hear them or not.

"Do it now," Rose said to her sister.

"No, not now," Jean said. "When we've been here longer."

"They could take us out of here any minute, Einstein, and then we'll never get to do it."

"I'm embarrassed."

"Then I'll do it."

"No, I can."

"Then what are you waiting for?"

Jean's eyes came up to meet Maggie's.

"Ma'am?"

"Yes?"

"We wanted to give you something."

"Well, that's very sweet," Maggie said. "But I hope you know nothing is necessary."

"We do, ma'am. We do know that. But this is just something we really want to do, and it would mean a lot to us if you'd take it."

The girl rose and walked closer to Maggie. The puppy thumped his tail from under the table.

Jean appeared to hold something clutched in her fist.

She opened her hand wide and Maggie saw a silver locket on a chain sitting on the girl's palm.

"It used to belong to our grandmother," Jean said. "Not the one we're about to go and see. Our good grandmother. The one on our mother's side. The one who died. It has pictures of us inside, because she loved us. She said she wanted to carry us everywhere. I was wearing it when the storm hit, so that's why I still have it. Except for the clothes we were wearing, this is the only thing we used to have that we still do. It got a little water inside so the pictures are damaged some. But you can still tell it's us."

"Are you sure you want to part with it?" Maggie asked.

She took it into her hands. Popped the delicate clasp. Rose and Jean smiled back at her from inside, a slight brown line of water across their faces. Maggie thought the water damage almost added something, since it was a marker of how the whole thing had come to be. But she knew it would sound strange to say it, so she didn't.

"Yes ma'am. Very sure."

"It's a lovely gift. I just don't want you to regret it later. You know. Giving away something so precious."

"No ma'am. We won't. We really want you to have it. So you won't ever forget us."

"Oh, honey. I never would have. I could never. But I gratefully accept the gift, if you're sure."

"Yes ma'am," Jean said. "We're just about as sure as we can be."

Maggie undid the clasp on the chain and reached behind her neck, securing the necklace in place.

"Thank you," she said. "It's lovely. And I'll think of you both every time I see it."

"That's all we ask, ma'am."

"I wish I could stay, but we'll have patients coming soon."

"That's okay, ma'am," Rose said from her spot at the table. "We were all done anyway."

Maggie rose and walked to the RV's door. Jean sat back down at her cereal, which must have been soggy.

Maggie opened the door, then paused.

She looked back at the girls, who looked up at her. Open. Unguarded. Not the tiniest bit jaded.

"You'll be happy again," Maggie said. "I know you can't see it now, but I really believe you will. I don't even know what I base that on, but I really believe it. In the middle of a thing like this it's hard to see beyond it. But time changes a lot of things. You don't have to believe me now. Just remember I said it. Just file it away in the back of your head: You'll be happy again."

The girls looked at each other, then into their cereal bowls for several beats. As if lost in thought.

Then Jean looked up into Maggie's eyes again.

"Thank you for saying so, Maggie," she said.

They returned to eating as the change reverberated through the small space.

Maggie stepped out into the bright sunlight and began to walk back. Then she stopped, pulled her phone out of her pocket, and dialed her ex.

"Dan," she said when he answered.

"How's it going out there?"

"Could be worse. Are the girls still around? Or have they gone off to school already?"

"Last day of school was day before yesterday."

"Oh. Right. They're out for the summer. Boy that came up fast. So, are they around? Can I talk to them?"

"No, they're at the mall."

Maggie listened to the birds as they spoke. They were chattering wildly in the trees over her head. The pressure of home settled back onto her nerves, and she realized it had been an enormous relief to step out from under it for a few days.

"Do they still seem upset?"

"About what?"

"Well, we had a massive fight before I left."

"I think maybe that was more performative than you think it was."

"Maybe," Maggie said, feeling around in whether that was better or worse. "Just tell them I called to see how they were and say hi."

"Will do," Dan said.

But, knowing Dan, he might or might not remember to relay the message.

Maggie clicked off the call and walked back to the clinic bus to face her long day of work.

———

"Hey, good news," Brad said when he saw her step into the bus. "The Bradshaw grandparents agreed to take the girls *and* the dog. They don't really want a dog, but they know the girls are attached to it."

The rest of the team was already there, watching and listening. Almost too intently, Maggie thought. As if awaiting her reaction.

"Him," she said.

"Him who?"

"The dog is a him, not an it."

"Oh. Okay. Fine, whatever. Children and Family Services is coming out today."

Maggie felt it like something hitting her belly at a great velocity.

"Today? I said I wanted the girls for a few more days."

"You said you wanted them as long as we're here. We're thinking of rolling out tomorrow. The hospital expects to be under capacity by then. I don't know if a social worker is actually going to *take* them today. But someone's coming. You can talk to them yourself when they get here."

"Fine," Maggie said, and pulled on a scrubs top over her sweater.

But it wasn't fine.

Lacey Bishop seemed to read her mind. She hovered over Maggie's station, clucking her tongue slightly.

"You wanted more time with those girls," she said. "I know."

"Not really something I want to talk about right now, Lacey."

She looked out the window to see two cars waiting. No hospital bus. Apparently the hospital had stopped sending a bus and just started telling stray patients where to find them. Another sign that their time here was winding down. Another painful twist to her already knotted belly.

"This is new," Lacey said, and reached out to touch the locket.

Maggie instinctively flinched away.

"It was a gift," she said.

"Should I even ask from whom?"

"No, Lacey! No, you should not!"

It came out much louder and angrier than Maggie had intended, and it drove Lacey back a step.

Seconds later Alex appeared, gently holding Lacey by the shoulders and steering her back toward her own station.

"I know when Maggie is overwhelmed and needs some time to process," he said. "And this is definitely one of those times."

He looked back over his shoulder at Maggie, and she mouthed the words *Thank you.*

Then the door opened and patients came in.

———

Maggie was treating an older man with a badly infected scraped knee when the social worker arrived. She was deeply involved in her work and didn't notice the woman coming through the door.

Her first clue was hearing Brad say, "Oh you'll definitely want to talk to Dr. Blount about that. She's pretty much taken the girls under her wing."

Maggie stayed true to her habit of not taking her eyes off the patient until the treatment was done.

When she had him properly bandaged up, his baggy pant leg rolled back down and a bottle of Cipro in his hand, she turned her attention to the social worker.

"I'm Dr. Blount," she said. "I'm sorry to keep you waiting."

"Evie Moskowitz," the woman said. "And no worries."

Maggie stood, and they walked outside together. The day was muggy and bright. The social worker was short and slight, with long, curly brown hair. She wore a smile, but her eyes looked worn down. Maybe even beaten down. Exhausted.

Maggie pointed to Alex's and her RV, and they walked side by side in the dappled shade.

"I hope this is okay," Maggie said, feeling unsure for the first time.

"You hope what is okay?"

"Having them in the RV. It's a bit less . . . conventional than a hospital room."

"Under normal circumstances," the social worker said, "sure. It would be odd. But after a hurricane like that one, nothing is normal. The hospital has no beds, and minors are unattended in those huge makeshift shelters. Normally I wouldn't take a day off work and drive two children to Mobile. I'd just call the grandparents and ask them to come claim the girls. But they don't drive anymore, and somebody has to get the girls somewhere. We're all doing the best we can, right?"

"That's a good way to look at it."

"Have you told them they get to take their dog?"

"I haven't seen them since then, no. If those are the first words out of your mouth I'm sure they'll be your biggest fans."

She opened the door to the RV. The girls were sitting at the table, their heads close. Talking about something, from the look of it. They blinked at the new visitor, but it was hard for Maggie to match an emotion with their faces. They looked calm, almost accepting. But Maggie could feel their resistance and fear.

The puppy crawled around in a circle under the table, pressing his face into a corner. Maggie thought if he could will himself right through the side of the RV, he would.

"Hi girls," the social worker said. "I'm Evie Moskowitz from Children and Family Services."

The girls only sat in a slightly stunned silence.

"I have some good news," Evie continued. "Your grandparents are going to let you bring your dog."

"Oh, that's great!" Rose said.

Since Rose hadn't spoken to Maggie until they'd known each other for a day or more, Maggie knew it meant a lot. Either they were coming up through the worst, most paralyzing phase of their trauma, or the dog just meant that much. More likely a combination of the two factors.

"Oh my, he's so thin," Evie said.

Jean opened her mouth to speak, but no words came out. Rose didn't even try.

Maggie decided to jump in to save them.

"They told me the puppy had worms and it was hard to talk their parents into paying for a vet visit. He's dewormed now, though. He just needs to gain back the weight he lost."

Maggie could see and hear both girls restart their breathing at the same time. She hoped it was less obvious to the social worker, who crouched down, looking at the dog.

"But I don't mean to speak for you girls," Maggie added. "I shouldn't do that."

The girls both shot her ridiculously grateful glances. Meanwhile Maggie marveled at how easily a lie slips out when it's for the benefit of someone who really needs a break.

"Just what she said," Jean told the social worker. "He's fine now."

"He was traumatized by the storm," Evie said. "Wasn't he?"

"Yes ma'am," both girls said, more or less at once.

"Unfortunately I'm seeing a lot of dogs acting this way right now. And people. Okay then. Dr. Blount, if you don't mind I'll sit down with just the girls and get some information, and let them know what to expect. And I'll start a file on them."

"Sure," Maggie said. "I'll be in the clinic. When do you think you'll leave?"

"Tomorrow morning."

"*Tomorrow morning?*" Rose blurted out. Then she clapped a hand over her mouth, as though she hadn't meant to say it. To say anything.

"I thought we got to stay longer," Jean said quietly.

"That's what I was thinking, too," Maggie said. "I thought I wanted to keep you under observation a little longer. But the hospital can handle the flow of patients now, so we'll probably roll out of here tomorrow and head home. I'll let you three talk."

Maggie stepped outside and almost headed for the clinic bus. But there were no cars beside it—or anywhere in sight—other than the social worker's minivan. And through the clinic bus's big windows Maggie could see her four colleagues sitting in a circle, resting or chatting or both.

Instead she sat on the fold-down outside steps of the RV and waited.

While she listened to the wind and the birdsongs, she gently attempted to process what she'd just felt from the girls. They seemed hesitant to move on, much the same way Maggie felt torn over letting them go. Did that mean they had bonded to her in return? And did that mean Lacey had been right all along, and she had only set them up for another loss? Or was it just the most basic and unavoidable human hesitation in response to change?

Or—and this was the most troubling idea—did they have doubts about their grandparents? Maggie remembered Jean calling her late maternal grandmother "the good one." Maggie hadn't dwelled on it much at the time, but one could read into that assessment.

It seemed like she had only been ruminating on the situation for two or three minutes, but the door of the RV opened and Maggie jumped up to allow the social worker to step out.

"I'll be back for them in the morning," she said.

The two women stood a few feet apart, and Maggie couldn't help noticing that the other woman kept her eyes cast down toward the dirt.

"Are you satisfied that they seem okay?" Maggie asked.

"But that's your department."

"I meant emotionally."

"Oh. Well . . . how much okay does one expect, considering their current situation? They had nothing but good things to say about you. You made them feel very safe."

"I'm glad I could," Maggie said.

They stood motionless for several seconds. Evie still had her gaze cast down. It took Maggie a second to tap into the other woman's feelings and understand why.

"You feel their pain, don't you?" Maggie asked.

The social worker's eyes came up to meet hers briefly. "The Bradshaw girls?"

"All of them."

Evie turned her head, gazing off toward the clinic bus and her own vehicle.

"I try not to," she said.

It was a flat statement, delivered with very little apparent emotion.

Evie didn't say how successful she tended to be. Then again, she didn't need to. It was all right there in the single sentence.

Chapter Nine

When Your Mind Is Transparent

When Maggie arrived back inside the clinic, there was Mexican food on one of the counters. A lot of it. Maggie helped herself to two tacos and set several aside for the girls. She did not ask where the food had come from. She was tired and hungry and just wanted to enjoy it.

She sat in the circle, balancing the paper plate of food on her lap.

"Lacey, I owe you an apology," she said.

Lacey's gaze shot up to meet Maggie's. It looked surprised.

"For . . . ?"

"I was short with you before."

"Oh, that? Oh, honey. Don't give that another thought. We're all on edge after a few days out in the field. And besides, I really am a pain in the ass, and don't for a minute think I don't know it."

"Preach," John said quietly around a mouthful of burrito.

"Hey," Lacey shot back. "You stay out of this. *I* can say it. *You* can't."

———

Maggie brought the girls two tacos each. She couldn't help noticing that they seemed unusually subdued.

"You okay?"

They nodded, but did not speak.

Maggie slipped her prescription pad and a pen out of her pocket and wrote her full name and phone number on it. She set it down on the table and slid it until it rested between the girls. They stared down at it but said nothing.

"We'll save our goodbyes for the morning," Maggie said. "But I wanted you to have this. If you're ever in trouble, or unsure, or not getting something you really need at your new home, I hope you'll give me a chance to help."

For a moment, there was only silence.

Then Jean reached out for the paper and slipped it into her shirt pocket.

"You've been so kind," she said. "I don't know what to say that's good enough to thank you. We're not gonna bother you unless it's something really important, but it's a nice feeling to have that. Thanks. And thanks for the tacos. They look really good."

"Try to get some sleep tonight," Maggie said.

And she walked out and left them on their own.

———

When Maggie woke in the morning it was light. Full-on light. Which meant it was much later than she normally slept.

Alex and the Bishops were sitting in their circle of chairs, eating breakfast. Talking in a whisper. Brad was nowhere to be seen.

Maggie blinked at her watch. It was nearly eight o'clock.

"Whoa," she said loudly, and everybody turned to look. "How did I sleep so late?"

"We figured you needed it," Lacey said, "so we just left you alone."

"I need to go say goodbye to the girls."

She sat up and swung her legs over the side of the makeshift bed. But before she could get to her feet, Alex was there in front of her. *Right* in front of her. Blocking her way, in fact.

"I'm sorry, Maggie," he said.

"What about, hon?"

"They're already gone."

"What?" Maggie bellowed. She hadn't meant it to come out as a shout, but it did anyway. She purposely lowered her voice and composed herself. "Why didn't you wake me?"

"It was already too late. We all slept until at least seven, and when I got up they were already gone."

———

Maggie stood alone in the RV, staring at the bed where the girls had recovered for days.

They had clearly done their best to leave the place in order. The sheets had been rolled up into a bundle, as if the girls had known the bedding would go straight into the laundry but hadn't been sure where the laundry might be kept. The pillowcases had been removed and must have been bundled in with the sheets. The blankets had been folded into neat squares and stacked at the end of the bed.

And yet, oddly, a paper plate stained with orangey taco grease had been left in the middle of the table.

She heard the soft sounds of someone coming in and felt the RV bounce lightly on its suspension. But she knew it was Alex, so she didn't turn around.

A few seconds later she felt him slide his arms around her waist and set his chin lightly on her shoulder.

"You okay?" he asked quietly near her ear.

"Pretty much. I mean, we did what we could for them, right? We released them to their fate. What else can you do? I just hope it's a good fate."

"They're strong girls."

"Yes they are," Maggie said. They continued to stare at the empty bed for a moment in silence. "Adversity makes us strong. Which makes me wonder why we're always trying to make sure that the people we love won't have any." Another silence. "Look how they cleaned up after themselves. In your wildest dreams can you imagine Gemma and Willa cleaning up like this?"

"No, I think they figure that's what maids are for."

She spun suddenly out of his arms, ready to stop feeling.

"But then they left this greasy plate on the table, which is weird."

She picked it up and hurried toward the trash with it. But before she could drop it in, Alex swept it out of her hand.

"I don't think you want to throw that out," he said.

"Why don't I?"

"It has a note on it."

Maggie held the plate out in front of her face, wondering why Alex had seen this and she had not. In her defense, the note was written in faint, soft pencil. Where the girls had found a pencil, Maggie didn't know. Maybe there had been one in the glove compartment, or one of the many drawers. And maybe, just maybe, it was time for Maggie to stop resisting reading glasses. But she pushed the thought away again for the moment.

On the plate was written, in a shaky hand, "We'll never forget you. Love, Jean and Rose."

Rose had obviously written her own name. The penmanship was different from the rest of the note.

Doing her best to feel nothing, Maggie carefully tore the paper plate, separating the words from the grease spots and throwing the non-note portions in the trash. She slid the note into the pocket of her sweater.

"I guess we should get ready to go," she said, purposely dragging her mind and heart back into the moment. "What all do we have to do?"

"Tons," Alex said. "We have to pack up everything that moves in the clinic, unless Brad gets back from wherever he is to do it for us. We have to go by the hospital and do some paperwork. We'll be lucky to get out of here before lunch."

———

It was a little after one in the afternoon when Maggie's cell phone rang. They had been on the road for nearly an hour, with Alex driving.

Maggie stared at her phone for a second or two. It was an unknown number. The area code seemed to belong to the part of Louisiana they had just left.

She picked up the call.

"Hello?"

"Ma'am?"

It was clearly Jean. Jean was clearly sobbing.

"Honey, what? Where are you? What's wrong?"

"We're on our way back to Lake Charles with the social worker."

"Why? What happened?"

"She wouldn't leave us there. They're gonna put us in a foster home, and we can't take Sunny. Will you still take Sunny? You told us you'd take him."

"Let me talk to the social worker, honey." In the silence that followed she said to Alex, "Find a place to pull over, love, okay? We've got problems."

A full minute later she heard Evie Moskowitz on the line.

"Dr. Blount?"

"Yes. What happened? Why can they not stay with their grandparents?"

"I had to make a judgment call," the woman said. "I have to consider the safety of the girls. The grandmother is suffering from dementia. Quite advanced. The grandfather seems like a nice man, and his mind is sharp enough, but he's just so physically frail. I don't even see how he can take care of himself, let alone his wife. Honestly, Dr. Blount, the situation is so bad that I called social services in Mobile to get that elderly couple a social worker of their own. I'm not at all sure they should be living alone. I think it would have been borderline elder abuse to drive away and leave those two to fend for themselves."

Maggie sighed deeply. Through the windshield she saw that Alex had pulled off the highway and stopped on the street near the end of an off-ramp. She had not in any way registered those movements earlier. In her peripheral vision she could see him watching her, as though trying to glean bits of the social worker's words from Maggie's reaction.

She clicked the call onto speaker.

"Are the girls having to hear all this?" she asked Evie.

"No. We're at a highway rest stop. I stepped out of the car to talk to you."

"Oh. Okay. Good. Now what?"

"We're hoping you haven't left yet, because they can't go into foster care with a dog. They're practically hysterical thinking what will happen to the dog if you've left already."

"Hang on," Maggie said.

She covered the speaker of the phone and looked at Alex, who looked back. Alex sighed and began the process of turning under the highway toward the opposite on-ramp.

"We're coming back for the dog," Maggie said into the phone.

"Oh thank goodness. The girls will be so relieved. I hope you hadn't gone far."

"Doesn't matter," Maggie said. "Talk to me about what happens now with the girls."

"We'll have to find them a foster placement."

"Which will be extra hard after a disaster of that magnitude."

"Of course it will. But you can count on us to see that they have some kind of roof over their heads."

Maggie winced at the mental picture. *Some kind of roof.*

"Go tell them I'm taking the dog so they can relax. We'll meet you back at that same campground. It'll take us an hour to get back."

"We're only half an hour out of Mobile, so I'm afraid we'll keep you waiting."

"Whatever," Maggie said. "We'll see you."

And they both clicked off the call.

She looked over at Alex, who did not look back.

"I'm sorry about this," she said.

"It's okay."

"Is it?"

"It's not exactly convenient, but it's no different from what I would have said."

They drove in silence for an awkward length of time. Nearly the whole hour. Maggie was lost in thought, mentally drowning in plans she talked herself into and back out of in rapid progression. But she did not feel ready to share those thoughts with Alex.

Alex knew her well, though. In time he broke the silence with a statement that made her think he was listening to the inside of her head.

"I know what you're thinking," he said.

"Do you? I'm not even sure *I* do."

But that was not entirely true. The direction of her thoughts was not clear and sure, but she at least knew what thoughts they were.

"Four girls is an awful lot to have on your plate."

"Oh," Maggie said. "Then you really do know what I'm thinking."

———

"Stay here with the girls, please," Maggie said to Alex when the dog and his half-full bag of puppy kibble had been loaded into the RV. "I want to talk to the social worker alone."

"Sure, no problem," Alex said.

Maggie gently took a bit of the fabric of Evie's sleeve and pulled her off into a spot under a stand of trees. The day was muggy and warm, and the social worker's face looked hard and braced, as if she had already decided she would not like what Maggie had to say.

"Talk to me about fostering when it's interstate," Maggie said.

She watched Evie's face change. Watched it soften and open.

"Are you thinking about fostering the girls yourself?"

"Maybe. I don't know. Don't say anything to them yet, okay? Because I don't know. I have to go home and talk to my own daughters. I'm sure they'll hit the ceiling, and I haven't decided how much to let that influence me. In some ways they'll have a fair complaint, but it's one we just may have to work through. I have to start by at least seeing if it's possible. From your standpoint, I mean."

"Oh, it's definitely possible. It happens all the time after a big disaster. People all over the country hear about orphaned children and want to take them in. There's a process you have to go through. A home course of training. Usually we require that the prospective foster family come out and meet the child, but since the girls are known to you . . . the Louisiana agency and the agency that's local to you would have to sign off on the arrangement, but I don't really anticipate any problems there. But we can find them some kind of temporary placement while you figure all this out. I know it's a big decision."

"It is," Maggie said.

But she had already decided, and she could feel it.

"But I have a feeling you already know what you want to do," Evie said. "If you think you're sure enough, tell them you're going to try. Not that you know it will work out, but just that you'll try. Yes, they'll be disappointed if it doesn't work out. But by that time they'll be used to their placement and far less terrified. This is the worst moment for them. They have no idea what to expect. Give them something to hope for at least. And it'll let them know you at least care enough to make that effort. Everybody needs something to hope for. It'll help them get through the next few weeks, and those are always the hardest."

———

"I'm really happy we get to say goodbye proper," Rose said.

Maggie resisted the temptation to correct her grammar.

They were sitting at a picnic table under gently swaying branches. The girls sat on the other side of the table from her, their faces lined with a fear they seemed to be carefully strapping down and holding inside. Maggie watched the shadows cast by leafy branches swaying back and forth over the scene.

Before she could answer, Jean broke open like a trapdoor and began spilling words. Lots and lots of words, all tumbling over themselves too fast.

"We wanted to say goodbye, ma'am. We told the social-worker lady it was really important, but you were all sleeping. Rose wanted to wake you up but I said no because I figured you were all working so hard these last few days and you needed all the sleep you could get. I just wanted to wait till you woke up on your own, but the social-worker lady, she said we didn't have that much time. We had to get going to Mobile. I sure hope you're not mad that we left without saying goodbye, it's just—"

Maggie placed her hand over Jean's hand, which jumped slightly at the touch. But it did stop the flow of words.

"Honey, nobody is mad at you. You don't exactly have control over the direction of your lives right now."

"We're kids," Rose said. "When do we ever have control?"

"We're not kids," Jean said.

"We're kids enough that we don't have control."

"Anyway, I sure wish she'd left us in Mobile. We could've taken care of Grandma and Grampy and we just have no idea what's going to happen to us now. She said some kind of foster home but we can't really close our eyes and picture what that means."

"I can," Rose said. "It means we go live with strangers."

"Maybe," Maggie said.

That just sat in the air for a few beats, and neither girl seemed to dare address it. Maggie took her hand back and sat up straighter on the bench.

"I wasn't even going to tell you this, because I'm not sure if it's going to work out or not, and the last thing I want to do with you girls is get your hopes up and then disappoint you. But Evie said it would give you something to hope for, and if it didn't work out at least you'd be used to the new place by then. I really hope this is not a mistake. But I'm going to look into the possibility that . . ."

Maggie stalled, doubting the wisdom of telling them. But the social worker knew about such things, right? She was the social worker. Then again, not everybody who worked in a given field performed their job with wisdom and good judgment.

But Maggie had to go in one direction or the other, and she had already gone awfully far in this one.

"That what, ma'am?" Jean asked, clearly nervous with the waiting.

"That maybe your foster home could be . . . my house."

Maggie was met with absolute silence. A kind of stunned-feeling silence.

Then Jean said, "Are you saying *you* would take us in?"

"I'm going to look into it. To giving you a home until you're old enough to be on your own. Which is just a handful of years. But I have to warn you. I have two daughters just about your age. And I don't expect them to like the idea. They might not be the kindest housemates if they're mad about it. And I'm pretty sure they'll be mad about it."

"I can't imagine them being mean if you raised them," Jean said.

"I'm not at all sure I raised them as well as you think I did."

"Still, if we had you, and the nice nurse man, and each other, and Sunny . . . I'm not sure what could bring us down. That sounds like heaven to me, ma'am."

Rose jumped in suddenly. "We'd have Sunny, right? When you said you'd take him, you meant to keep, right? Not to give away? I was afraid to even ask."

"I meant to keep."

A brief silence. The girls seemed to be soaking in the new possibility for the direction their lives might take.

"I think the social worker was right, ma'am," Jean said. "We were feeling so lost and like we had no idea what was coming next, and now I feel like something great could be right around the corner. And if it doesn't work out, well . . . maybe I shouldn't speak for my sister but I'm gonna do it anyway . . . if it doesn't work out we'll still love you forever for at least wanting to try. That's more than anybody's done for us in as long as I can remember."

"That's more than anybody's done for us ever," Rose said.

"Your parents kept you and cared for you."

"That was their job," Rose said. "It's not your job, but I'm not gonna argue."

———

Maggie popped awake in the passenger seat. It was dark outside the RV's windows. She only sat a moment, feeling the familiar humming vibration of the road under their wheels.

She turned her head around to check on the puppy, who was curled up under the table. He looked asleep, but he seemed to feel her gaze land on him. He looked back at her in the dim light and tapped his tail submissively.

"You still okay to drive?" she asked Alex.

"For another couple of hours, yeah."

She looked out the window at the highway shoulder streaking past, even though there was nothing much to see in the dark. Just a white line glowing in their headlights, but she watched it. For how long, she wasn't sure.

"Am I crazy, Alex?"

Alex smiled a crooked and slightly sarcastic smile. It was one she'd seen before and always enjoyed. It made a spot in her belly feel warmer.

"Absolutely yes," he said. "But in a very high-quality way."

Chapter Ten

Two Out of Five Ain't Great

They drove straight through, trading off driving instead of stopping over for a night.

When they arrived home it was the middle of the following night. They unloaded a few things from the RV, but only what couldn't wait until morning. The food from the fridge, the laundry. Things like their phones and laptops, which they might need.

As Maggie was locking up the RV for the night, Alex came back down the walk quickly and spoke up.

"Aren't you forgetting something?"

"Am I? I give up. What am I forgetting?"

He waited a moment on the dark sidewalk, apparently thinking she'd get there on her own. But she was just so tired. Her brain just would not stretch.

"Here's a hint," he said. "It has four legs and low self-esteem."

"Oh," she said, and smacked herself on the forehead. Harder than she'd meant to.

She unlocked and opened the RV's door again and called to the dog. Quietly, so as not to disturb her neighbors.

"Sunny, come."

She heard the slight tap of his tail, but he did not come.

"Sunny, come!" she said, a little louder.

"He might not know that command," Alex said. "He might not even know his name is Sunny."

"What do I do with him? Should I just leave him with some food and water and let him stay in the RV for the first night?"

She was hoping he would say yes. Exhaustion was overtaking her, and her uncertainty over the problem felt like too much to cope with in the moment.

"He might need to go out in the night. We might wake up to a mess in there. I would think he'd be better off in the yard."

"But there's no doghouse or any type of shelter back there."

"It's warm enough weather, though. Tell you what. You go get a couple of those old blankets out of the garage and I'll coax him out."

When she got into the yard with two of the blankets that had been saved for use as drop cloths, the dog was hovering in a corner of the fence in the dark. Alex had the hose going and seemed to be washing off his arms and shoes.

She made a nest of the blankets and then joined Alex near the hose.

"He was more afraid of me than I realized," Alex said quietly. "He wouldn't come to me, so I made the mistake of trying to pick him up. He got so scared he peed all over everything. The RV. Me. Everything. The RV I'll deal with in the morning. You can get him some food and water and I'll head straight for the shower. I'm so ready for this night to be over."

"Amen," Maggie said.

———

They lay awake for the better part of half an hour, listening to his plaintive whimpers at the sliding glass door to Maggie's bedroom. It wasn't until he tipped his head back and let out a full-volume, blood-freezing howl that Maggie jumped out of bed and shrugged into her robe.

"Clearly I hadn't really thought this through," she said on her way to the door.

"I'm not sure thinking would have helped much. These are just the problems you get into when you bring a new dog home."

"I meant the decision to agree to take him in the first place."

"Oh," he said. Just as she threw the door open, he added, "It might set a bad precedent to let him in when he howls."

But by the end of the sentence the door was already open and the puppy was skittering under the bed.

"Not sure what choice I had," she said, listening to him repeatedly thump the bottom of the bed frame as he tried to get comfortable under there. "The neighbors want to sleep as much as I do. Well, maybe not as much as I do. I'm not sure anybody on the planet can beat me in that contest tonight. They can only hope for a tie. But the neighbors want to sleep, and since they're not the ones who were foolish enough to arrive home in the middle of the night with an almost entirely undomesticated puppy, they probably deserve a chance to try."

She threw off her robe, tossed it at the end of the bed, and climbed back under the covers. But now she was agitated, which was not conducive to sleep.

"He's probably not housebroken," she said to Alex, who also seemed not to be anywhere near the edge of sleep.

"Not likely."

"I worry for the Persian rug. So expensive. So much history. It was my grandmother's."

"So valid, as worries go," Alex said.

"You think he did whatever he needed to do while he was out in the yard?"

"Hard to know."

"Maybe he should sleep in the bathroom," she said.

"But to get him into the bathroom you'd have to get him out from under the bed. And as my experience has so unfortunately proven, when you go to grab him, he's going to pee everywhere."

"Maybe I could coax him out with food," she said.

"But he just ate his fill out in the yard."

"I'm not sure Sunny has a fill. Maybe he'll find it sometime in the next year or two, when the memory of all that starving begins to fade some. You think the girls will be happy to see a dog?"

"That's a tough call," he said. "A real crapshoot."

"They used to ask me for one all the time."

"They probably wanted to go pick out something pretty at the breeder. A purebred Afghan hound or something."

Maggie sighed deeply. All her resistance to this current crossroads in her life seemed to flow out with the sigh. If her life sucked in this moment, it just sucked. She had no energy or will to do anything about it before a good night's sleep.

"That sounds like my girls all right," she said. "I'm going to go to sleep. I'm going to hope for the best for the rug. I guess that's what professional rug-cleaning services are for."

"I promise to sleep with my fingers crossed," Alex said.

———

When she woke in the morning to light streaming through the curtains, Alex was still asleep. She didn't have to raise her head and look at the rug. She could smell it. But she raised her head anyway, just to absorb the damage. She saw a loose, barely shaped mound of stool in the corner of the rug, half on the light-colored fringe and half on the hardwood floor. It was surrounded by a yellowish puddle.

She dropped her head back onto her pillow, feeling defeated.

Alex stirred.

Before he even opened his eyes, she saw his nose working the air.

"Oh, that can't be good," he said.

From under the bed, the puppy thumped his tail nervously at the sound of a human voice.

"Oh, it's not."

"Tell you what. You go make coffee, and I'll clean this up and roll up the rug and I'll take it by the cleaners on my way home."

"You're a prince. I swear I don't know what I'd do without you."

But for the moment, nobody moved. Several seconds ticked by. It might even have been a minute.

Then Maggie said, "This is how much it turns our lives upside down to bring home a dog, and here I am thinking of adding two human girls to that equation. And I'm not the least bit sure I'm even doing a decent job with the two human girls I've already got. I feel pretty silly right now for thinking I was up to this task."

Alex seemed to mull that over for a moment before answering.

"Just to play devil's advocate, though, the two girls you're thinking of fostering know how to live in a house. They know how to be someone's daughters. They're not even young children. They're mostly grown. From what I've seen of you with Jean and Rose, they seem to support you more than they draw from you. The dog is new to all this. I think we need to cut him some slack. And you need to cut yourself some slack for taking this on. The first night with a new puppy is never easy, but that doesn't mean it won't work out in the long run. Dogs tend to, if you stick with them."

Maggie sighed, and ran her fingers through the curly hair that spilled down over his forehead. She trusted him to recognize it as a gesture of appreciation.

"Nice to know that two of the five individuals in question know how to be what we want them to be. I'd better get up and get this day started. Dan will be bringing the girls back soon, and I need to be full of coffee and wide awake for what's about to follow."

———

Willa was stomping through the living room when she saw the dog through the huge plate-glass window. She stopped cold and stared for a worrisome length of time. The dog stared back meekly.

Maggie leaned in the kitchen doorway and watched her daughter stare. She wasn't sure where Gemma was—maybe still unloading her things from Dan's car—but in that moment she wasn't anxious to multiply her problems by two.

"What. The hell. Is that," Willa said. No part of her words sounded like a question.

"I'm tempted not to dignify that with an answer," Maggie said, her voice as even as possible.

"I don't deserve an answer to a basic question?"

"I don't feel it was a straightforward question. It felt disingenuous. You know that's a dog. I think a more honest and direct question would be why he's here, not what he is. And that would be a valid thing to wonder. But by phrasing it the way you did, you made sure your judgment came through, which I didn't especially appreciate. Yes, I realize it's a big change, and I realize you're probably feeling like I should have run it by you first, and there's certainly validity to that. But it just came up, the need to take him, and I'm asking you to please accept him. You always wanted a dog."

Willa had not moved, but her heavy leather duffel, with its long strap slung over her shoulder, had drifted down until it was resting on the ground. She was wearing a wildly colored knee-length sweater that Maggie had never seen before. Dan, or Dan and his new girlfriend, must have taken her shopping, or given her money to spend at the mall.

"I wanted a purebred Pomeranian puppy from Jessa Northrup's mother's breeding dog. I don't know what that thing is. A dirty, scruffy no-breed from the look of it."

"I wonder sometimes," Maggie said, pushing off from the door-frame and walking closer to her daughter, "if people think about how it sounds when they say things like that about a dog. Like only pure bloodlines make for value. Imagine if that was a person you were talking about."

"Well it's not. And nobody thinks like that. Nobody's like that. Besides, all I'm saying is that he's ugly."

Maggie felt it as a little stab, and she wasn't sure if that meant she was attached to Sunny already. Or maybe it just meant she was attached to the young woman passing the judgment, which was a given. Sunny was not ugly. Not at all. He just wasn't fancy-looking, and his coat was not a pretty color.

"Imagine—again—if that was a person you were talking about when you say only beauty has value."

Willa turned her hard gaze onto her mother for the first time since arriving home and opened her mouth to argue. She stopped, and stared at a spot near Maggie's collarbone.

"What is that? That heart thing around your neck? You never had that before."

"It was a gift from a patient."

"Oh. Kind of old-fashioned looking."

"That's one of the things I like about it."

Willa opened her mouth again to speak. Before she could, Gemma came trudging through the living room, dragging her heavy suitcase across the rug. She stopped cold when she saw the dog through the window.

He had shimmied a little closer now, which Maggie found encouraging. He was lying on the mat in front of the sliding glass patio door in a straight sphinx position, his gigantic hips poking up above his back.

"What the hell is that?" Gemma said.

"Mom says it's a dog," Willa said, "but I'm not so sure. She says we always wanted a dog so she figured we'd want *that*."

"I wanted one of those puppies that were half white Siberian husky and half wolf."

And that was just what we needed to be keeping around the house, Maggie thought. She thought it in that moment, and she'd thought it back when Gemma had first asked. *A nice wolf is just what we need to round out this challenge.*

"I want to sit down with you girls and talk about some changes," Maggie said.

"Well, duh," Willa said. "We're living with *that* now."

"He's not part of the changes I had in mind."

"There's *more?*" Gemma fairly shrieked, a metallic edge to her voice that actually hurt Maggie's ears.

"Yeah," Maggie said. "There's quite a bit more. In fact, you should probably sit down."

———

It would be a wild understatement to say that the family meeting didn't go the way Maggie had imagined. She was braced for a lot of yelling and histrionics. She expected every sentence of her explanation to be interrupted.

Instead she was met with only silence. Weirdly abnormal silence. She paused between sentences and heard only silence. She rattled on for five or six sentences longer than necessary because the silence felt so unbalancing.

Finally she stopped, having said everything that needed saying. She listened to all that nothingness and just waited.

Nothing happened.

She glanced at the girls' faces, which looked absolutely blank. Willa was blinking too much.

"I think . . . ," Maggie began, "that this is the part where one of you says something."

But for several seconds there was only silence. And a lot of blinking.

"You're risking my taking your lack of objection as acceptance," Maggie said.

"Is this one of those things," Willa said, her voice uncharacteristically tentative, "where you tell a person something that isn't real just to shake them up and scare them?"

"No," Maggie said. "It's real."

Gemma opened her mouth suddenly.

"This is a three-bedroom house," she said, sounding desperate.

"Yes. It is. Having bought it, and lived in it for seven years, I know that about it."

"Where do you figure you'll put two extra girls?"

"In the long run," Maggie said, "I thought I'd bring in the contractor to fix up the basement. I mean, really fix it up. With nice interior walls, and heat and air-conditioning, and a new bathroom. And there's plenty of room down there for two bedrooms. But that'll take months."

"And in the short run?" Willa asked.

"Not everyone will have their own room."

"You want us to share a room with *strangers?*" Gemma shrieked.

It was the closest anyone had come to the reaction Maggie had expected.

"No. I want you to share a room with each other for a few months."

More silence. The girls looked at each other for an extended time. They seemed to be having a conversation using nothing but their eyes.

Then she saw Willa nod slightly to her sister.

"We're going to go live with Dad," she said calmly, turning her gaze to Maggie. "We've been talking about it anyway. This decides it."

"You said you hated it there."

"We hate it here more."

Maggie let that sit for a moment while she settled on her reaction.

Under no circumstances could she allow herself to change course based on the threat. If she did, the threats would never go away. It would be one thing after another. Also, she didn't expect the move would last. Maybe the best bet would be to let them go. Let them see that they wouldn't get everything they wanted there, either.

It hurt to think of them out of the house, but she didn't figure it was wise to let that knee jerk of pain influence her decision.

"Well, I'll miss you. A lot. And I'll be hoping you change your mind and come back. In the meantime I don't want to feel like we're no longer a family, so I'll insist on—at very least—Sunday dinner here every week." *And maybe some family counseling,* Maggie thought. She decided not to spring that on them just yet. "But if that's really what you want . . ."

Both girls looked positively dazed. It dawned on Maggie that it had never occurred to either one of them that she might call their bluff.

In time they stomped up to their rooms with no more words exchanged.

Maggie made herself a cup of tea and tried to let the prickly daggers of emotion settle out. Then she found Evie Moskowitz's card in her purse and called on her cell phone.

"Sorry to get you on a weekend," she said, "but start filling me in, please, on what I'll need to do to get the process started."

———

"How does that *feel* to you?" Alex asked her in bed that night.

"Terrible," she said. "I feel like a terrible mother. Like a failure. Like I'm losing my babies. But I just can't imagine the alternative is any better. They're faking me out. I know they are. They didn't think I'd call their bluff. They hate it at Dan's. They'll come back. I just know they'll come back."

"And meanwhile Jean and Rose have a little time to settle in before the great war."

"And I didn't do it on purpose, but we talked about how maybe a shake-up in their lives could shift their direction. And how my mother always says, 'If nothing changes, nothing changes.' Well . . . something changed."

"You can say that again," Alex said.

Maggie heard a tone from her phone. A text. She pulled the phone off the bedside table.

It was from Dan.

"Don't worry," the text said. "It's performative. They'll be back."

Chapter Eleven

The Only Parents Who Don't Worry They're Terrible Parents

When Maggie arrived home from her first day back at her medical practice, there was a moving van in front of the house.

She felt it like something being literally, physically torn out of her belly. Something that belonged there. Something that was trying, hard but unsuccessfully, to hang on.

The front door of the house was standing open.

She stepped inside to see Willa following a beefy mover as he carried two boxes down the hall. Her mood seemed tight and proprietary, as if the big man could not possibly be trusted with her two boxes.

"Family dinner Sunday," Maggie said. "We're clear on that?"

She kept her voice straightforward and unemotional. In other words, she tacitly lied about how she was feeling.

Willa stopped, and the man with the boxes walked on without her supervision.

"Sure, I guess," Willa said. She raked a hand through her long hair, close to her scalp, to sweep it back from her face. "Whatever."

"And I was thinking about counseling."

"Counseling?" Willa asked. She sounded genuinely confused by the word, as if she'd never heard it before.

"Therapy."

"Good," Willa said. "I think you should."

"I meant—"

But her daughter gave her no time to say what she meant.

"Oh, right. I get it. You mean us. You mean *we* have to go. Because *we're* the problem. It couldn't ever possibly be *you*."

"I meant all three of us," Maggie said. "I'm not saying you need to be fixed or I need to be fixed. I mean we need to fix the way we relate to each other. And it means I'll own up to my part of the problems. I would think you'd like the idea. It means you get to tell me everything you can't stand about the way I treat you."

"I'm not sure I believe you," Willa said.

"About which part?"

"The part where you don't think it's all our fault."

Maggie sighed deeply, and felt something deflate inside her.

"It's true, though," she said. "I haven't been the best mom. I've been busy with my practice, and I didn't help you girls as much as I should have after the divorce. I keep wanting to talk more about things, but now you're angry, and your anger backs me down. I should stand up in the face of it and help you more, but somehow I'm failing in that. Over and over."

Willa jumped out of the way of two movers who were crossing paths in the hall.

"Good idea," she said. "About telling you everything I can't stand about the way you treat us. I'll start now. You can't just go out and get two new daughters. You can't just replace us with two other girls. Do you have any idea how that makes us feel?"

"I'm not replacing you," Maggie said. "I'm adding two more children to the family. I know that's a tough concept for the two I've already got, but I just want to go to therapy and work through it."

Gemma appeared suddenly behind her.

"Who *does* that?" she fairly shrieked.

"Actually . . . it's done all the time. Parents—parents of both bio-logical and adopted children—adopt more children. Or give birth to more children. People add new children to the household all the time, and the ones they've got don't tend to like it at first. There's a period of adjustment. I won't even tell you what your sister used to say about you in the first year or so. But she accepts you now."

"Barely," Willa said. "So listen. Mom. We've been asking each other this question a lot, and now we're going to ask you. Do you even care that we're leaving? Because you seem fine with it."

"Honey," Maggie said, "it's killing me."

She expected an angry response, but it never arrived. Instead Willa stared down at the hall carpet and Gemma sniffed the way she tended to do when she was trying not to cry.

"We'll see you Sunday," Willa said.

The girls began to move toward the door.

"You never answered me about the counseling."

The girls stopped.

"What counseling?" Gemma asked her sister.

"She wants all three of us to go."

"Do we have to?"

"No idea," Willa said.

"It doesn't sound like very much fun."

"Oh, I don't know. We get to tell her everything we're mad about."

Gemma spun on her heels in the hallway and looked into Maggie's face. Granted, it was from a fair distance, but Maggie's sore gut was seized with the idea that she was seeing underneath that angry, jaded exterior to a more vulnerable Gemma. That her little girl was still in there somewhere.

"Do we get to think about it?"

"Of course," Maggie said.

Then the two girls walked out the open front door.

Maggie locked herself into her bedroom because she didn't want to cry in front of the moving men.

———

She called Dan's house a couple of hours later, when she had pressed cold, wet washcloths on her eyes for long enough that she felt presentable. Because she had not thought to bring her phone into the bedroom with her when she locked herself in.

She figured the movers were gone. She hadn't heard them lately. But she also figured Alex must be home.

"Already?" Dan said in place of hello.

"I miss the girls. Can I talk to them?"

"Which one?"

"I don't know. Pick one. Both, but it's pretty much got to be one at a time, right?"

"Or I could just put the phone on speaker. Hang on."

Maggie closed herself and her phone back into the bedroom while she waited.

What felt like several minutes later Dan's voice came back on the line.

"They're watching TV and they're not too keen on the idea."

"They won't talk to me?"

"I don't know if I'd go that far. They say they just barely got here, and they want to know why you don't miss them so fast when you're out on the bus."

It was an interesting question, and it stopped Maggie from answering. She did miss them when the team set out on the road, but not usually after a couple of hours. Maybe because she knew their rooms at home were still full of their belongings, and that the girls would be there, living at home, when she got back.

"They're angry," she said, her voice sounding a bit dull to her own ears.

"Gee," Dan said. "Ya think?"

A long silence fell. Maggie thought maybe he wanted the conversation to be over.

"You know," he said, "you could always change course."

"Meaning what?"

"Not foster two more girls."

"They were already angry before that idea came up."

"Oh," Dan said. "Yeah. I guess that's true, isn't it?"

"Just tell them I love them," she said, her voice breaking. Then she hurried off the phone.

———

She found Alex sitting in the backyard, eating a sandwich. The pup sat by his side, waiting for the little scraps of bread Alex was occasionally breaking off and giving to him.

She watched without announcing herself for a time. It filled her with a feeling that at least two someones in her world were getting along, and she needed that feeling.

In time she stepped outside and sat in the chaise longue by his side.

"Interesting choice before dinner," she said.

"I missed lunch. I couldn't possibly have waited. Trust me. I'll still eat. You want to order in?"

"Sure. That sounds easy."

He pulled a piece of turkey out of his sandwich, streaked yellow with mustard, and fed it to the puppy, who jumped for it like a hungry shark.

"You look like you've been crying," he said.

"And there's a reason for that."

"I take it the girls are finished moving."

"Yeah. They're at Dan's."

"You don't have to follow through with this, you know."

"Except . . . except for the fact that I think I do. They need to do better with making adjustments. It's a life skill we all need to be happy.

And you don't help someone learn to make adjustments by seeing to it that there are no adjustments to be made."

"I'm just thinking about your happiness."

"I know you are. I know you always do."

"I trust you to know what you're doing," he said, slipping the dog a piece of bread.

"I wish I trusted *myself* to know what I'm doing. But I'm second-guessing my own parenting a lot. I think I'm going to go ahead and find a therapist and start seeing him myself. Or her, as the case may be. If the girls are willing to join me later, that's good. But either way I'm sure we can find something to work on."

———

MFCC Scarlett Silverman was barely Maggie's age. More likely a little younger. It had been a surprise when Maggie had first met her. She hadn't sounded that young on the phone. It made Maggie vaguely uneasy, as if age were the only determining factor in life experience, and maybe Maggie should be counseling *her*.

She tried to push that thought away again.

She had recounted the background of her situation in quite a bit of detail, and now she found it had left them barely five minutes of session to discuss it. Then again, this was only the first session. Probably these things took time.

"I'm still not sure if the girls are willing to come to counseling with me," Maggie said. "And, if not, I don't know if I can compel them to."

"You can compel them to be in this room with you. But if they're unwilling to participate in therapy, they won't. You can't compel them to be forthcoming in a way that will be helpful to the process."

She was wearing jeans and a blue silk shirt, a very casual look, and she had a truly impressive head of long auburn hair that swept off to one side as if she had commanded it there. It was that natural look that some women could attain by rolling out of bed and others took hours trying to achieve. Maggie wasn't sure which category her new therapist fell into, but she suspected the former.

"In other words, I can lead my two horses to water . . ."

"Something like that," Scarlett said.

"Well. Whether they do or whether they don't, I'm still going to be here. I feel like I'm going to need this."

"And when are the foster girls coming?"

"Remains to be seen. There's a process. Lots of paperwork. At least one home visit. Background checks, I assume. I haven't been given a date yet. But they could definitely benefit from some therapy. One at a time, together, with me. I don't know."

"Maybe all of the above. Are you looking forward to their arrival? Or dreading it?"

"It's scary, but I'm really looking forward to it. But then I feel like maybe I shouldn't feel the way I feel. Maybe I shouldn't enjoy their presence while my own daughters are in exile. Or at least I figure that's the way it seems to them. I don't know. Everything is kind of a sickening whirl in my head these days."

"Sounds like you're doubting your choices," Scarlett said.

"Oh, that comes through, eh?"

"It really does. But it's pretty normal."

"But I might be doubting myself more than is normal," Maggie said.

"You're worried you might be a terrible parent."

"Oh. That comes through, too?"

"Not exactly. I just happen to know that most parents worry they might be terrible parents. Maybe not constantly, but at one time or another. In fact, the only parents I know who never once worry they might be terrible parents are terrible parents. Seems to be related to the Dunning-Kruger effect. People who aren't able to recognize incompetence in themselves never worry. They just figure they're doing great. Which may explain why they're not. They never hold their own feet to the fire to do better. People like you keep holding yourself to a higher standard. That's a good sign."

Maggie sat back in her chair for the first time and felt something almost related to a little smile play at one corner of her mouth.

"Oh, I think we're going to get along just fine," she said.

PART TWO

A DIFFERENT TWO GIRLS

Chapter Twelve

When a Dog Makes a Joke About a Tree

When Maggie first saw them again, they were walking down a long airport hallway toward the baggage-claim area. A middle-aged woman in a flight attendant's uniform was walking with them, smiling and talking. Maggie didn't know if it was an airline rule that the girls be accompanied until they were met by an adult or if they had simply made friends on the plane.

The girls looked up and saw Maggie, both at almost exactly the same time. Their faces lit up like Christmas morning, and they waved wildly.

Maggie waved back.

A spot in her gut was warmed by their greeting, and her mind reacted with guilt. It felt good to be wanted—to have two girls actually look thrilled to see her—and she couldn't help wondering if that made all of this a selfish thing to do.

They ran to her and hugged her, both at once, and the flight attendant waved to Maggie and peeled away.

"We need to get your luggage," Maggie said near the ears of the girls, who were almost as tall as she was.

They stepped back and looked at her with slight confusion.

"What luggage?" Jean asked.

"You didn't check anything?"

"Not sure what we would check," Rose said. "We have these backpacks."

They slipped the shoulder straps off and brought them around in front of themselves and showed Maggie. They were dark blue with a lighter-blue border, about as big as a medium-sized book bag for school.

"That's everything?" Maggie asked, not meaning to sound shocked. She sounded shocked anyway.

"Heck, we thought that was a lot," Rose said. "That social worker took us out and bought us a few things. When we first met you we didn't have anything but wet clothes and that locket Jean was wearing. Oh! You're wearing it. You're wearing that locket we gave you!"

"Of course I am. I love this locket."

"You didn't just put it on because you were about to see us?" Jean asked, sounding painfully vulnerable.

"No, I've had it on every day. Well . . . come on then. We'll go home and get you fed, and let you have a good rest if you need one, and then we'll go shopping. You need to own more than just what fits in those little backpacks."

———

The girls didn't want to talk much on the drive, and Maggie struggled with whether or not to be concerned about that.

She tried to keep some conversation going.

"How was that temporary foster home?" she asked.

Jean was in the passenger seat beside her, Rose in the back. Maggie turned her head slightly to make it clear she was speaking to both of them.

"Foster home?" Rose asked. "You mean where they had us before we got to come here?"

Maggie couldn't imagine what other foster home Rose might think she was referring to, but she only nodded as cheerfully as possible.

"It was okay," Jean said.

"Just okay?"

"Yeah. Pretty much just okay. I mean . . . the lady wasn't mean to us or anything. She gave us a room and food and all that. She was just sort of . . . quiet. She didn't talk to us much. It's like we never really knew what she was thinking."

"Not like *you* at all," Rose added.

More silence fell, and lasted several miles.

"You both seem awfully quiet," Maggie said.

In fact, they seemed somewhere between worried and downright scared, but Maggie wanted to approach the subject gently.

"We're okay," Jean said, staring out the window. Avoiding Maggie's eyes.

"Liar," Rose said from the back seat.

"Talk to me," Maggie said.

Jean turned her face toward Maggie, as if to look into her eyes. But her gaze never made it quite that far. She ended up appearing to address the dashboard.

"We're nervous to meet your daughters," she said.

"Oh. Well, you can put that on the back burner for now. You won't meet them for another week."

Jean briefly met her eyes, then spoke to the dashboard again.

"Where are we gonna be until then?"

"You'll be at home with me. They won't. They'll be at their father's."

"Oh," Jean said. She sounded quite relieved. Surprised, but relieved. "I guess that's nice for us, to have a little time to get used to everything. How much of the time are they at their father's?"

"All the time, except for Sunday dinners."

"I don't understand."

"They live with their father now."

First, only silence. In her peripheral vision, Maggie could see Jean chewing over this new information. Then the girl's eyes flew wide.

"Because of *us?*"

"Because of a lot of problems that started a long time before I met you."

"Were we any of the problems at all?"

Maggie struggled briefly with how much honesty felt appropriate. She noticed her grip had grown abnormally tight on the steering wheel. It made her knuckles look white and translucent.

"There's always a period of adjustment with a thing like this."

"Oh no," Jean said, her head in her hands. "Oh no, oh no. We can't put them out of their *home*. That's not right."

"You didn't put them out of their home. I'd like you to move that thought out of your head right now, and keep it out. They are perfectly welcome in their own home any time they want to come back, and they know it. This was their decision. And they *will* come back. I really believe they will. They're just learning to deal with changes, and other things that don't suit them well."

Everyone was quiet again for several miles.

Then Jean said, "I still feel really bad for them."

"It's kind of you to feel that way," Maggie said. "But I honestly believe we'll work it out."

———

"Sunny!" Rose shrieked. She ran to the sliding glass door, threw it wide, and fell on her knees in the grass in front of the dog. "Sunny, I missed you so much!"

Sunny had a way of showing that he had missed Rose, too. He leaped straight up into the air and then landed on his paws again. Almost to the level of the kneeling girl's head. Over and over and over he jumped. He began to yip, and the yipping turned into cries that sounded almost like a dog shrieking in fear or pain, but it was clear to look at him that he was happy and excited.

"The neighbors are going to think we're stepping on his paws," Maggie said quietly to Jean, who was standing close to her side in the living room.

"I see what you mean. He looks wonderful. You took good care of him."

"Well, I fed him plenty. And Alex and I go out and spend time with him. We haven't had him in the house much, because he's not housebroken. But if you can housebreak him you can have him inside."

Still the dog screamed his excitement in the background.

"Not sure how to go about housebreaking a dog," Jean said. "We were never allowed to have one before."

"I could get you a book on dog training," Maggie said. "Or if that's not enough I could even bring a trainer in."

The yelping calmed. Maggie watched the puppy melt into Rose's arms and settle. When she looked back at Jean, the girl was staring directly into her eyes, her face soft.

"You're just the nicest person," she said. "I'll never know how we got so lucky as to meet you."

Maggie opened her mouth to verbally struggle with accepting such a compliment, but Rose interrupted the moment.

"He got so big!" she called in through the open door.

"Puppies'll do that," Maggie said.

"And you can't even see his ribs! He's really happy here. He told me so."

———

She tried to show them to her girls' bedrooms, but they were having none of it.

"But aren't these your daughters' rooms?" Jean asked, backing up in the hallway as if facing a physical threat.

"But they chose to live with their father."

"But they're coming back. You said yourself they're coming back."

"It's just temporary," Maggie said. She moved into Willa's room, hoping the girls would follow. They stood their ground in the hall. "The long-term plan is to get the basement fixed up into a really nice couple of rooms with a bathroom."

"We don't need two rooms," Rose said. "We never had two rooms."

"Wouldn't you be more comfortable though?"

"Oh no," Rose said. "Not at all. We wake up and talk all through the night. If you gave us two rooms, one of us would just get up and go in with the other."

"Can we see the basement?" Jean asked.

"Well yes. Of course you can. But it's nothing right now. Just a concrete floor with a water heater and a washer and dryer."

"If we had a concrete floor we could let Sunny sleep inside with us," Rose said. "Couldn't we?"

"Yes, I suppose you could. But it's really not a good enough space the way it is now."

"But can we see it?" Jean asked again.

They walked together to the basement stairs and Maggie led them down, stopping to flip on an overhead light. It was a huge, unadorned space that looked cold and unwelcoming to Maggie.

"This is plenty good enough!" Rose said in her most emphatic voice.

"It's really not," Maggie said. "It doesn't even have ducts for the heat and air-conditioning."

"So? It's California. It doesn't get very cold. And it's not hot at night. Besides, you're right by the ocean. It's summer, and we're down here now, and it's fine."

"What's the pushback here?" Maggie asked. "Be really honest for a minute. Why wouldn't you want two nice rooms in the house? Is it a deservingness thing? Some kind of feelings about how much you feel comfortable taking?"

For a moment there was no response. Jean was looking down at the concrete floor and Rose was gazing through one of the high, small windows.

Then Jean spoke, her voice quiet. Even for Jean.

"But those are their *rooms*."

"Which they've chosen not to live in right now."

"But when they come home. You know. They'll know we've been in their rooms. They probably resent us already and I just know this couldn't help. People are weird about their rooms."

"Here's the thing, though," Maggie said. "I'll have to have my contractor and his guys come down here and put in a bathroom and real walls and floor, and heating and air-conditioning ducts, and you won't be able to be down here while all that construction is going on."

Another silence fell, and the girls' anxiety was palpable to Maggie. Especially Jean's.

"We don't need all that stuff," Rose said.

"Be that as it may," Maggie said, "*I* need you to *have* all that stuff."

"Maybe just a nice couch while the work is being done," Jean said. "I'll bet your couches are more comfortable than our beds at home used to be."

"One other possibility," Maggie said. She led them up the stairs, through the kitchen. Down the hall to her home office. "I could put a couple of cots in here in the short run."

"Don't you need this space though?" Jean asked.

"I could move the important stuff into my bedroom."

"I'd rather sleep in the basement," Rose said. "Because then we could bring Sunny in."

"But then the workers need to be down there, genius," her sister said.

"Maybe by then we can housebreak him. Didn't she say we could bring him in if we could housebreak him? I thought I heard her say that."

They both turned and looked at Maggie to say the final word. It made her feel overwhelmed and overloaded.

"We'll move the beds down to the basement tonight and work out the rest as we go along," she said.

Dinner consisted of deli sandwiches from Merv's, which was unarguably the best food in a thirty-mile radius, along with their famous potato salad and coleslaw. Alex had been kind enough to pick it all up on his way over after work.

"I hope it doesn't seem weird having sandwiches for dinner," Maggie said to the girls.

She had been watching them, especially when they weren't watching her watch them. They no longer seemed nervous. They looked almost . . . happy. Or at least externally elated, even if there were other losses brewing below. Maggie had never gotten any such feeling from them before, and wanted to explore it further, but she wasn't sure whether to hit the subject straight on.

"I'll eat anything anytime," Rose said, cutting off her sister before she could speak. "Breakfast for dinner. Pizza for breakfast. I love it all. Besides, these are *good*!"

"They really are," Jean said.

The table fell silent again. Pleasantly silent.

"You girls seem happy," Maggie said after a while.

"Oh we're just so relieved," Jean said quickly, despite her mouth being full. She chewed and swallowed, then elaborated. "I was just thinking that it was like that book. Remember that book, Rose?"

"I was just thinking that!" Rose shouted.

"What book was this?" Alex asked between bites.

"Rose and I both read this book, and there was a happy family in it. You don't usually read about that. Usually families are unhappy in books, I guess so the characters have a challenge and you root for them to be happy in the end. But this family was really happy all along and the conflict was coming from outside the house. Anyway, they all got together every night for dinner and they talked and laughed and everybody enjoyed being together. They had these running jokes. I know we haven't been telling jokes yet. But it still just reminded me of that happy family."

"I was just thinking that!" Rose shouted again.

"I'm glad," Maggie said, feeling a warm pressure build inside her gut.

"What kind of jokes?" Alex asked.

"These running jokes that were all sort of on the same word," Rose said excitedly. "Oh, I'm not explaining it very well. Give me a word. Just any word. But probably it should be a thing. You know. Like a noun."

"Tree," Alex said.

"Okay, great. Tree. And then the father would say, 'I think we'd be better to leaf that one alone.' And the mother would say, 'Or at least branch out into some other conversation.'"

"I get it," Alex said.

"I know it's corny," Jean said.

"No, it's fun," Alex said. "I'm just trying to root around for one of my own."

The girls laughed.

Maggie wanted to jump in, but couldn't think of anything. She wanted to use the word "bark" but was stuck digging around for a context.

Before she could think of one, Sunny weighed in. He was watching them through the dining-room picture window. Apparently he had reached the end of his mental tether regarding seeing food he couldn't eat. He let out one loud, sharp bark that made everyone jump.

"Sunny wanted to play!" Maggie cried out. "Did you hear that? He said 'bark.'"

Everyone laughed. And laughed. And then, without seeing it coming, and for reasons hard to pin down, Maggie started to cry. She tried to hide it, but it picked up steam quickly and got out of hand.

"Ma'am?" Jean said, suddenly worried. "What's wrong, ma'am?"

Maggie dabbed at her eyes with her napkin.

"I don't think you should call me ma'am, honey," she said. "I think we know each other too well for that, or if we don't we're about to. You should call me Maggie. And later down the line, if you feel like you want to, you can call me Mom. But if that's too hard after just having lost your own mother, that's okay. I understand. And maybe it's even premature to say it. But at least Maggie."

"But why were you crying?" Jean asked.

"Did we do something wrong?" Rose added.

"No, of course not. Nothing's wrong. It wasn't that kind of tears. I've been a little emotional since my girls moved out and it really did feel like a happy family just now. And I'm not used to that. I guess I'm not explaining it very well."

"It's okay, ma—Maggie," Jean said, stumbling over what to call her. "We get it just fine."

They didn't talk much for the rest of the meal, but it was still a happier meal than Maggie was used to having.

———

Alex disappeared after dinner, saying he was going to move cots down to the basement. The girls absolutely insisted on doing the dishes.

When Alex hadn't come back to find her after longer than it should have taken to move cots, Maggie wandered down the basement stairs.

"Oh my," she said when she saw what he had done.

He was arranging roses in a vase of water. He had made up the two cots nicely with pillows, sheets, and blankets. He'd brought a bedside table down from one of the girls' rooms and set it up between the beds, where it currently held the vase of roses. Over the beds he had hung a tapestry she'd kept rolled up in the garage. A lamp from her office threw a warm glow on the scene. It was all set up on a Persian rug, also from the garage.

He looked around when she spoke.

"I cut some roses from the bushes on the side fence," he said. "I hope you don't mind."

"Of course I don't mind."

"The rug wasn't my best thinking. They wanted to have the unhousebroken dog down here with them. That was the whole point of being down here instead of in your office. I can put it back in the garage if you want."

"No, it's okay," she said, crossing the basement to sit next to him on one of the cots. "It's not an heirloom or anything. It was in the garage. If he ruins it I'll get a new one, if I even decide I need one. This is so nice, what you did."

They sat quietly for a minute or so. Maggie felt like crying again, but she managed to keep it inside.

"Is it good enough for them?" she asked after a time. "It's still a basement."

"In the short run. I think so."

"Will their social worker think so?"

"If you tell her you offered them two rooms upstairs and they refused, probably. Maybe we'll even have it all remodeled down here by the first home visit."

"I feel like they deserve more. And I wish *they* felt that way."

"That won't happen overnight, though. That'll happen over time."

"I suppose you're right." She slid an arm around his neck and kissed him on the temple. "Thank you for doing this."

A sound made them look around. The girls were standing at the top of the stairs, their mouths open and eyes wide.

"You made it so *nice* down here!" Jean said.

"Well, Alex did this," Maggie said. "But . . . of course. You girls deserve nice."

———

Maggie tucked them into bed that night, kissing each girl on the forehead.

Rose only said good night and rolled over to sleep, but Jean had something on her mind.

"Ma'am?" she said tentatively. "I mean . . . Maggie?"

"What, honey? What is it?"

"Maybe I shouldn't say anything about this because maybe your daughters aren't any of my business, but I just can't imagine your girls not being the nicest girls in the world. Because they're your girls."

Maggie sighed, and sat on the bed near Jean's hip.

"I guess it's just more complicated than that. I thought it was simple. I thought you just give your children everything they want and they'll be happy. But now I think getting everything you want doesn't make a person happy at all. Because things don't mean as much if you've never done without them. And because the world isn't a place that will always go your way, and I probably shouldn't have set up the expectation that it was. I'm not suggesting that's the only factor. Their father and I divorced, and that's always hard on children. It was hard on me too, and I've made a lot of mistakes since then. I threw myself into my work and wasn't there for them, and when they tried to tell me I wouldn't listen because I didn't know how to change. I wanted to be a good parent but now I'm not even sure I know what that is."

"I think you're doing fine," Jean said.

Maggie gave her a second kiss on the forehead.

"Try to get some sleep," she said.

And she let herself out.

Chapter Thirteen

The Double-Edged Nature of Water and Everything Else

"You have a *pool!*" Rose shrieked.

Maggie was sitting at the breakfast island in her kitchen with Alex when Rose and her enthusiasm spilled into the room. Jean was nowhere to be seen. Probably she was still in the basement, or outside with the dog.

"We do," Maggie said.

"I love swimming! I want to go swimming! I want to go swimming *right now!*"

"Knock yourself out," Alex said.

"But I don't have a suit."

"Oh. Well. We'll get you one," Maggie said.

"But I want to go swimming *right now!*"

"Okay. You can swim in your underwear."

Rose's eyes darted briefly to Alex, and she blushed slightly.

"But there's a *boy* here."

"Okay. How about your underwear and an oversize T-shirt?"

"I've got T-shirts that will cover you much more than a suit would," Alex said.

"That might work," Rose said.

"I'll get her one of yours," Maggie said to Alex. "And I'm going to move this breakfast outside. Until I know more about her swimming skills, I think we should have a lifeguard on duty."

"I'm a good swimmer," Rose said.

"Just being safe," Maggie said.

"I'll bring your bagel out when it's done toasting," Alex said.

———

She was sitting on a chaise longue next to Alex, eating her bagel and waiting for Rose to change and come out. It was maybe seven in the morning, and a Sunday. Nobody had to think about work. The air was already warm and had a dry, summery feeling.

That was when Alex said that thing he said. The one Maggie wasn't expecting.

"We could get married," he said, "if that would be better for adopting the girls."

Maggie couldn't quite muster a response on short notice. There was a lot to unpack in that one sentence, and it caused her brain to go in several directions at once. Good directions. The whole thing had a warm, comfortable, welcome feeling to it. But it was a lot all the same.

"You told me you want to adopt them," he said.

"I've actually looked into it. It might be something that could be done in six months or so. No guarantees it would be that fast, but it can be. The trick will be running the idea past Willa and Gemma. But, anyway, back up a minute. Did you just propose to me?"

"Not exactly. Not literally. If I really propose for real I'll get down on one knee, or take you out to a restaurant and hide the ring in the dessert, or propose on the Jumbotron at some big sporting event, or one of those other corny things guys do."

"We never go to sporting events, but I appreciate the stickiness of the sentiment. I didn't know you were thinking in those terms."

"Which is why I brought it up. I just wanted you to know it's an option."

"You realize you'd be taking on four instant kids."

"Or, seen another way, they all sleep through the night already and in a handful of years we'd be empty nesters."

"I regularly wonder what I did to deserve you," she said. "I'm going to start making some calls."

He opened his mouth to say something, but she never found out what it was. At that moment Rose came running through the backyard and dived into the pool. And Sunny started barking. And he didn't stop.

They watched her swim for a few minutes without speaking. It would have been hard to be heard over the dog anyway.

Maggie reached over and squeezed Alex's hand so he would know how she was feeling. So he wouldn't think her lack of opportunity to say yes was any kind of cue to her mood, which was some variety of warm elation.

Jean came over a moment later. Probably she had come outside to see what the dog was barking about.

Rose was swimming lap after lap in her dress-length T-shirt, and Sunny was running beside the pool, back and forth, back and forth, barking wildly. Whether he thought Rose was in danger or was simply frustrated by not being able to go where Rose went was unclear. But whatever his issue, it was clearly important to him, since he was paying no attention to the half-eaten bagels.

For reasons she could not entirely explain, Maggie's mind shifted to sending the girls to school when it reopened in the fall. She wondered if the California students would tease them about their Louisiana accents.

"We're all here," Jean said. "Why are we all here?"

"I thought Rose should have somebody nearby while she swims," Maggie said, speaking up to be heard over Sunny's barking.

"Rose is a good swimmer."

"I'm beginning to gather that. But I hope you understand my thinking."

"Of course," Jean said. "You're taking good care of us." She ran up to Maggie's chaise longue and offered her an awkward hug around the neck. "I have to go make the beds," she said.

Then she ran off before Maggie could tell her the maid would do it. Likely that wouldn't have discouraged her from doing it herself anyway.

Rose hoisted herself out of the pool and sat on its edge, shushing the dog. He fell silent immediately and began licking the pool water off the girl's face and neck, making her giggle.

Maggie heard a tone from Alex's phone, signaling a text coming in.

He pulled it out of his pocket and read silently. Maggie watched his face fall.

"Bad news?" she asked.

"Very."

"What is it?"

"It's John Bishop."

"Oh no. What about him? Is he okay?"

"No. He had a massive coronary."

"Is he going to be okay?"

"No," Alex said.

He didn't elaborate. Or need to.

"I'm surprised she didn't tell you first," Alex said. "Or at least at the same time."

"My phone is in the house."

She heard her own words as if she were standing outside herself. As if someone else had spoken them. She seemed to have removed herself from the situation to experience it from a remote distance. She was an onlooker, thinking, *Yes, there's been a tragedy.* But for the moment it almost felt like somebody else's tragedy. Knowing it would catch up to her in time, she didn't attempt to force herself out of the feeling.

She looked up to see a dripping Rose standing over her.

The girl sat down on the edge of the chaise longue with her and began squeezing water out of her long hair, leaning away to avoid splashing Maggie. She did not seem to be looking at either of them, and Maggie saw no indication that she had picked up on their mood. She was off in her own little world.

Sunny was busy licking pool water off Rose's arms, and the silence was blissfully welcome.

"Do your daughters have a pool at their dad's house?" Rose asked, still looking at the dog.

"No. No pool."

"They must miss it."

"They never use the pool. Never. I put it in because they begged me for one, but they haven't used it in years."

"That's the first time I've been in water since . . ." Rose began. "Well. You know. Since that thing happened that had to do with water."

"How did it feel to you?" Maggie asked. "Did it feel mostly good or did it mostly bring up terrible memories?"

It felt nice to go in an unrelated direction from the Bishops, conversationally. To spend a minute in a world where the lovely John Bishop had not just died.

"It's weird," Rose said. "It felt weird. Because I love water so much, and it's such a good thing. And it still felt like a good thing, even though I know in my head what a bad thing it can be. Even though I still remember that day so well. How can something be so good and so bad at the same time, Maggie?"

"Pretty much everything in life is," Maggie said.

"It is? What else is?"

"Well. Everything. Fire. If you're huddled around a fire, and it's keeping you from freezing, you think fire is the best thing ever. If your house catches fire, it's the worst. Knives. They're great for cutting your food but they also cut *you*. People. People are as wonderful as they are terrible and as terrible as they are wonderful."

As she spoke, she watched Alex in her peripheral vision. He was staring off into space. Probably processing the ways in which the world had just changed for them.

"I thought people were more terrible than wonderful," Rose said. "I think most people think that."

"No, I don't think so," Maggie said. "I don't think that's possible. People are like coins with two sides. Heads and tails. People are capable of evil to the same degree as they are of good. One side of a coin can't be larger than the other."

"Huh," Rose said. "That's a weird way to look at a thing. What's wrong with Alex?"

Oddly, Alex showed no visible response to hearing his name spoken out loud, if indeed he had heard it. He seemed to remain a thousand miles away.

"A good friend of ours just died," Maggie said.

That got Alex's attention, and he seemed to snap back into the moment.

"Oh, no," Rose said. "That's awful! What did he die from?"

"He had a heart attack," Alex said. "He was one of the doctors who used to go out on the road with us. You met him."

"That nice older man? Dr. Bishop?"

"Yes," Maggie said, feeling now like the tragedy was more her own.

"Oh, no. That's so sad. That makes me really sad."

She looked sad, too, Maggie noticed. In fact, she looked instantly devastated. As if she'd known John all her life and his death had emotionally destroyed her. But Maggie knew the death that had destroyed her was probably not John's.

"Can you still do what you do with two doctors and a nurse?" she asked, seeming to shake herself out of it.

"Not sure," Alex said. "We wouldn't expect his wife to go out on the road with us anytime soon. She'll have a big adjustment to make. I don't know if one doctor and one nurse make the trip worthwhile. It's something we'll have to think about."

"Knowing Lacey the way I do . . ." Maggie began. But it didn't seem worth finishing the thought. It was all just speculation. "Well. We'll see, I guess."

They all sat without talking for what might have been a long time. It was hard for Maggie to judge.

Then Rose said, "Why do people have to die?"

"I'm not sure I know," Maggie said. "Except that I don't suppose it would work to have every person who was ever born all living on the earth at the same time. Competing for resources. But I don't expect that was the answer you wanted."

"Not really," Rose said.

"I was thinking about counseling for all of us. As a family. Maybe those are the kinds of questions we could talk about together. We could help you and your sister deal with the losses you've had."

Rose seemed to chew that idea over for a time.

"I don't really know anyone who's had it," she said. "So I don't know what I think about it. But I guess if you were there it would be okay with me. And it *would* be nice to talk to somebody about what happened."

They sat silently for a time. The sun had risen enough to be visible over the wooden board fence, and it shone into Maggie's eyes.

Sunny sat with his chin on her knee, fixated on the last of her bagel. Licking his lips.

"Just out of curiosity," she said to Rose, "why did you name him Sunny? He wasn't the most cheerful little guy in the world when we met him."

"Because there was that terrible storm," Rose said, "and it was the worst storm in the world, and everything was bad. And then Sunny came along and it felt like the storm was over. Like the sun might actually come out again. He was the end of our storm."

———

"I finally got through to Lacey," Alex said, walking into the bedroom at the end of the day.

He sat down next to Maggie, who was already under the covers in her nightgown.

"Had she turned her phone off or was it just constantly busy?"

"Some combination thereof. The memorial is Sunday. Except they're calling it a celebration of John's life."

"That's so soon."

"I know. Did you tell the girls?"

"Willa and Gemma, you mean?"

"Wow. Huh. You're right. We're going to have to stop saying 'the girls.' It doesn't narrow things down enough anymore. Yeah, that's who I meant."

"No, I thought I'd go over in the morning before work. I thought in person would be better. I kept starting to call, but the phone just didn't feel right."

"You think they'll take it hard?"

"I have no idea how they'll take it. None. I've been thinking about it a lot, and it's just not one of those things you can guess about. They've known the Bishops for most of their lives, but I'm not sure young people have as much attachment to their parents' friends as we'd somehow like to think. And I've made up my mind I'm going to leave them free to feel whatever they feel about it and no more. Nothing obligatory. Hell, people three and four times their age don't know what to feel when somebody dies. And also I feel like I've slipped into the role of their chief antagonist lately, which is not exactly comfortable for anyone involved. I'm not going to antagonize them over this. The only thing I plan to ask is that they come to the memorial with us."

Alex's brow furrowed. He stood, unbuttoned and pulled off his shirt. Put it in the clothes hamper.

He wandered off toward the bathroom.

Just before he stepped inside he said, "All four girls are going?"

"I'm not going to insist that Jean and Rose go, but I expect they'll want to. They have a lot of gratitude toward the Bishops for those four days in Louisiana."

"You realize that will be the first time all four girls are ever in the same room with each other."

Maggie hadn't realized that, actually. At very least she hadn't taken much time to ponder the ramifications. And her brain sank into instant overwhelm when she tried.

"Cross that bridge when we come to it," she said.

Alex disappeared into the bathroom, leaving Maggie to do the brow furrowing. She could hear him brushing his teeth.

When he emerged he had changed into pajama bottoms. He climbed under the covers bare-chested, as he tended to do, and they sat quietly for a few minutes with the light on.

"Are we going to try to get another volunteer doctor?" Maggie asked him after a time.

"I don't know," he said. "I've been thinking about it a lot, but I just don't know. I don't know if Lacey will want to hang it up for good now, or if she'll completely immerse herself in the volunteering. That could go either way. I don't know what we'd do for another RV. I don't know if Lacey could do all the driving on her own. There's really only one thing I feel like I know at this point. Getting a new volunteer doctor is not going to be as easy as you think. You have no idea what I went through to get three yeses. Or one yes and one double yes, however you want to count that. That's more a part of how you and I ended up together than you might know. When you said yes, I started looking at you in a new light. I thought, '*This* woman is *different*.' And then I guess I never stopped looking."

She said nothing, so he reached over and turned off the light.

After a minute in the dark, Maggie said, "I think we *should* get married."

He turned on the light again and they looked into each other's faces, which was hard for Maggie to do with most people.

"Did that come from someplace special?" he asked.

"Well. The inside of my head."

"I think you know what I mean."

"I guess . . . ," she began, "I guess I think the reason we should get married is because life is shorter and less predictable than we'd like to think. We all act like we'll live forever and so will the people we love, and we think we have plenty of time to do all the things we plan to do someday, but we don't really know. It's days like this that you know how much you don't really know."

"I suppose that's a decent reason," he said.

He turned off the light again.

"Wait," he said into the darkness. "Did you just propose to me?"

"Possibly. Should I have gotten down on one knee?"

"Oh no," he said. "You're not getting off that easy. I want the Jumbotron."

Chapter Fourteen

*The Elusive Sweet Spot between Civil and
Gracious*

In the morning she knocked on Dan's door. Unannounced.

Unfortunately his girlfriend answered.

She was young, and a bit brassy, with hair an unnatural shade of bright red and oddly white skin. She looked Maggie up and down, seeming unimpressed by what she saw.

"Oh," she said. "You." Then she peeled away from the door, leaving it standing open. "Dan!" she bellowed. It actually hurt Maggie's ears. "It's your ex."

Dan wandered to the door a minute or two later, still in his bathrobe, both hands buried deep in his robe pockets. His thick dark hair was almost comically uncombed.

"Wasn't expecting *you*," he said.

"Is that her normal level of decorum?"

"Well, you know," he said. His mouth twisted into a crooked smile at one corner. "Nobody exactly loves the ex."

"I need to talk to the girls."

"There's always that telephone thingy."

"John Bishop died."

His expression changed suddenly. And radically. As if it were his own mortality being discussed.

"Oh, no. That's too bad. They're eating breakfast. Come in."

She followed him down a long, dim hallway. Almost to the kitchen. Then he peeled away and up the stairs, and she stepped into the kitchen on her own and sat at the table with her girls. Whom she had missed. The whole middle of her torso felt hot and under pressure from how much she had missed them, and from how nice it was to see them now.

"What are you doing here?" Willa asked, still staring down into her cereal bowl.

"I have to tell you girls some sad news." She paused briefly, in case they had a reaction. When none reached her, she continued. "John Bishop . . . passed away."

"Oh, I'm sorry," Willa said.

She seemed to mean it, but it was hard for Maggie to gather much from her face.

"That's too bad," Gemma said. "How's Lacey?"

"I haven't been able to get through to her. Alex talked to her yesterday, briefly. I can pretty much tell you, even without knowing firsthand, that she's okay and she's not okay. Both at the same time. I didn't want to tell you on the phone. I know you knew the Bishops pretty well, and for a really long time, but I also know they were generations older, and my friends more than yours. I'm not telling you what to feel about it. I'm just going to ask that you come to the celebration of his life at their house on Sunday."

"Okay," both girls said, a bit weakly, and more or less at the same time.

Maggie sat in silence for a time while Willa ate her cereal and Gemma pushed hers around in the bowl with her spoon. Maggie was wondering if that was all, and if she should just go. She wanted it to be more like a visit. But she hadn't scheduled or announced a visit, so maybe that was too much to ask.

Willa's face changed suddenly. As though she'd been sleeping with her eyes open and something had startled her awake.

"Wait. *They* won't be there, right?"

"Jean and Rose? Yes, they *will* be there."

"Why? They didn't know him."

"They did know him. They spent four days at the clinic with us, remember?"

"We knew him a lot longer than four days," Gemma whined. "It's not fair."

"It wouldn't be fair if I were taking them and not taking you. But I'm only suggesting that everybody has a right to be there. Those four days were a terrible time for those girls. Their parents had just drowned and they were very sick and they had no idea what their future would look like. The people who helped them through that time took on an outsize importance to them. Remember when I told you I wasn't going to tell you what to feel about John dying? Well, we're not going to tell *them* what to feel either. Nobody is going to tell you to feel more or tell them to feel less. We're just going to get together and honor his life, and anybody who wants to be there can be there."

Another silence rang.

Willa pushed her bowl of now-soggy cereal away, as if stressing that her appetite had abandoned her.

"Do we have to talk to them?" she asked Maggie.

"You don't have to talk to them more than feels comfortable to you, no. But I do expect you to be somewhere between civil and gracious at all times. If you have problems with them, or the whole situation with them, the memorial of a dear friend is not the time and place to air them out."

"I guess we can get along for an hour," Willa said, her eyes trained down to the table.

"Plan for two," Maggie said. "And afterward we'll have the usual Sunday family dinner. Except it'll be the first one with all four of you girls together."

"Yeah," Willa said quietly on an outbreath of laugh. "Usual. How very usual."

She got up and left the kitchen.

Maggie looked at Gemma and Gemma looked back.

"We miss you," Gemma said.

Maggie tried not to show how much it surprised her to hear it. Not that it didn't seem possible that the girls had been missing their mother. More that it seemed astonishing to hear such a thing expressed. It sounded almost like a confession.

"I miss you both, too," Maggie said. "You know you can come home anytime you like."

"No we can't. You gave away our rooms."

"They're not in your rooms. They're in the basement."

"Well, but when the contractor comes to fix up the basement . . ."

"Then they'll be in my office. They didn't want to stay in your rooms. They thought you would mind if they did, because they're your rooms. They were quite adamant about not wanting to do that."

Maggie watched her daughter squirm under this sudden news. Clearly it was something that made it hard not to like Jean and Rose, and Maggie could see the resistance it created.

It didn't seem that Gemma would answer, so Maggie spoke up.

"Are you happy here at your dad's?"

Gemma shrugged. Then she jumped up and left the table. Maggie was left with a vague impression that her daughter might have been about to cry, and didn't want any witnesses to that outpouring of emotion. But it all happened fast, so it was hard to say for sure.

Maggie let herself out and drove home.

———

"I'm nervous," Jean said to Maggie as they walked toward the door of the old-fashioned ice-cream parlor.

The girls were walking one on either side of her, and she put an arm around each of their shoulders.

"I understand, honey," Maggie said. "But you'll all get used to each other after a while."

"What if they're mean to us?" Rose asked, sounding genuinely scared.

"I won't let them be."

That seemed to settle everyone's rattled nerves a bit.

They stepped inside.

Dan was already there with Willa and Gemma, holding the biggest table for their arrival.

Maggie sat down and looked up to see Jean and Rose standing nervously, the way one might jump to their feet and stay that way when someone important stepped into the room.

"Sit down, girls," Maggie said. "It's okay."

Willa turned a scathing look onto her father.

"You didn't tell us *they'd* be here."

"You didn't *tell* them?" Maggie asked.

She was shocked by the news, and her voice did nothing to hide it.

"Why would I?" Dan said. "So they could say no?"

Maggie shrugged. "I would've gone a different way," she said.

"Well, I'm the one making decisions for the day-to-day stuff now," Dan said. "And this was my decision."

"And they're pissed about it."

"Oh, they're pissed about everything."

"Hey!" Gemma objected.

"Okay," Maggie said. "Let's start over. Willa and Gemma, this is Jean and Rose. We thought we'd introduce you before the memorial on Sunday. Give you a chance to talk and get to know each other. Because, as I've stressed before, Sunday is not the time for any conflict. That wouldn't be fair to Lacey."

The girls said nothing.

After a brief silence Dan said, "And where's Alex? Wanting to stay out of the cross fire?"

"Parking the car," Maggie said.

Before Dan could even mount a reply, Alex appeared at her left shoulder, and sat. He looked around and smiled. A bit tentatively, Maggie thought. Maybe even nervously.

"How are we doing so far?" he asked.

Willa grunted a nonverbal reply. It was the only response to his question. At a table of seven.

A very young waitress came to the table and handed them menus.

"Ooh," Rose said. "They *wait* on you? I've never been to an ice-cream place where they *wait* on you."

"That's one of the reasons we like it here," Maggie said.

They stared at their menus for a time in silence.

Then Rose gasped. It was loud enough and sudden enough to make everybody jump.

"They have root-beer floats here! I haven't had a root-beer float in . . . forever. I know what I want!"

Jean leaned closer to Maggie and spoke quietly.

"Are we supposed to just get . . . you know. Ice cream? Like a scoop of ice cream?"

"No, she can get a root-beer float."

"I meant me. If I wanted something big, like . . ."

"Get whatever you want, honey."

"Even if it's really big, like a banana split?"

"Of course. What about you girls?" Maggie asked, projecting her attention across the table. "Do you know what you want?"

Willa turned her head toward her father and spoke to him instead.

"I don't even know why you brought me here. You know I'm on a diet."

The words felt like something sharp piercing Maggie's heart and gut.

"Oh honey," she said to Willa, "you *so* don't need to go on a diet. You're already so thin. It worries me."

"Not compared to the girls I go to school with I'm not," Willa said.

Dan spoke up. "You won't win on this one," he said in Maggie's direction. "Peer pressure versus Mom's advice? You haven't got a chance."

The waitress came by, and they placed their order.

Dan ordered only coffee. Fairly predictable for a man dating a much younger woman, Maggie thought. Willa ordered a single scoop of sorbet. Gemma asked for a single scoop of chocolate-chip mint.

"I'm going to have the banana split," Maggie said, perhaps a bit too loudly and cheerfully. "It sounded so good when Jean mentioned it." She purposely did not directly look to her daughter Willa for feedback. "Two banana splits. One root-beer float. And what are you having, Alex?"

"Mocha almond fudge," he said. "Two scoops."

The waitress gathered up their menus and left. A silence fell. It felt heavy and dense. Something that might prove stubbornly hard to break. It lasted for a full minute or two, if not longer.

Then Maggie decided she was the adult—or at least one of them—and she should step in. But before she could even open her mouth, the very brave Jean spoke up. Her voice was mousy and quiet, but she dared to address Maggie's daughters.

"We sure didn't mean to push you out of your house or take your mom away or anything like that. I know you're not too happy about things and I understand how you feel."

"I'm not sure if you do understand how we feel," Willa said, sounding listless. "Unless your parents ever brought a couple of new kids home. Did they?"

Maggie gave her daughter a stern look, but Willa shrugged it off.

"What? It's a reasonable question."

"I guess I didn't say that very well," Jean said, her voice even smaller. "I should have said I can imagine how you must feel."

Willa only grunted.

Another long silence fell.

Surprisingly—no, astonishingly—it was Gemma who broke it. And not with a complaint, either.

"Thank you for not moving into our rooms," she said, her eyes trained down to the fifties-style Formica tabletop. "That would have been weird."

"Of course," Jean said. "We knew that would be weird for you."

Maggie breathed deeply, thinking the ice had been broken. But another painfully long silence fell.

The ice cream arrived, and they ate in excruciating silence for what must have been five or ten minutes.

This time it was Rose who broke it, bravely attempting to speak to Maggie's daughters.

"Are you looking forward to going back to school in the fall?"

Both Willa and Gemma looked up from their ice cream for the first time since it had arrived. They looked at Rose as though she had just spoken a sentence in Swahili or Klingon.

"How could anybody look forward to school?"

"We do!" Rose said brightly.

Willa only grunted. She went back to eating her sorbet. A moment later her head shot up in alarm.

"Wait," she said. She turned her attention suddenly onto Maggie. "*Where* are they going to school?"

"We've discussed it," Maggie said, "and they're okay with public school."

"Better," Rose said. "We don't need anything fancy."

Willa turned her gaze back down to her nearly empty bowl and said nothing. But she looked relieved. It was obvious enough that no one could miss, or fail to notice, how much she didn't want Jean and Rose at her school.

Everyone said nothing. For a truly uncomfortable length of time.

Finally Willa dropped her spoon into her empty dish, startling everyone with the clanging noise. She looked over at Gemma, who was only dragging her spoon through melted leftovers.

"Can we go?" she asked her father. "We're done."

"I guess," Dan said.

He looked to Maggie for confirmation on the decision, but the girls were already halfway to the door.

"Well they didn't kill each other," Dan said. "That's something."

Then he got up and followed them out.

———

"Did we do okay?" Rose asked on the drive home.

Alex was driving, so Maggie was able to turn around in her seat and address the girls directly.

"You did great," she said.

"I feel like I should've talked more," Jean said.

"Yeah, I feel that way myself," Maggie said. "But it was a tough situation and we did our best."

Chapter Fifteen

Fear of Grief and Other Human Emotions

Maggie saw Lacey standing alone at the deck railing, staring off toward the ocean. Utterly alone, which seemed odd with more than a hundred people in the house.

Gemma and Willa were cruising the buffet table with Dan, and Jean and Rose were hanging close to Alex, who was talking with three familiar doctors.

Maggie quietly let herself out through the sliding glass door and onto the patio.

Lacey glanced over her shoulder, but looked satisfied when she saw who was there. It was clear by the puffiness around her eyes that she had been crying. Not that anyone would expect otherwise.

She also appeared to be smoking a cigarette, which *was* a surprise.

Maggie joined her at the railing.

"I haven't started smoking again," Lacey said.

"Well you definitely fooled me, then."

"It's an herbal cigarette." She took a drag and blew a cloud of it in Maggie's general direction. It smelled spicy and good and definitely not like your average cigarette. "No tobacco. I haven't completely gone off the deep end. I have to confess, though, honey . . . ever since John died, it's the first thing I think of every morning and the last thought in my head when I go to sleep at night. But I'm not going to."

"Good," Maggie said, and stared out at the ocean with her. "I'm sure that's not what John would have wanted."

"Oh, to hell with what John would have wanted!" Lacey spit out, surprising them both. "Oh, I'm sorry, honey," she added quickly. "I know that is *so* not what I'm supposed to be feeling."

Maggie draped an arm around the older woman's shoulders.

"This might be a good time to suspend the whole 'supposed to' concept."

"Heaven knows I loved that man," Lacey said, her voice more measured. "And I don't even blame it on him. He didn't tell me I had to live my whole life based on what he wanted, but now that it's over I can look back and see clearly, and that's exactly what I did. Maybe it's the way I was raised, I don't know. Or maybe that's just me. It'll take me more than a week to figure *that* whole thing out."

"What are you doing out here all by yourself? There are, like, a hundred people in there."

"I just needed a minute to breathe."

"Yeah, I get that. Of course. I just couldn't figure out why everybody but me was letting you."

"People find me intimidating," Lacey said. "Did you really not know that?"

"Who finds you intimidating?"

"Apparently everybody."

"*I* don't."

"You're not easily intimidated. It's one of the things I like about you. Besides, I'm grieving. Even those who aren't normally afraid of me are afraid of that emotion. Other people's grief is not so much fun for anybody. They don't know what to say." Lacey looked around over her shoulder, peering through the sliding glass door into the house. "Where are the girls? You did bring them, right?"

"Which girls?"

"All of them."

"Yeah, they're all here. Dan brought Willa and Gemma and he stayed. He wanted to be here. I hope that's okay."

"Of course it's okay. Anybody who cared about my John should be here, and I'm not going to tell them they cared any less than they say they did." She took a long drag of the herbal cigarette before speaking again, pushing smoke out with the words. "How are the girls getting along?"

"Hard to say. This is only the second time they've met."

Lacey's eyes remained glued to the horizon, but Maggie saw her brow furrow.

"Explain that to me."

"Willa and Gemma are living with their father right now."

"You didn't tell me that. We've talked . . . what? Three times since Louisiana? Four times? You never brought that up. That seems like some pretty big news."

"It's not my favorite subject."

"Got it," Lacey said.

"Today was going to be the first day they met, but Dan and Alex and I were a little worried about that. We weren't sure it was such a good idea. If there were going to be any initial fireworks we figured today was not the right venue. That's why we took them all out for ice cream this week."

"And how did that go?"

"Quietest twenty-five minutes of my life. Nobody had anything to say to anybody. Jean and Rose tried to say a sentence or two, but when they got mostly half-audible grunts in return they gave up fast. Gemma thanked them for not moving into their rooms, and I could have kissed her for that. But then that was it. That was all they had to say to each other. And there was so much ice cream left. We just ate in this excruciating silence. I was thinking I should have been the one to keep some conversation going, but I got frozen up too. It was just hard."

"These things take time. What are you going to do with the new girls when you go back out on the road again?"

"I wasn't even sure we *would* go back out on the road again. Nobody wanted to put you on the spot by asking."

"Honey, I would give my left arm to get back out there. This house is so damn empty and quiet. I'd kill for a good disaster right about now. I scour the paper every morning looking for a hurricane or an earthquake and then I feel bad because I shouldn't be wishing that on anybody. But what a relief it would be. Anyway, you must have thought about it when you first took them in. Before . . . you know."

"I figured they could stay home. They're sixteen and fourteen. They should be okay."

"You never left your own girls at home."

"My own girls would have thrown the party of the century and probably burned the house down in the process. I don't have any such worries about Jean and Rose."

"No," Lacey said. She crushed out the cigarette on the sole of one sensible shoe and, after examining it to be sure it was entirely out, dropped the butt into the bushes. "They don't seem like the partying type. If it's still summer, and school is still out, why not bring them? I think they'd like it, and they'd probably be a lot of help to us. They're what we used to call do-gooders. Nowadays you hear people saying that word like it's a bad thing, and I'll never in a million years understand that. Why would you make a person out to be wrong for doing good? It makes no sense."

"If you're not doing good yourself you're going to want to take shots at the people who are. It's easier to make them wrong than to change yourself."

"Now that's a theory," Lacey said. "I've got plenty of room if you and Alex want your space all to yourself at night. Our RV sleeps six. I mean . . . *my* RV. That'll take some getting used to."

"Can you handle all the driving on your own?"

"Jean could help with that, too."

"I don't think she knows how to drive."

"No one knows until they know. Until someone teaches them. She's sixteen."

Before Maggie could answer, the patio door slid open and Jean and Rose stepped outside. They were wearing dresses that Maggie had bought them, though of course she'd allowed them to pick out their own. Both were in a deep navy blue because they were afraid of appearing inappropriately cheery. Jean's was much more feminine-looking.

"Is it okay if we say something to Dr. Bishop?" Jean asked.

"Of course, honey," Lacey said. "You girls just come right on out."

The girls walked up to Lacey and stopped. They looked at each other, apparently making a silent deal as to who would go first. Then Rose stepped in and embraced Lacey.

"We're really, really sorry about the other Dr. Bishop," she said, her voice genuinely sorrowful. "He was such a nice man. We've been crying about it a lot, and Jean says maybe it's because we weren't done crying about our own parents. That's probably right, but it's not *all* about that. He really was a nice man."

"Thank you, darling," Lacey said. "It's nice to talk to someone who understands grief from the inside, though I'm sorry you have to at your young age."

Then Rose stepped back and Jean stepped in, hugging Lacey and saying something Maggie could not make out.

Through the window Maggie saw her two daughters watching. They did not look pleased.

She made her way back inside, where they pretended to be interested in the buffet again.

"If you want to go say something to Lacey," Maggie said, "nothing is stopping you. Just go say it."

"I'm not sure what to say," Gemma said.

"Just maybe what you thought of John, or that you hope she's okay."

"We'll try to think of something and then we'll talk to her," Willa said.

"And while you're at it," Maggie added, "I think it might be time to tell Jean and Rose you're sorry they just lost their parents. Both their parents drowned right in front of them, just a few weeks ago. A condolence would be in order."

"Yeah, okay," Willa said. "We'll try."

"I appreciate the effort," Maggie said. "And I know they'll appreciate it too."

Lacey came back in and joined the crowd shortly after. In time Willa and Gemma did approach her, but Maggie was too far away to hear what they said.

They did not embrace her. They looked embarrassed and awkward. They couldn't have said much, because the exchange only lasted seconds.

They never spoke to Jean and Rose as far as Maggie could see.

———

"We're not coming to Sunday dinner," Willa said as they all filed out to their respective cars.

Maggie stopped dead. Willa stopped too, and looked directly into her mother's face. The others walked on ahead. Maybe purposely. Maybe to give them privacy to talk, or maybe they just wanted to have no part in the conversation that would follow.

"*Why* aren't you?" Maggie asked. "I thought we had a firm understanding about that."

"We talked about it. Gemma and me. And the reason we agreed on Sunday dinners is because you wanted to see us a little bit every week. But you've seen us plenty this week. There was this memorial today, and then that thing we got tricked into at the ice-cream place the other day."

"It wasn't my decision to spring that on you."

"Whatever," Willa said. "I'm just saying we've spent plenty of time with you this week. If it was just you and Alex we'd probably come, but it's *them*, and we'd have to talk to them, and that's hard for us, and we've done as much of it as we can for right now."

"Why, you've barely talked to them at all."

"Which should show you how hard it is for us."

Maggie broke off her daughter's gaze and looked down at the pavement of the path from the Bishops' front door. She could feel no drive or energy to insist, and if she were being honest with herself, she had been dreading another session of watching the four girls struggle to coexist.

"Fine," she said. "Okay. Next week then."

"Whatever," Willa said.

They walked toward the cars again.

It felt like a relief to Maggie, not to have to brace for another four-girl meeting. And the sense of relief made her feel deeply guilty.

———

They were pulling out of the Bishops' driveway, Alex driving, when Rose spoke up.

"Will we ever get to go down there?" she asked.

Maggie looked to see where the girl was looking. Rose was gazing out the car window to the west, but that didn't help much.

"Define 'down there,'" Maggie said.

"The ocean. We've never seen the ocean. I mean . . . we've seen the gulf. Does that count? I guess it's sort of an ocean. Part of one. But we've definitely never seen the Pacific Ocean before, except from way up here where the houses are."

"Of course we can go down to the beach," Maggie said. "I'm sorry. I should have asked if that would interest you. I didn't really think about the fact that you're not used to it the way we are. Sure, we can go."

Alex made a left onto the street at the end of the driveway. West, away from home.

"Oh, I didn't mean now," Maggie said. "They don't have their bathing suits."

"I just want to *see* it," Rose said. "I'm not sure about swimming in it anyway. I've heard stories. I've heard the waves are really big and they can hold you down and drown you."

"Still, it's going to be really crowded on a Sunday in the summer."

"It's almost five," Alex said, showing her the face of his watch. "The crowd should have thinned out nicely by now."

"Fine," Maggie said. "I'm okay with going now."

Jean, who had been quiet, spoke up for the first time.

"It would be nice, after . . . you know. That was so sad, what we just did. It would be nice to do something that feels cheerier."

———

They all took off their shoes in the parking lot and left them in the car.

Alex carried a blanket from their trunk, and they found a nice spot, and he spread it out on the sand. They sat and looked around. There were maybe twenty other groups on that little section of beach, which was definitely a thin crowd for a summer Sunday.

The sun had slanted well to the west, and the girls shaded their eyes to look out to sea.

Other than a few voices and some laughter, the overriding sound was the surf, which Maggie found comforting. She felt suddenly grateful for the idea to change the mood to something less somber.

"People are going to think we're weird," Jean said. "For being down here with our good clothes on."

"Do you care what they think?" Maggie asked.

"I guess not."

"I'd like to just dip my feet in," Rose said. "Wade in just enough to see how cold it is and how the waves feel. But I don't want to get my nice new dress wet."

"Those dresses have belts," Maggie said. "Don't they? Let me show you a trick."

They all stood, and Maggie showed the girls how to reach through between their legs and grab a piece of the back hem of the skirt, then pull it forward and up and tuck it under the belt in front. The result was something like a puffy pair of shorts, with all the fabric well above their knees.

They ran to the edge of the water together.

"Should I roll up my pant legs and go down there?" Alex asked. "They've never been in the ocean before."

"I don't think they're going in very deep."

They sat and watched the girls for a time. Watched them jump and wiggle when a wave slid in around their feet. They were nearly silhouettes in the late-afternoon sun.

Then Alex said, "I think I'm going to anyway. Looks like they have the right idea, getting their feet wet."

He rolled up the legs of his good pants almost to the knees, showing off those hairy, well-muscled calves Maggie liked so much.

She watched him trot down the sand to the girls. Watched them stand together in shin-deep water, waiting for the next wave. Alex stood between Jean and Rose, and they both moved closer to him and grabbed onto his arms when a wave caught them. Maggie couldn't hear them laughing, but she could imagine it.

They looked like a wonderful, close family, and it filled Maggie with a deep satisfaction to see it. And her satisfaction made her feel guilt again. She'd been feeling guilty a lot lately. For being so happy.

In time Alex came trotting back.

"They're fascinated by the way the water takes the sand right out from under their feet as it pulls in and out. They just can't get enough of that."

They watched in silence for a very long time, but the girls still could not get enough of that. They showed no signs of wanting to come back.

Maggie figured it had been over an hour, based on the change in the position of the sun.

The air was much cooler now, and the ocean breeze made the late afternoon feel almost cold. Maggie looked around and saw that only two small families and one couple had stayed on the beach with them.

"Do we just let them stay?" she asked Alex.

"I guess. It's not like there's anywhere we need to be. Are you getting hungry?"

"Not even close. I ate so much at Lacey's."

They watched for what might have been another half an hour.

Then Rose seemed to spot something on the sand near her feet as a wave slid away. She held it up. Looked at it closely. Showed it to her sister. It looked fairly large, but Maggie couldn't see much more from the distance.

Rose turned, and shouted out something before she had even fully spun around to face them.

"Mom!" she called. "Mom. Look what I found!"

But by then she was looking right at them. Both her arms fell to her sides again, and she seemed to sag. She dropped whatever she'd been holding, and both girls walked back to the blanket, looking sad and defeated.

The closer they got, the more Maggie could feel their sadness. It was big and weighty, and felt like something solid and heavy in Maggie's gut.

"I don't know why I said that," Rose said, flopping down on the blanket.

"I told you to call me 'Mom' whenever you were ready."

"That's not what it was, though."

"Oh."

Of course Maggie wanted to ask what it was if it wasn't "that," but she thought it might be better to give the girl time to volunteer it on her own.

She glanced sideways at Jean, who smiled sadly and looked away.

"What was it you found?" Maggie asked instead.

Rose didn't answer. She seemed lost in her own little world. Unreachable.

Jean answered for her.

"It was a starfish. It was kind of orange. Really cool-looking. But I told her it might still be alive and it would be nicer to put it back in the water."

They sat in silence for a while longer. Both girls looked cold, and their legs and feet were coated with sand. But nobody made a move to go.

"I wasn't calling you 'Mom' because you said we should," Rose said suddenly. "I wasn't exactly talking to you. I mean, I was. I sort of was, but . . . I don't know how to explain it."

Maggie only waited. What felt like several minutes ticked by.

"My brain played a little trick on me," Rose said. "Just for a second I forgot how everything wasn't the way it always used to be before."

Maggie reached out and put a hand on the girl's shoulder. Gave it a little squeeze.

"I know I must have said this already, but I'm really so, so sorry you girls had to go through that loss."

Rose took the conversation in an entirely different direction.

"Can we stay and watch the sunset?"

"We can watch the sunset from the house, genius," her sister said.

"It's different from the beach, though."

"The sun doesn't set until after eight this time of year," Maggie said. "And I think we'll all be hungry and cold by then. But we can come down again after dinner with jackets if you want."

Rose got up and brushed sand off her legs.

"No, that's okay," she said. "It's good from the yard, too. We should go home now. Thank you for taking us down here."

They gathered themselves up and walked back to the car.

The feeling of sadness did not lift.

———

Just as they were driving out of the nearly deserted parking lot, it struck Maggie that an empty lot like that one would be a great place to teach somebody to drive.

She turned around and looked at Jean in the back seat. Jean returned her gaze questioningly.

"Ever had driving lessons?" she asked.

"No ma'am. I mean . . . no, Maggie."

"You're old enough to learn if you want to."

"Well sure! Of course. Who wouldn't want to?"

Alex braked to a stop.

"Now?" he asked.

"No," Maggie said. "Not now. It's tempting. But she doesn't have a learner's permit. We should wait and do it right."

Alex accelerated again and they headed for home.

"Still nice of you to think of it," Jean said.

"It was actually Lacey's idea. She thought you girls might like to come with us next time we go out on the road again. She thought you'd be a big help. And she doesn't have John to share the driving anymore, so she thought if you got your license you could even help with that."

"Cool!" Rose said.

"We'd love to go," Jean said. "When are we going?"

Maggie laughed slightly in her throat.

"Well, we need a big disaster first. We don't know when that's going to happen. And we can't wish for that."

"No," Jean said. "We'd never wish for that."

Chapter Sixteen

The People Who Think They're Better Fear They're Worse

Maggie sat in Scarlett Silverman's office while Jean and Rose read their books in the waiting room outside. Maggie had scheduled back-to-back sessions and the girls had gone first. She had waited for her turn with a surprising amount of nervousness. Far more than she had been set to expect.

"How are you feeling?" Scarlett asked.

"Guilty," Maggie said.

It came out without pause and without the slightest thought. The first she realized she was poised to confess to her guilt was the moment she heard herself say it out loud.

"Interesting," Scarlett said. "I just heard the same answer from the girls."

Maggie opened her mouth to ask what they had to feel guilty about but was stopped by a thought.

"I'm not sure I understand the whole therapist-and-client confidentiality agreement as it relates to minors," she said instead.

"It's more of a gray area, certainly, than treating adults. Parents—including foster parents—have a right to know enough to decide on treatments and such. In most cases they don't have access to the actual notes. But in this case, even though I'm not sending you home with the notes to read, the girls have made it blazingly clear that they have no secrets from you. They said anything they say in session can be shared with you, and that they intend to go home and tell you every detail of our time together anyway."

This news filled Maggie with the feeling she'd experienced so often since the girls had arrived. Unfortunately it was the feeling that brought up all the guilt.

"Well then . . . I guess I'll go ahead and ask. What are they feeling guilty about?"

"They're happier than they've ever been. Mind you, they're still suffering from the trauma of losing their parents in such a sudden and horrible way, and it'll take a long time and a lot of healing to unravel that. And likely it will never completely unravel. But on a day-to-day basis they're happy with you in a way they've never been before. And that makes them feel like they're disrespecting their parents' memory."

"Ah," Maggie said. "That makes a great deal of sense."

"Now we know why *they* feel guilty. What about you?"

"Much the same, but with no deaths involved. I'm happier than I've ever been. At least in as long as I can really, clearly remember. Living with Jean and Rose is like this intense happy-family experience. We talk and laugh at the dinner table. They're never on their phones. Well, they couldn't very well be, could they? They don't *have* phones. I wanted to buy them phones, but they weren't the least bit interested. They wanted more clothes instead. They listen when I talk, and they throw their arms around me and tell me they love me on a regular basis. Which is kind of . . . what I expected when I had children of my own."

"Right," Scarlett said. "Definitely not the first time I've heard that. There's this myth of the happy family, and real-life families never seem to live up to the hype."

"This one, though . . . I'm not trying to suggest that the girls are perfect, though they're certainly amazingly humble and kind compared to most teenagers I know. Part of it might be because they're so new to me. I think they feel like I pulled them out of this terrifying abyss and

me. I think they feel like I pulled them out of this terrifying abyss and just at the moment I can do no wrong. I haven't stopped them from doing anything they wanted to do, or enforced any rules they don't like, because there hasn't even been time for that."

"That could certainly factor in," Scarlett said. "But that kind of gratitude tends not to wear off completely. I take it you're telling me you feel guilty because you're enjoying a happy family with two teens other than your own."

Maggie squirmed slightly in her chair and shifted her gaze out the window. She didn't confirm that her therapist was right, because it really didn't require confirmation. The situation was obvious.

"What I'd really like," she said after a time, "is to have all four of them together. Of course part of me dreads that, because it would look a little something like World War Three. But I still want my girls home. I still want to try to make a blended family out of all of us. Hard as I know that will be. I miss Willa and Gemma something awful, but at the same time there's all this peace and love and all these good feelings in the house, and until I can bring them home I can't help enjoying that. And so there's all this guilt. Is there any way around that?"

"Around what?"

"Guilt."

"You're asking me if there's some way to avoid human emotions? I'd have to say no. I mean, people *try* to avoid them all the time, in a variety of ways. I'd even go so far as to say my job depends on those efforts. But in the long run, the emotions tend to have their way with us. And if they don't, I really don't recommend the life people have to lead to keep what they're feeling at bay."

"Got it," Maggie said. "I guess I knew that, really. I'm hesitant to even go here, but now that I've told you much more about my parenting since the divorce . . . I'm having trouble wrapping this up in words. I was so appreciative of your telling me everyone is worried they're a terrible parent. But some people actually are, and I'm afraid I've made it clear I fall into that category. The divorce was hard on all of us, and it was so hard on me that I didn't help them enough. It was like I didn't know how to. I didn't even know how to help myself. I threw myself into my work and didn't give them enough time, and now I'm blaming them for being awful teens, but they're angry, and I'm why they're angry. Now it's this vicious cycle. The angrier they get the less I want to spend time with them, and it just keeps going around. And I'm the adult. If that's not being a terrible parent, I'm not sure what is."

Scarlett set down her pad and sighed. She looked directly into Maggie's eyes, but Maggie couldn't quite hold her gaze. She was too worried about what was about to come flying in her direction.

"Parenting is not a zero-sum game," Scarlett said.

"Meaning?"

"All parents make mistakes. Did you make more than the best of them? Probably. Did you make more mistakes than average? Not sure. The average is pretty high. But instead of calling yourself a terrible parent, maybe let's think of you as a flawed parent. Welcome to a club with an astronomically large membership. If there's room for improvement, which it seems clear there is, think in terms of improvement. It doesn't do much good to just pronounce yourself terrible. The message there seems to be 'I failed. I'm giving up.' How about we change that to 'I made a lot of mistakes but now I'm vowing to do better.'"

Maggie breathed for what felt like the first time in a long time. A lot of toxic feelings seemed to flow out on the exhale. She wondered why she hadn't sought out this kind of help much sooner.

"I can do that," she said. "Thanks."

She spent the balance of the session talking about John Bishop, because the other situation was just too hard.

Sure, that's how you know you're in a bind, she thought. *When it's more comfortable to talk about the death of a longtime and much-loved friend.*

At the end of the session the therapist asked, "Are Willa and Gemma ever going to come?"

"Hard to say," Maggie said. "When last we discussed it, they wanted time to think it over."

"Which is okay," Scarlett said. "But I hope they do. Either just the two of them, or a shared session with you. What would really be great would be to get all four of the girls and you in this office together. But that's probably more of a pipe dream at this point."

"My world is full of pipe dreams at this point," Maggie said.

———

They drove home together, in silence for the first couple of miles.

Then Maggie said, "Did you girls feel comfortable with Scarlett?"

"Who?" Rose asked.

"The therapist."

"Oh, Mrs. Silverman," Jean said. "She was very nice. I think we should all just go in together next time. Because everything we want her to know we want you to know too. And that way we don't have to say it all twice."

"I just thought you might want to speak to a therapist privately."

"That was very nice of you to think of that," Jean said. "But we don't. We don't have any secrets from you. Did she tell you what we talked about? I told her she could."

"She told me about the guilt you were feeling, and about the trauma around losing your parents. But not much else. Was there more?"

They drove in silence for a few blocks. Maggie saw the ocean come into view from her driver's-side window. She felt drawn to it, maybe for much the same reason the girls had been drawn to it after John Bishop's memorial—as a way of washing the mood clean.

"We're worried this might come out wrong," Jean said.

"I think . . . just say it. I'm thinking whatever you say will be okay."

"But it's about your daughters."

"That's all right. You're entitled to a complex set of feelings about them."

"Not entirely sure I know what that means," Jean said. "I mean . . . I get the gist of it. Anyway, here goes." But for several seconds nothing went. "We feel like they're looking down on us."

Maggie felt her grip on the steering wheel tighten.

Yes, probably her daughters were looking down on the new foster girls from Louisiana. And it was probably best not to deny Jean and Rose's experience with their attitudes. Then again, she didn't want to solidify and validate the impression if it would make them feel even worse.

It was hard to know how to proceed.

"If they are," she said after a time, "it's more a reflection on them than it is on you."

Both girls seemed to chew that over for a few beats. They had both opted to sit in the back, maybe because they liked to sit close together, and Maggie glanced in the rearview mirror and watched them briefly.

"We're not really sure what that means," Rose said.

"It means . . . you're not 'less than.' You're not less than anybody. You're not beneath anybody. If anybody treats you like you're somehow not as good as they are, that shows a problem with them, not with you. Most of the time when somebody acts like they're better than you it's because they're afraid they're not as good. Or maybe all the time."

"Really?" Jean said. "That's an odd thought. I never looked at it that way before."

"Okay, but think about it. Let's say a person is happy and confident and sure of who they are. Say they're sure they're a good person, pretty much just the person they want to be. Why would they want to make anybody else feel small?"

"Hmm," Jean said. "I guess that does kind of make sense. But why would your girls worry they're not as good?"

"Well . . . they know I've been a bit concerned about their behavior lately—that I feel like they're being selfish and spoiled. And they've probably picked up on the fact that you two are just about the polar opposite of selfish and spoiled. And they must know I appreciate that about you . . ."

Maggie looked up to see her own house. To see that it was time to turn into her driveway. It struck her how much she'd been driving on autopilot as they spoke. How much the car had seemed to go home almost of its own accord.

"Wow," Jean said. "That's a lot to think about. When's my first driving lesson? Can we do a driving lesson today?"

"You have to get your permit first."

"I got it today. Alex came home at lunch and took me to the DMV. I thought he would've told you. There are some things I'm supposed to do before I get a private lesson, but it's up to you . . ."

"I haven't talked to him since lunch."

"So . . . today?"

"Tell you what. Here's what I think we should do. For your very first lesson I think a huge empty parking lot would be a good idea. Let's wait till morning and we'll go down to the mall around seven o'clock before any of the stores are open. And we'll have acres and acres of parking lot all to ourselves."

———

"We drive with one foot," Maggie said. "Our right foot."

She sat in the passenger seat of her car in the empty sea of mall parking, watching Jean stare at the dashboard in fascination and horror.

"That seems odd," Jean said. "There are two pedals and I have two feet."

"I'm just teaching you what I was taught. Most cars today have automatic transmissions. But someday you might want to drive a stick shift. And if you ever do, you'll need your left foot for the clutch. It's a very hard transition to make for people who've been two-footed drivers."

"Oh," Jean said. "Okay. I want to learn right."

"Take your right foot and feel where the gas pedal is and where the brake is. The brake is the wider one."

The engine revved slightly when Jean touched the gas pedal, and it made her jump.

Maggie turned to look at Rose in the back seat. She looked even more nervous than her sister. Maggie caught the girl's eye and smiled, and that seemed to put her more at ease.

She turned her attention back to Jean.

"Release the hand brake. That's right. Now put your foot on the brake and shift it into 'drive.'"

"Okay," Jean said. She struggled briefly with the gearshift, then seemed proud and relieved to see the letter D illuminated. "Now what?"

"Just take your foot off the brake. Don't even press on the gas yet. Just release the brake and the car will roll forward a little."

Jean moved her foot and the car moved.

"Well, this is not so bad," Jean said.

"Now brake gently. Good. Now release the brake again."

"This is easy enough."

"Now very gently give it a little bit of gas."

"Oh. Right."

Jean pressed the accelerator, but it was too much, and the car lurched forward.

"That's okay," Maggie said. "It was your first time."

"Where's the brake? Where's the brake?"

"You don't need it yet. Just ease off the gas a little and keep going forward. There's nothing out here to hit."

"There's that light post," Jean said, and pointed.

"Just steer around it."

"Which way?"

"Either way. Just turn the wheel and go around it."

Jean steered right, and they passed the pole with a good twenty feet to spare.

"And let me tell you something about where you're looking," Maggie said. "Be careful where you're looking. Don't look at your hood. Look out beyond it. And look where you want to go, not where you don't want to go. If you're looking at a light post, there'll be a tendency to steer toward it without meaning to. We tend to end up where we're putting all our attention. A good lesson for life as well as driving."

"I'm not sure about the life part," Jean said. "I don't get what you mean by that."

"That's probably a more adult concept. Don't worry about it. Okay, the brake is just to the left of where your foot is now. Find it and gently stop. Good. Now give it some gas again."

They repeated the simple process three more times. Stop, go, steer around any oncoming light post.

"Rose, look!" Jean said. "I'm driving a car!"

"I can see that, dummy. I'm *in* the car with you."

Jean stopped the car without having been asked. She sat a minute, staring through the windshield, her face darkening. Her eyes clouded over with whatever she was thinking.

"But this is a *car*," she said.

"Not sure where we're going with this," Maggie said.

"That's an RV. How big an RV?"

"Not too big as RVs go. But you'll have plenty of time to get used to this first. Probably Lacey won't turn the wheel over to you unless it's straight highway driving all the way through."

Jean stared through the windshield a minute longer, blinking too much.

"That's so much responsibility," she said, her voice barely over a whisper.

"You don't have to do it if it feels like too much."

"But she needs me to do it."

That was when Maggie noticed that the girl was shaking. It came up suddenly, and in just a matter of seconds it turned violent. Like a full-on panic attack. Jean seemed to try to talk, but by then her breathing had grown labored and desperate, and she couldn't speak.

She shifted the car into "park," pulled on the hand brake, and jumped out.

Maggie stepped out into the parking lot and tried to address Jean over the roof of the car, but the girl was hunched over, holding her own knees. Maggie could feel the panic flowing off the girl in waves. Or maybe it was her own. Or both. It was impossible to tell.

Maggie ran around.

"You want me to take over?"

Jean nodded silently.

"You want to go home now?"

An even more emphatic nod.

"Are you okay? Is there anything I can do for you?"

No answer.

"Just home?"

Jean nodded. She stumbled around to the passenger side and Maggie got in behind the wheel, and they headed for home.

"Try putting your head between your knees," she said to the girl. "And breathe as deeply and evenly as you can."

Maggie looked at Rose in the rearview mirror and Rose looked back.

"Does she have a history of panic attacks?"

"Not so much before the storm," Rose said. "But after that . . . after our parents . . . a couple times, yeah."

"Anything I can do for her?"

"I think she just wants to go home."

They drove home in a strained silence punctuated only by Jean's desperate breathing. She was obviously trying to follow directions and breathe deeply and evenly, but it was not easy and not entirely working.

When they arrived home Jean leaped out of the car and ran inside. Rose followed.

Maggie walked through the house to see where they had gone. She looked in their room in the basement, but it was empty.

She found them out in the yard with Sunny. Jean was sitting on the grass and hugging the dog tightly, and he was licking her ear in return. Rose was sitting close by with one hand on her sister's shoulder.

"She'll be okay," Rose said. "It's getting a little better. She told me so."

"Did she say why it got so bad?"

"It dawned on her that people are depending on her and she can't say no to people if they're depending on her and it felt like she was supposed to be the one taking care of a thing, like the driving-the-RV thing, but she's just a kid and she's used to our parents taking care of everything."

"Got it," Maggie said.

She sat on the other side of the girl, and she and Rose both held Jean until the shaking subsided.

Chapter Seventeen

Why It's Not Great

Willa called on a Friday morning, about nine months after she and Gemma had moved away. Which was unusual enough on the face of the thing. The girls had rarely called Maggie since leaving home, and had not betrayed much openness when Maggie called them.

"We want to come to dinner *soon*," Willa said. "Sooner than Sunday."

"Why, do you have something you want to do on Sunday?"

"Um . . . yeah." But she didn't sound all that convincing.

"It's already Friday. How much sooner were you thinking?"

"Like tonight," Willa said.

"I wasn't planning anything very special for dinner tonight. I was going to make spaghetti, and I know you're not a fan."

"It's not that. I don't *not* like it exactly. It's just so much carbs, and I'm on a diet, which you would know if you kept track of me or were interested, or cared, and I'm not supposed to have carbs on my diet."

"Willa, you *so* don't need to lose weight. It worries me. I really wish—"

"Mom," Willa said, cutting her off. "Don't start."

"Fine. I could get takeout if you prefer. I could get Alex to bring home dinner from Merv's."

"Yeah, that would work."

"But you know Merv's sandwiches also have carbs."

"Yeah but Merv's sandwiches are worth breaking over for. We'll be there at six thirty."

Maggie opened her mouth to ask if Dan was planning to drive them, but her daughter had already clicked off the phone.

———

Her daughters arrived at nearly seven, and they arrived alone. Which set things off on a very bad footing.

Jean and Rose had put on two of their nicer outfits in anticipation of Willa and Gemma's arrival—which Maggie had tried hard to convince them was not necessary—and they jumped to their feet and stood nervously as the two girls came through the door.

Willa looked at Jean and Rose. Looked them up and down as if adding a column of numbers in her head. But then she looked away again and said nothing. Not even hello.

Gemma nodded at them glumly.

"Why didn't Dan come in?" Maggie asked.

"Because he's home," Willa said.

"Who drove you here?"

"I did."

"Wait. You have your license?"

"No, but I have a learner's permit."

Willa threw her purse on one of the chairs by the door. Literally threw it, as though throwing it *at* the chair.

"A learner's permit requires an adult to be in the car with you at all times. And I'm not sure, but I think it also restricts you from driving after dark."

"It's not *dark*," Willa shouted, rolling her eyes.

"But it will be by the time you drive home."

"Could you let it go, Mom? Can you ever let anything go? Dad said it's okay."

"Then I'll take it up with your dad."

Willa made a huffing sound. Then she and her sister went off to look into their old rooms. As if the rooms might have been stolen in their absence.

———

"Should we tell them the good news?" Alex asked over dinner.

There had been no previous discussion about any of it, and Maggie suspected he had brought it up only—or mostly—because he couldn't stand another minute of the strained silence.

"What news is that?" Maggie asked, though she was ninety percent sure she knew.

Alex touched the ring finger of his left hand, and Maggie nodded. "Go for it," she said.

"Unless you'd rather."

"No, it's all yours."

Alex wiped his mouth on his napkin and set it on the table next to his plate. A bit formally, Maggie thought.

"Your mother and I are getting married."

"Whoa," Gemma said. "When were you planning to tell us that?"

"We told you just now," Maggie said.

"It's great!" Rose said, her voice nearly squeaky with excitement.

"It's not that great," Willa said back, her voice quiet and thin.

"Why is it not great?" Rose asked.

Willa only stared at the table.

"Yeah," Maggie said. "I'm a little curious myself. Why is it not great?"

While she was waiting for an answer she glanced at Alex, who looked crestfallen. In fact, he looked almost seasick.

"Nothing," Willa said. "Never mind."

"No, really," Maggie said. "Now I want to know. Why is it not great?"

"It's fine," Willa said. "I'm sorry I ever brought it up."

Maggie turned her attention to Gemma, who was picking the fat off the corned beef in her sandwich.

"You haven't weighed in on this, Gemma."

For an extended moment Gemma continued to pick apart the meat without answering. Then, still staring at the sandwich, she said, "It's not great because it means you and Dad are never getting back together."

Maggie felt it in her gut like a bowling ball, accidentally swallowed.

"Oh, honey," she said. "I'm so sorry. I had no idea you thought we ever would."

"Well, we didn't think you *would*. Exactly. But I guess we sort of thought you *might*."

"I'm sorry. To both of you. I wish I'd known. I would have cleared up the misunderstanding long before now. But believe me, whether Alex and I got married or not, that was never going to happen."

They all ate for a minute in silence.

Then Willa said, in Alex's general direction, "You didn't even get her a ring?"

"We're working on it," Alex said. "It was a recent decision."

Maggie recognized the overly measured tones Alex fell into when he needed to work to hold his temper around the girls.

Willa set down her sandwich and drilled her gaze straight into his face. He looked back with something that looked like a cross between defiance and dread.

"Let me ask you this, then," she said. "You're about to be our stepfather, so I want to know where you stand. Is there anything wrong with me driving over here with just a learner's permit?"

"Of course there is," Alex said. "You're supposed to have a licensed adult in the car with you at all times."

Willa rolled her eyes again.

"You two *should* get married. You're perfect for each other. Nerds of a feather."

"Where did you hear that?" Maggie asked, thinking it sounded more imaginative and clever than she expected from Willa, not to mention based on an old saying she doubted the girl would know.

"Nowhere. I made it up."

"She saw it on TV," Gemma said, "and thought it was funny."

Willa shot her sister a scathing look. Then she turned her attention to the new girls across the table. She drilled her gaze into Jean, who looked back with a face full of utter panic. Maggie wasn't sure if Jean was even breathing.

"What about *you*?" Willa asked.

"What *about* me?" Jean asked in a tiny, thin voice.

"You're sixteen, right?"

"Yeah."

"Have you got a learner's permit?"

"Yeah."

"If your mom or your dad said it was okay to drive alone with it, would you do it?"

Jean cleared her throat nervously and glanced sideways at Maggie, as if sending out an SOS call. But then she bravely took on the question.

"The only mom or dad I have are right here at the table. And they've already said they wouldn't want that."

"But if they did?"

"If it's not legal, I wouldn't do it."

"Great," Willa said, in a tone that made it clear that she did not find it great.

"I think it's time to shut down this entire line of conversation," Maggie said.

But even as the words were leaving her mouth she sensed that the conversation had died a natural death on its own.

They ate in silence for several minutes before Maggie noticed some kind of quiet negotiation going on between her daughters. It started with weighted glances and nods or shakes of their heads. Soon it spilled into whispers, mostly loud enough for Maggie to hear.

"I don't want to do it now," she heard Willa say. "It'll never work. This'll be just as bad."

"Okay," Maggie said. She spoke loudly, and the whispering halted suddenly. "I sensed an agenda when you called and pushed dinner up to tonight. Now we're hearing whispers of it. I think it's time to let everybody know what's going on."

For an almost painful length of time nothing was said. Her daughters stared down at the table as though caught in the act of . . . well, Maggie didn't know. Something bad, anyway.

It was Gemma who finally piped up.

"We hate it at Dad's," she said weakly. "We want to come home."

That just sat on the table for a moment in stunned silence. Even the figurative echo of the words seemed stunned.

Despite the slight feeling of shock, it was not a complete surprise to Maggie. After a month or so at their dad's they had begun to hint that they were not happy there. Then Maggie had sat them down and gently broken it to them that she had filed to adopt Jean and Rose, and they had grown silent again—and more distant, if such a thing were possible.

"Of course," Maggie said. "It's your house. You were always welcome back here. I never wanted you to leave in the first place. You're both agreed on this?"

"I want to talk to Mom privately," Willa said.

They both rose from the table, and Willa followed Maggie into the kitchen.

"I *was* sure," Willa said. "But now I don't know. I can't get along with them. I can't even talk to them. I don't understand them at all. Do I have to talk to them?"

"I would say," Maggie began, leaning her back against the kitchen island and crossing her arms, "that the same guidelines apply as they did for John's memorial. You won't be forced to talk to them more than you want to, but when you do talk to them I expect you to be somewhere between civil and gracious. And in case you're wondering where that line is, you've been on the wrong side of it for most of tonight."

Willa seemed to brush the criticism aside.

"They'll be in the basement, right?"

"To sleep. During the day they can be in any part of the house or the yard they like. And week after next the contractor is coming with a few of his guys to start fixing it up down there, so they won't be able to go down there at all till it's done."

"I'm not sharing a room. That would be a total deal-breaker."

"They'll be in my office during the construction. I thought I told you that already."

"It's our house. They shouldn't be able to chase us out of our own house."

"Oh, wow," Maggie said, feeling her ire rising. "There is just so much wrong with that sentence. First of all, you know I'm in the process of adopting them, so it's their house too. Except to the extent that it's *my* house. You're my daughters, so it's yours too, but let's not forget who pays the mortgage. And nobody chased you out of anywhere. Those girls have been nothing but friendly to you and Gemma. You decided to leave. Everybody wanted you to stay except you. That's the kind of attitude I'd like to see you working on. You can do better than you're doing right now. I know you can. I've seen you do it."

Willa stood in silence for a time, gazing out toward the dining room. As if the correct answer might waft in to her from there.

"Okay," she said. "I'll really try."

Maggie breathed a deep sigh of relief. Really breathed fully since her girls had first walked in the door. She was getting her daughters back. And she could feel a sense of elation about it. But underneath that was the cold, hard knowledge that the happy family she'd been guiltily enjoying was now over. Home would be a challenge from this moment on.

It was almost painful to feel two such conflicting emotions so strongly, and at the same time.

"Thank you," she said. "You don't know how much that means to me."

She put her arm around her daughter's shoulder, and they walked back to the dining room together. All eyes rose to their faces.

"It's official," Maggie said. "The girls are moving back home."

PART THREE

ALL FOUR GIRLS

Chapter Eighteen

Introduction to Sushi

"Oh my God!" Maggie heard one of the girls shout. It sounded like Gemma.

It was a relief to identify the voice as one of her biological daughters, and they tended to get upset over very small things, even now, after almost three months of living together. Nearly nonexistent things, in most cases. Such an exclamation from Jean or Rose would have meant actual trouble.

Maggie moved in the direction of the sound and bumped into Gemma in the hallway.

"Look at this!" Gemma shrieked, hurting Maggie's ears.

She held out her purse—a soft pink leather bag that she tended to wear cross-body.

"What about it?"

"Look at it! It's ruined!"

"How is it ruined? I don't even see what you're seeing."

"Here. Look. Look right here. That awful dog chewed it to shreds."

Maggie took the purse in her hands and looked more closely. Near one of the straps she saw a few soft teeth marks.

"You seem unclear on the concept of shreds," Maggie said. "Walk and talk. My toast is about to burn."

Gemma followed her into the kitchen, still seething.

"What is somebody going to do about that dog? Why was he even in my room? It's my room. He can't just go in there and destroy my things."

"Well, you're in luck," Maggie said, "because the dog trainer is coming again this morning."

"Why didn't you hire one sooner?"

"We wanted to see what Jean and Rose could do on their own with three books on the subject."

"Oh well. At least we have one now. You think she can stop him?"

"I think puppies go through a chewing stage and you have to make adjustments for them. Have you considered leaving the door to your room closed?"

"How is he a puppy? He's huge!"

"But he's still a puppy on the inside until he's at least two."

"It gets hot in there. The AC vent in there isn't nearly big enough."

"Okay. I'll talk to the contractor about putting in another vent. Or a bigger vent. And in the meantime, maybe put your things up where Sunny can't reach them."

The coffee maker beeped, and Maggie took down two mugs, one for herself and one for Alex, and poured.

"I shouldn't have to do that!" Gemma whined. "It's my house and I shouldn't have to do that!"

Maggie felt herself grow angry. Truly angry, for the first time that morning. She looked over at her younger daughter, taking a few seconds to breathe before speaking. Reminding herself that she had promised to do better.

Alex came trotting down the stairs and into the kitchen. He took one look at Maggie's face and switched into retreat mode, grabbing one of the coffees without stopping.

"I'll just have my coffee out by the pool with Jean and Rose."

"How do you know they're out by the pool?"

"Because they're always out by the pool."

She watched his retreating back for a moment or two, then turned back to her daughter.

"When you girls were little, I had to babyproof the entire house. For years. Do you have any idea how much work that is? Every cupboard, every drawer had to have a special latch that you couldn't work, except I could barely work them myself. Even the toilet seats had to be locked down. Everything had to be out of your reach, but then you started climbing, and everything had to be locked away. Period. And not once did I say 'This is my house and I shouldn't have to do this.' I made adjustments for you. Because that's what you do. That's how you take care of a young living thing. And in time you grew out of it."

Gemma was standing with her hands on her hips. Defiantly. Clearly Maggie's speech was not having the desired effect. It was not softening Gemma.

"That's entirely different."

"I don't see why."

"Because I'm a *person*."

"So? Why is that so different? People and animals both go through stages when they're young."

Maggie had planned to say more, but before she could gather her thoughts the doorbell rang.

"That would be the dog trainer," Maggie said.

"Good," Gemma huffed.

"Go let her in, okay? You can complain to her instead of to me."

———

Maggie bumped into the dog trainer in the kitchen about half an hour later. The woman was standing at the kitchen sink washing her hands.

She was a sturdy-looking woman in her late thirties with a quick smile and a no-nonsense short haircut. Unfortunately, Maggie had forgotten her name.

"Coffee?" Maggie asked.

"No, I should get going. I just wanted to catch you up on our progress."

"Please," Maggie said. "I've been wondering. I'm sorry, I've forgotten your name."

"June."

"June. Of course. How could I forget that in the month of June?"

June dried her hands, and they sat together at the island-style table.

"Is there hope for the little guy?" Maggie asked.

June seemed caught off guard by the question.

"Oh, he's a *wonderful* puppy. He'll be a really nice dog. Shy, and still showing that he was traumatized, but you'll be amazed how they come around if you love them. Dogs drop their bad pasts a lot better than we drop ours. He's very sweet and seems to love everybody. Not sure he'll ever be a watchdog, but at least you don't have to worry about him biting anybody. Rose said he's only had one accident in the house this week, so if those are the straight goods it's excellent progress."

"Rose is pretty honest."

"That's my impression too. He's eager to please. He'll be a great family dog. I have no idea what went wrong with the family—or person—who had him before, but they don't know what they gave up."

"We just figured he never had a home."

"He's already neutered," June said.

That forced a moment of silence while Maggie let that settle in her head. Whoever had owned him must not have had him long, because she thought most people waited until at least the age Sunny was when they'd found him—if not longer—to spay or neuter. And they couldn't have treated him well.

She remembered Rose saying, in the RV in Louisiana, that Sunny had told her nobody ever cared about him. Then again, the fact that somebody had owned the dog didn't necessarily mean they cared. Had they abandoned him? Or treated him so badly that he'd run away from the only home he'd ever known? Was a puppy even sufficiently independent-minded to do that? Maggie didn't know enough about dogs to decide.

"I never thought to check about that," she said. "I figured we'd have to do it soon. I thought we'd already put it off longer than we should have."

"Somebody saved you the trouble."

"And it would seem that's the only thing we can thank them for. Did you talk to my other two daughters at all? Gemma was mad at him this morning."

"Yeah, she told me he chewed her purse to shreds. And then she showed me the purse."

The corner of June's mouth was trying to twist into a wry smile and she seemed to be attempting to control it.

"I know, right? I already told her she seemed unclear on the concept of shreds."

"I talked to her a little about puppy-proofing."

"And what was her reaction?"

"She seemed receptive."

"Weird. I told her the same thing and she exploded."

"I'm not her mother though. I'm glad I caught you at home so I could tell you how things are going. I thought you'd be at work."

Maggie frowned. She hadn't meant to, but she could feel herself do it.

"I took a leave of absence," she said. "I haven't worked since school let out for the summer again. I wasn't too sure about leaving the four girls home alone all day. You know. Especially now, with school out and everything. When I go back I might have to get some kind of nanny. Or just skip the formalities and hire a referee."

June laughed.

"I've got to tell you," June said. "I work with some pretty rambunctious clients. One is over two hundred pounds. Most are way too full of energy, and a couple of them bite. And I still wouldn't trade places with you for all the money in the world. Four teenagers who don't get along? I don't know how you do it."

Maggie opened her mouth to say she wasn't sure how she did it, either. Or that she wasn't sure if she even *was* doing it. But at that moment her phone rang in her pocket.

"I should write you a check," she said to June.

"End of the month is fine. I'll see myself out."

Maggie slipped her phone out of her pocket and was stunned to see that the caller ID read "Eleanor Price." She only stared at it for a moment as it rang, wondering what possible reason the TV host would have to call her. Then she realized the only way she could answer that question would be to pick up the call.

"Hello," she said, in a generic tone that did not betray that she knew who was calling.

"Maggie? Eleanor Price."

"Wow. I must say I'm surprised to hear from you. What can I do to help you?"

Maggie stood and walked over to the sliding glass window as they spoke and stared out into the yard. Jean and Rose were practicing obedience with the dog. Commanding him to sit and then lie down. Her own daughters were nowhere to be seen.

"First of all," Eleanor said, "I heard you and Alex are engaged, so congratulations."

"Wait. How do you *know* that?"

"The same way I knew about you in the first place. My makeup person's niece is a nurse who works with Alex. Did you not know that?"

"I . . . don't think I knew it, no. I wasn't sure how you happened to hear about us. Maybe Alex told me during one of those times when I was holding too much in my overloaded brain. Sometimes someone will put something in my head at the wrong time and it drops right back out again."

"I hear you. Well, let me cut to the chase, hon. I'm interested in this thing about you coming back from Hurricane Mina with two more girls. Amazing human-interest story. Now you have four teenagers? How's that going?"

"Don't ask," Maggie said. "You'll only get me started."

"I'd like to do a segment on it if you're open to the idea. But we might not be able to get your two new daughters on camera, what with them being fosters."

"They are *not* fosters," Maggie said with an invisible swell of pride. "They have been successfully adopted."

"So fast?"

"It took about eight months from the time we started the paper-work. But yes, that's a good outcome. It went very smoothly. Still, I'm not sure about having all four together in an interview."

"Great human-interest story."

Out the window the training session seemed to have ended. Rose was playing chase games with the dog, trading back and forth regarding who chased whom.

"Wouldn't it be a better human-interest story if they all got along?" Maggie asked into the phone.

"Not really. Happy families don't fill a whole segment. The meat of a story is when people have obstacles to overcome."

"Oh, we have obstacles. But I don't know, Eleanor. All four girls would have to be on board with it, and I really doubt my girls would play along. Jean and Rose would do it if I asked them to, but I'd have to be sure it's really the best thing for them. Maybe it's too vulnerable to go on national TV and talk about your birth parents drowning right in front of you. Willa and Gemma . . . if they know I want them to do it, they probably won't. They're mad at me these days."

"I don't know, though. You'd be surprised. Teenagers like to see themselves on TV."

"I'll ask. Of course I'll ask. How soon do you need to know?"

"No strict time limit on it, really. Call me, love. Call me either way, please. So I know."

"Will do."

Maggie opened her mouth to say thank you, but the call had already ended.

———

Maggie walked outside an hour later to talk to the two newly adopted girls about a TV appearance, but the subject was changed immediately.

Jean was sitting on the edge of a chaise longue, crying. Rose was hovering over her with one arm around her shoulder, and Sunny was attempting to lick her face.

The girls' pain hit Maggie in the gut like those battering rams police use to break down doors. Or, at least, that was how she imagined it.

"Oh, no," Maggie said. "What happened?"

Jean straightened up immediately, swiping at her eyes as if trying to wipe the situation away.

"Nothing," she said. "It was nothing."

Maggie sat next to the girl, and Sunny began trying to lick Maggie's face too. Not instead of, but also. His head swept back and forth as though he were watching a game of tennis, but with licking.

"Really nothing? Like, literally nothing happened and it's more like something that happened a while ago coming up and making you cry? Or nothing as in something happened but you want me to think it's no big thing?"

Jean opened her mouth, but for an extended time—several seconds— no sound emerged.

"They were making fun of our accents," Rose said.

"Willa and Gemma?"

Rose nodded.

"I don't think they knew I could hear them," Jean said, as if excusing them.

"Which *so* does not make it okay," Maggie shot back. "I'm going to go have a talk with my girls."

She rose, but Jean's hands reached out to grab her wrist.

"No, don't! They'll know I ratted them out and things will get even worse!"

"If you can overhear them, so can I."

Jean's hands slowly released their grip on her, and Maggie stomped into the house.

She found both of her daughters in Gemma's room, sitting on the bed. Their heads were close together and they were laughing about something. Maggie leaned in the doorway, and the girls looked up at her face and registered alarm over what they saw there.

"Having a merry little laugh over the way other people speak?"

Maggie watched the color drain from her daughters' faces.

"You heard that?" Willa asked. "We didn't think anybody heard that."

"Ah. So you were making fun of people behind their backs. That's so much better."

"You're being sarcastic," Gemma said. "Right?"

"Very."

"*They* didn't hear, did they?"

"In fact, Jean's out in the backyard crying right now."

"Oh," both girls said at once.

Suddenly Gemma's bedspread became a source of fascination. The girls couldn't take their eyes off it.

"Which is better?" Maggie asked, her voice hard but calm. "California or Louisiana?"

"Is this a trick question?" Willa asked.

"If I told you that, it would ruin the trick."

"I guess we're supposed to say they're the same," Gemma said.

"Actually, you're supposed to *believe* they're the same. But clearly you don't. Clearly I've raised a couple of California chauvinists."

"I thought that was a feminist thing," Willa said.

"Those are male chauvinists. These are California chauvinists. A chauvinist is anyone who thinks what they are is better. I never taught you that. Where did you learn it, then?"

"We . . . live in the world?" Willa said.

"Right. Got it. Well, here's the deal. Think what you have to, but if it's a form of looking down on your adopted sisters, then you just keep those thoughts to yourself. Completely. Even if you're pretty sure they're not listening. Are we clear about that?"

"Yes Mom," they both said, weakly, overlapping one another rather than in unison.

———

Rose stuck her head into the dining room as Maggie was setting the table for dinner.

"Ooh, dinner," she said. "Great. I'm starving. What are we having?"

"Oddly," Maggie said, "I have no idea. Alex is coming home in about ten minutes and he's bringing takeout with him. But I don't know what kind."

"Alex is already home," Alex said.

She turned to see him standing in the dining-room doorway with a positively massive bag of food.

"Sushi Palace," Maggie said, reading the stamp on the bag. "Willa and Gemma will be thrilled. Not sure how Jean and Rose will feel."

Maggie turned back to Rose, whose face looked lost and confused.

"We never had sushi," Rose said. "But we'll try it. We'll try anything."

"I purposely brought a ton of salmon-skin rolls and California rolls," Alex said.

"Is that good?" Rose asked.

"Those are two kinds of sushi that aren't raw," Maggie said. "Think of it as beginner sushi."

"I'll go get Jean," Rose said. Then she stopped. Turned back to Maggie. Her mind seemed to be turning. It showed on her face. "Should I get Willa and Gemma too?"

"I'm guessing you mean do you dare?"

"Something like that."

"I think they can handle your telling them dinner is served. If not it'll be a learning opportunity."

———

"What's the green stuff?" Jean asked, pointing with her chopsticks into the miniature tub of wasabi. "Is it an avocado thing?"

"No!" Maggie said. "Whatever you do, don't put that on your food like it was something mild like guacamole. It's wasabi, and it's a type of horseradish. Very, very hot."

Jean scooped a tiny bit of the green paste onto her chopstick and licked it cautiously. Maggie watched the girl's eyes open wide, and she coughed three times.

"Maybe I'll just skip that," she said.

"This ginger stuff is good," Rose said. "Can we pick up the salmon-skin rolls with our hands?"

"Absolutely. You're supposed to. But you can pick up anything else with your hands, too, if you're not used to chopsticks."

"I want to try them though," Jean said.

She reached out and tried to grasp a section of California roll, but the chopsticks slipped and crossed each other, and the sushi dropped onto the serving plate again.

Willa and Gemma laughed. Or anyway, they started to. But Maggie shot them a truly withering gaze and their faces turned stony.

They ate in silence for a time, Maggie watching Willa unwind her yellowtail roll so she could eat the fish and leave the rice.

Maggie opened her mouth to float the Eleanor Price idea. But before she could, Willa spoke.

"I'm sorry about what happened earlier," she said.

It was clear by context that she was speaking to Jean and Rose, but she continued to stare down at the tablecloth and carefully avoid their eyes.

"Thank you," Jean said quietly.

"And I know we should have said this a really, really long time ago, but it totally sucks how you lost your parents that way, and we're sorry that happened. Aren't we, Gemma?"

"Yeah," Gemma said. "We wouldn't wish that on anybody."

It was an unfortunate turn of phrase, because it made it sound as though her new sisters were far down on the list of those she'd seek to protect.

But it was progress, and Maggie didn't want to mess with progress. So loath was she to disturb that delicate moment that she decided to save the Eleanor Price question for another time.

———

"Okay, go ahead and tell me. What did the girls say about it?" Alex asked her as they climbed into bed that night.

"About the TV thing with Eleanor Price?"

"The exact thing in question, yes."

"I actually haven't had a chance to broach the subject with them yet. It's surprisingly hard to get them all together in one room."

"And then when you do," Alex said, breaking into a wry smile, "you kind of wish you hadn't."

Maggie matched his smile.

"That too. But I was going to say something more like 'When I do, things tend to go in a different direction and it's hard to stop them.' The four of them can get things off track pretty fast. But maybe it's a mistake anyway."

"The TV thing?"

"Right. I mean, does it kind of smack of . . . airing our dirty linen in public?"

"I see nothing dirty about our linen. Blended families are hard."

"The dirty part of our linen is that Willa and Gemma are being less than magnanimous, and we'd be putting that all across the country for people to judge. I can't imagine they'd want that. But I do agree that any blended family would have issues." She paused, nervous about the next part. Then she added, "Is this all too much for you?"

She tossed it off like a light comment, but honestly, she had been worrying about it.

"I had nine brothers," Alex said. "Commotion is as natural to me as breathing. Don't you worry about me. And as to the TV thing, I don't think you should stress too much about whether it's a good idea or not. They'll probably refuse anyway. But either way their answers will solve the problem for you."

Chapter Nineteen

I Can't Drive with You Staring at Me

Maggie was sitting at the breakfast table with Jean and Rose, sipping coffee and watching them eat cereal, when construction began in the basement.

"Whoa," Rose said, her mouth still full.

"Yeah, it's going to be bad for a while. But then it'll be such a nice area for you girls."

She looked up to see Willa standing in the kitchen doorway, still in her silk robin's-egg-blue pajamas. Her hair was wildly uncombed, her face positively seething.

Maggie opened her mouth to say that she had something she wanted to discuss with all four girls as soon as Gemma was up.

She never got to say it.

"Why is it seven o'clock in the morning?" Willa bellowed.

"I think it pretty much is once every day," Rose said, apparently trying not to smile.

"That's not funny," Willa said.

"I thought it was funny," Maggie said.

"You know what I meant. Why are they making all this noise at seven o'clock in the morning?"

"I'm sorry," Maggie said. "That's just when construction people start."

"And we're supposed to be blasted awake at this hour for how long?"

"If we're lucky, maybe . . . a month?"

Willa dropped her head back. Rolled her eyes. Then she squeezed them shut for an extended time.

"Why didn't you do this a long time ago?"

"They kept saying they didn't want it or need it. But after the adoption came through I decided they were getting it anyway."

"I need coffee," she said. "Is there coffee?"

"I didn't even know you drank it," Maggie said.

"Yeah, well, there's a lot you don't know about me. *Is* there any or not?"

"Sit down," she said. "I'll pour you a cup."

Maggie had to get up anyway to make another pot. Otherwise there would be none for Alex when he got out of the shower.

"I know it's inconvenient," Maggie said. "And I'm sorry. But I want to have decent rooms for the girls."

For a moment Willa just sat there at the table with her face in her hands.

Then, through her fingers, she said, "The girls. Right. Of course. I remember when *we* were the girls."

Jean and Rose carefully concentrated on their cereal.

"I apologize for the phrasing," Maggie said. "But also . . . be careful to stay on the right side of that line."

She set a mug of coffee in front of Willa, who never replied.

"When Gemma gets up," Maggie said, "I want to talk to you girls about something. Where *is* Gemma? She couldn't possibly sleep through all this."

"Gemma can sleep through anything," Willa said. "It's like her superpower."

A long silence fell. At least, if one could call that level of construction noise silence.

Just as Maggie was sitting down again to let the coffee brew, Jean looked up into Maggie's face. She looked hopeful and shy.

"You think I could have a driving lesson today?"

It was a positive sign, because Maggie hadn't been sure Jean would ever want another lesson after the panic attack of the first one all those months in the past. But she decided it was better not to address that issue in front of Willa.

"Um . . ." Maggie tried to force her mind to focus on the day, but couldn't really bring any plans into clear focus. "I guess. Yeah. We should do it soon, though, before the mall opens."

"Hell*o-o*," Willa said, putting a sarcastic emphasis on the last syllable. Her arms were spread wide as if to indicate the size of the world to all those present. "I *also* have a learner's permit. And you're not asking me if *I* want a lesson."

"You drove yourself and your sister over here for dinner with no adult present. Some time ago. I would hope that means you've had all the lessons you need."

"I need to learn to parallel park. I didn't need it to drive over here because I could just pull into the driveway. But I'll need it for the test."

"Okay," Maggie said, "come with us."

She expected that to settle the matter, but Willa's jaw only dropped, leaving her mouth hanging wide open.

"Come with you," Willa said flatly.

"Wasn't that what you wanted?"

They spoke with voices raised to be heard over the construction.

"And sit in the back while she takes her lesson."

"Right."

"And then she'll be sitting in the back while I take mine."

"Right."

"Staring at me."

"You can't see someone staring at you when they're behind you. Even if she was going to stare. Which I doubt."

"I could look out the window," Jean said.

Willa swept all of that away with no apparent consideration.

"I can't drive with a stranger staring at me."

"First of all," Maggie said, "she's not a stranger. She's your adopted sister. You've been living together for months. Second, and more importantly for your driving future, you know who's *actually* a stranger? The guy at the DMV who gives you the test. And guess what he does the whole time you're driving?"

Maggie was interested to hear what kind of comeback Willa could possibly mount, but she never found out.

Instead Gemma came stomping into the kitchen, fully dressed.

"Why. Is. It. So. *Noisy!*"

The last word was a full-on shriek.

"They've started the construction on Jean and Rose's area in the basement," Maggie said, careful not to repeat her mistake of calling them, simply, "the girls."

"Ah," Gemma said. "Jean and Rose. Of course."

There was subtext there. Maggie was weighing whether to address it when Alex walked into the kitchen, freshly showered and shaved.

He walked straight to Maggie and kissed her briefly on the lips.

"Your mother is coming," he said.

"Excuse me?"

"Your mother. Coming here. For a visit."

"How do you know this and I don't?"

"You left your phone upstairs on the bedside table. I picked it up because I saw Bess on the caller ID. I was trying to tell her to hold on while I carried the phone down to you, but she insisted I just give you the message instead."

"Great," Maggie said. But it was clear by her tone that she did not find it great.

"You don't like Grandma Bess all of a sudden?" Willa asked.

"I love Grandma Bess. She's my mother."

"But you don't like her?"

"I like her fine. I like her *and* I love her. It just seems like a lot. Two adults, four teens, one dog, and about six workmen making a racket by day. I'm just not sure about adding one more person to the fray."

"What's a fray?" Gemma asked.

"*This* is a fray!" Maggie shouted to be heard over the banging. "What we have right here this morning. Now, everyone who wants a driving lesson, pack it up. We're leaving."

———

Maggie shifted the car into "park" and looked behind her at the two girls in the back. Willa had wanted to sit in the front, and had been quite unyielding on the matter. Jean had of course wanted to let Willa do as she pleased. But it seemed wrong to Maggie to allow Willa to dominate her new sister, it had turned into a terse squabble, and the only solution seemed to be to give the privilege to no one.

"Who's going first?" Maggie asked.

"I'm thinking me," Willa said. "But probably now you're going to tell me I'm being rude to *her* and so I don't get to drive at all."

"'Her' has a name," Maggie said.

"Fine. You'll say I'm being rude to Rose."

"This is Jean. Do you honestly not know their names by now, or is that just a little bit of purposeful disrespect?"

"She can go first," Jean said.

"We'll flip a coin." Maggie opened the car's ashtray, which she kept filled with quarters for parking meters. She pulled one out. "Call it," she said.

"Which one of us?" Jean asked.

"Heads," Willa said.

Maggie flipped the coin, knowing that if she missed it, it would end up under the car seat for all of time. She caught it.

"Tails," she said.

"Great," Willa said. "Even the coin likes her best."

———

"Okay, I think I remember," Jean said. "Foot on the brake before you shift into 'drive,' use your turn signals, look in both of the side mirrors . . ."

"You don't have to put on your turn signal," Willa said from the back of the car. "The mall is closed and there's nobody out here."

"I want her to get into good habits," Maggie said.

"For that matter she doesn't even need to look in the mirrors."

"She needs to look in the mirrors."

"Why? There's nobody here."

"There could be somebody here," Maggie said, feeling her irritation rise. Trying to cap it tightly. "*We're* here."

"The chances are like one in a hundred. More."

"So probably no one will be here, but every now and then somebody might be. What do you suppose is the best way to tell which way it's going to go this time?"

"Look in my mirrors," Jean said.

"Well said."

Jean looked left and right, behind her in the rearview mirror, then cautiously pulled forward.

"You're going so slow," Willa said.

"It's only my second lesson." Jean tossed the words over her shoulder in what struck Maggie as a baby step toward actually standing up for herself.

"Are you familiar with the concept of a backseat driver?" Maggie asked Willa.

"No, what does it mean?"

"It means hush up and let me drive," Jean said.

Her words were followed by a stunned silence. Even Jean seemed stunned, and she was the one who had said it. She snuck a look over at Maggie from the driver's seat. She looked nervous, but also slightly pleased with herself. She looked like she was trying hard not to smile.

Maggie gave her a small approving nod.

"You're oversteering when you see a light post," Maggie said. "It's almost like you're apologizing to them for getting less than twenty feet away. I'm not suggesting you cut it close, but try using a light touch on the steering wheel. You know that old saying 'A miss is as good as a mile.'"

"I do know that saying! My mom used to say that."

"It's partly just nervousness. You're really new at this. But I can already tell you'll be a good driver. Just go around a few more times and try to gauge how much you need to turn the wheel."

They drove in silence for a few minutes. Maggie was so confident in Jean's risk aversion that she found her mind wandering.

"You know," she said after a time. "I'm sure you and Rose could come with us if we ever end up going out in the mobile clinic again. Even if you don't feel ready to drive the RV."

For a beat or two, Maggie heard only silence.

Then Willa exploded from the back seat.

"Wait, *what?*" she bellowed.

It startled Jean, who swerved wildly. She quickly braked to a stop and just waited, as if unsure what to do next.

"What's the issue?" Maggie asked.

"They get to *go* with you? When you go out in the rolling clinic? You never once asked us to go with you. Not *once*."

"Honey, they'd be coming along to help. It's work. It's not a vacation in a five-star hotel. I never once dreamed you or Gemma would want to."

A long silence fell.

"*Do* you want to?" Maggie added.

"Well. No. But that's not the point. At least you could've *asked*."

"I don't think I want to drive anymore," Jean said weakly.

"Ever? Or this lesson?"

"This lesson. Let Willa take her turn."

"That was a pretty short lesson."

"Please?" Jean said, barely above a whisper. "I just really want to be done."

———

"You're staring at me," Willa said, burning her withering gaze into the rearview mirror.

Jean opened her mouth to defend herself, but all that came out was a confused stammer.

They sat in the car in front of the local coffeehouse, Willa in the driver's seat preparing to try her parallel parking on a fairly long open space of curb.

"Willa, be kind," Maggie said.

"What? What did *I* do? She said she wouldn't stare at me."

"She was looking through the windshield."

"She said she'd look out the window."

"The windshield is a window. Leave—" Maggie stopped herself. She had been about to say "Leave your sister alone," but she was afraid Willa would howl loudly and rudely at the idea that Jean was her sister. And that was something they could all do without. "Focus off Jean and just park. We're holding up traffic. People are having to go around you."

"So? They can go around me."

"They have to cross the double yellow line to pass. They have to wait for a break in oncoming traffic. You need to do this thing. Pull up a little more so you're ahead of the driver's door of this parked car. Now put it in reverse. Go slow now. Back up until your steering wheel is about level with his, and then start cutting the wheel toward the curb. Slower!"

"I'm going slow!" Willa shrieked.

"Not nearly slow enough! Brake!"

But if anything, Willa seemed to hit the gas.

The car flew backward at an awkward angle and hit the parked car behind them. They felt the jolt and heard a kind of grinding thump.

For a brief moment they only sat in silence. The thump seemed to echo, underscoring that slight shock of something objectively bad having dropped into their lives.

"Uh-oh," Jean said.

Willa turned that burning gaze onto Maggie. "You distracted me. You were yelling."

"Pull up a little and put it in park. We have to get out and go back there and see how much damage there is."

Willa sailed out of the driver's seat before Maggie could even get her seat belt unbuckled.

Before Maggie could get the passenger door open Willa was back. It seemed faster than Maggie would have expected for just a quick trip to the rear bumper and back, not to mention surveying the damage.

"It's fine," she said, jumping in. "It's an old banged-up car anyway. Let's just go home."

She shifted into "drive" and pulled out of the space.

"Willa, you stop this car *right now*!" Maggie bellowed.

It was the loudest voice she had ever used in front of Jean or Rose. It might have been the loudest voice she had ever directed at one of her daughters.

Willa slammed on the brake and stared at Maggie with her eyes wide, her mouth open. She appeared genuinely wounded.

"You never talk to me like that."

"You've never hit someone's car and tried to drive away before. Now back up. Slowly. Park in that space. I'm going to get out and see what's what."

Willa silently did as she'd been told.

Mark this day on your calendar, Maggie thought.

Before she got out of the car, Maggie glanced into the back to see how Jean was doing with all this. She was holding her book open on her lap—an apparent defense against the staring accusations—and her face was noticeably white. She was gazing into space and didn't seem to notice Maggie checking in on her.

Maggie stepped out of the car and walked to the car behind to assess the damage. It was not terrible, but it was not fine. The front fender was noticeably dented, and spotted with a few traces of the midnight-blue paint of Maggie's car. True, the car was older and had several dents and scratches. But this one was their responsibility.

She reached back into her car and grabbed her purse, rifling around for something resembling paper.

An older woman with suntanned skin and wild white hair stepped out of the coffeehouse and headed directly toward her.

"Oh, is this your car?" Maggie asked.

"Such as it is, yes," the woman said.

"I was just about to write you a note. I was trying to teach my seventeen-year-old daughter to parallel park, and we had a little problem."

"Well, let's take a look," the woman said.

She bent at the waist and stared at the dent at a surprisingly close distance, brushing it with her hand. Then she straightened.

"Well, if it was the only damage on the car that might be a shame. But look at it." She indicated the full length of the vehicle with a dramatic sweep of her right arm. "Do I strike you as someone who's afraid of a few little dents or scratches?"

"Are you saying . . ."

But Maggie drifted off. It sounded as though the woman was letting them off the hook, but she was afraid to say it. Afraid her guess was too extravagantly optimistic.

"I'm saying go have a nice day and don't worry about it. I have four children and I had to teach them all how to drive. What a trial! You're lucky you just have the two teenage girls."

"Actually," Maggie said, "I have two more at home. And two of the four are fosters we just newly adopted."

"Oh my. Then you have bigger problems than a dented fender. Go on. Just have a good day."

"You're a very nice woman," Maggie said.

But the woman only waved the compliment away as she climbed into her car.

Maggie glanced at her own scraped bumper and then opened the driver's door of her car.

"Move over," she said to Willa.

Willa scrambled wildly over the center console and then dropped into the passenger seat.

Maggie sat a moment, hands tight on the wheel, listening to the ringing silence.

"You got incredibly lucky," she said, her voice quiet and tightly controlled. "She's not holding you responsible for the damage to her car. But my bumper will need to be repainted. And that's coming out of your allowance."

Willa's mouth dropped open.

"But you have insurance!" she shrieked.

"Car insurance has deductibles for collision. You'll need to learn these things if you plan to operate a car. And now . . . another thing. I think your professional instruction should be next and then I think a driving teacher who isn't me would be a really good idea for both of you."

Maggie waited for some feedback on that proposal, but none came. She shifted into "drive" and they headed home in absolute, stunned silence.

———

After a cooling-off period of several hours, Maggie found Willa in her room. Willa was lying on her bed, staring at the ceiling. Her expression was decidedly sulky.

"Should we talk about it?" Maggie asked.

"You already did. Right in front of *her*."

Willa never took her eyes off the ceiling.

"I'm sorry. I know I shouldn't do that. But it just all happened so fast."

"You're always telling them how good they are. You never say nice things about us."

"Honey, I'd love to shower you with some praise, but first you have to do something praiseworthy. And a hit-and-run fender bender isn't it."

"What do I have to do to get your praise?"

"A really great way to start would be by accepting your two adopted sisters. I promise if you can even make a good start on that I'll praise you to the heavens and beyond."

"Define 'accepting.'"

"Understanding that it's going to continue to be this way. Not making them feel bad if you can help it."

"Fine," Willa said. "If that's what it takes, then I'll try."

Chapter Twenty

Remember Those Girls?

Maggie came home from dropping Willa and Jean at the driving school only to find her mother on the living-room couch having a conversation with Gemma.

She stepped closer, eyes wide, and her mother raised her gaze to Maggie's face and smiled that signature smile. The one that had been rumored to stop trains.

She had cut her straight white hair to just above shoulder length, and looked especially tan. It struck Maggie that there was a resemblance between her and the woman who had let them off the hook for the fender dent.

The jowls she had begun to develop were magically gone. Apparently she'd had work done.

"Hello darling," Bess said.

"Mom?"

"Yeah, it's Grandma Bess!" Gemma squealed.

It was a misreading of the question, because obviously Maggie knew this was her mother. But Gemma sounded so childlike and excited. It was a joy to hear.

"You act like you're not sure," Bess said.

"I just . . ."

"You knew I was coming, right? Alex gave you the message?"

"Yeah. I knew you were coming. But somehow I pictured you following up with a date and time. Maybe a flight number, so I could pick you up at the airport."

"I'm perfectly capable of taking a cab from the airport. I'm not dead yet. Now, where are my two new granddaughters? I'd like to meet them."

"Mom."

"What?"

"They've lived with me for a year."

"Yes, but now they're adopted, so they're really yours, and it's permanent. So I thought I should meet them."

Maggie sighed. This was so typical of her mother, to take actions that made no sense to Maggie and then attempt to sort them out with words that didn't help much.

"Jean is out taking a driving lesson. And I just got here, but if I were a betting woman I'd wager that Rose is in the pool."

"Run along, Gemma," Bess said. "Give your mother and me a chance to talk like grownups."

Gemma stood, but did not immediately leave.

"But you brought us presents, right?" she asked her grandmother.

"Gemma!" Maggie barked. "That's rude."

"Oh, it's no such thing, darling," Bess said, "it's just human." Then, turning her attention to her granddaughter, she said, "Of course I brought you presents. Don't I always? But we don't give out presents until all four of you are here. Why do you think they call them presents?"

"Huh?" Gemma asked.

"Never mind. You got it, right, Maggie?"

"Oh yeah. But then I grew up with you."

"Wait," Gemma said. "Till *all four* of us are here? You didn't bring presents for *them*, did you?"

"Well of course I did. I wouldn't leave them out."

"But you don't even *know* them," Gemma whined.

"It's very common to give someone a gift when you first meet them. It sets you off on the right foot."

"I guess just so long as it's not more than what *we* get," Gemma said.

"I didn't bring them a monetary gift the way I do with you, dear. That's considered crass. I only do it for you and Willa because you made it ever so clear that you know exactly what you want and I don't. Now run along, dear. The grownups need to catch up."

———

"I could use a glass of wine," Bess said when they were alone.

Maggie glanced at her watch.

"It's not even one thirty in the afternoon."

"Which is four thirty Florida time. And it was a long flight. I hardly expect you to begrudge me a glass of wine."

"Oh, I don't. I'd join you, except I have to go pick up the girls soon."

"Half a glass, then," Bess said.

"Yeah, maybe."

But she poured one large glass only—for her mother—and sat with her on the couch.

"I'm curious as to what you got Jean and Rose," she said. "Is it okay to ask?"

"I'll show you."

Bess rummaged around in a woven fabric purse the size of an overnight bag and pulled out a small box—like a jewelry box—with a blue ribbon tied in a bow.

"Oh, not if it's gift-wrapped," Maggie said.

"It's just a box with a bow. I can slide the bow right back on."

She slid the ribbon off the corners, opened the box, and handed it to Maggie.

Maggie pulled out a small, old-fashioned-looking silver locket. She heard her own breath suck in.

"How did you know? *Did* you know?"

"I asked you where your locket came from last time we had a video chat, remember? And you told me the story."

"Huh. I have no memory of that. Weird."

"You've been up to your ears in teenagers. If you try to put too much into your brain at once something will drop out again."

"I suppose, but . . ."

Maggie trailed off. She pressed the tiny latch with her thumbnail and let the locket fall open. Inside was a picture of Maggie on the left, and one of Bess on the other side.

"I wanted them to know who their new family is. But in a way that loops in the old one."

Maggie opened her mouth to speak and almost felt that her breath was abandoning her. She had to collect herself for a moment.

"This is . . ."

But then she couldn't immediately find the word for what it was.

"I give up," Bess said. "What is it?"

"It's . . . amazing. Mom, this is so thoughtful."

"Don't sound so surprised. Did you not think I was thoughtful?"

"I think you're extremely thoughtful, but this is like two or three levels up from extremely. This almost makes me want to cry."

Before Bess could answer, the dog came bounding into the room. He put his paws up on Bess's lap and tried to lick her face.

"Rose?" Maggie called.

"I'm right here."

She popped into the room in her green one-piece tank suit and a towel, still dripping slightly. Maggie quickly closed the box and tucked it under her thigh so as not to ruin the surprise.

"Sunny, come!" Rose commanded.

The dog obeyed immediately.

"Sit. Lie down."

Twice more, Sunny complied.

"Oh my," Bess said. "You've done an outstanding job with him."

"Yeah, he's a good boy," Rose said.

"Rose," Maggie said. "This is your adopted grandmother."

Rose's eyes grew wide.

"Really? I get a grandmother too?"

She stepped in and held out her hand to shake, but Bess was having none of that.

"Oh no you don't. I want a hug, young lady."

"But I'm wet."

"Well, I'm your grandmother now and I don't care."

The two embraced for several seconds, Maggie picturing the chlorinated pool water soaking into her mother's expensive clothes. She could see the side of Rose's face. The girl's eyes were pressed tightly shut and she looked as though she were smelling freshly baked cinnamon rolls first thing in the morning.

They stepped apart.

"I'm gonna go take a shower and get dressed," Rose said. "Okay?"

"Fine, dear," Bess said. "We'll be right here."

"Wait. What do I call you?"

"Grandma Bess is fine. Now run along for now. Your new mom and I are going to drink some wine."

———

"Remember when they were little?" Maggie asked her mom.

"I assume you must mean Willa and Gemma. What about it?"

"They were so sweet. And so kind. And so . . . open. And I think I was loving with them. I certainly hope so. And I'm looking back now, and I just can't seem to figure out at exactly what moment our train went off the tracks."

She gazed out the window at the pool. Sunny had been put back in the yard while Rose showered. He was sitting by the edge of the pool, staring in. As if he couldn't imagine why there were no girls in there.

"Oh, the train is fine, darling. They're teenagers."

"Jean and Rose are teenagers."

"Right, but they've been through a terrible trauma that knocked them back on their heels. And your relationship with them is newer. They haven't had a decade and a half to build up resentments. They need somebody to cling to just at the same time your own daughters need to push away from you and be their own people."

Maggie glanced at her watch, just to be sure she wasn't late picking up the girls from their driving lesson. But she had almost fifteen minutes.

"Was I that bad when I was a teenager?"

"No. But that was different. You didn't have to go through a divorce. And you didn't have the advantage of being beautiful. Or maybe it's a disadvantage, I'm not sure. I'm not trying to insult you. You grew into a pretty girl. But you had braces on your teeth forever, and that lazy eye that we might have waited too long to fix. And your late father's nose—that the surgeon wouldn't touch until you turned sixteen. No matter how much you begged."

"Begged? I was afraid of the surgery. You and Dad talked me into it."

"If we pushed you it was only because the other kids were so hard on you. And you may have been afraid, but you wanted it. You were tired of being teased. And then after your father died you gained almost sixty pounds . . ."

"I'm not sure where we're going with this," Maggie said, feeling uneasy.

"What I'm saying is that you couldn't skate by on your good looks. You had to learn how to be likable. You had no choice. The world wouldn't just roll over for you because you were beautiful. And in a lot of ways I think that's a good thing. Beauty fades. Knowing how to treat people lasts forever. But look. I know you're at the end of your rope with them. They know it too. But those sweet, kind girls you were asking me to remember are still in there somewhere. Trust me on that."

Maggie sighed, and gazed out toward the pool again. Sunny had given up and gone elsewhere.

"I sure hope you're right. I should go pick up Willa and Jean. And—listen. It's almost two o'clock, and in a minute the workmen are going to get back from their lunch break. And the noise in here will be unbearable."

"Oh dear. Thanks for the warning. I think I'll go freshen up at my hotel."

"Should I drop you?"

"I'll take an Uber. I don't want to be a burden."

———

They stood by their places at the dinner table—Maggie, the four girls, and Grandma Bess—waiting for Alex to come down the stairs and join them.

"There's that handsome hunk," Bess said loudly.

Alex walked into the room and embraced Bess.

"I swear," Bess said, letting him go, "if I were thirty years younger . . . oh, and if you weren't engaged to my daughter. There's *that* little inconvenient detail."

They sat at their respective places at the table.

"I don't know what you did to deserve him," Bess said in Maggie's direction.

"I tell him that all the time," Maggie said.

"Well, figure out what it was and keep doing it."

"You cooked," Alex said, sounding approving and a little surprised.

"She did!" Rose said excitedly. "She made lasagna and garlic bread and salad. I made the salad, actually. And I buttered the garlic bread."

"Well, it looks marvelous, dear," Bess said.

They began to pass the food around. Maggie cut the lasagna and lifted squares of it onto plates, which she handed to Alex to pass around.

"I'll cut right to the chase," Bess said. "I'm thinking of moving here, if you'll have me."

Maggie stopped cutting and lifting for a couple of beats.

"You don't like Florida?"

"I really don't. It's too humid. But that's not the main thing. I'm not making friends there like I thought I would. I have a daughter and four grandchildren here."

Willa's head came up sharply. "You have two grandchildren," she said.

"No, I have four. Look around you and count, dear."

Willa scanned the faces and apparently decided not to press the issue.

"You know we don't have room here in the house," Maggie said.

"Oh, I didn't mean I was going to *live* with you, darling. I'm far too independent for that. I figured I'd sell the condo and try to get something within a half-hour drive of here. I'd be helpful. You know. With all these young people. I could stay with them while you go out on the road."

"That's . . . actually true," Maggie said.

"So I'm approved?"

"Of course you are, Mother. You can live wherever you like."

"Good. Then it's settled. Time for gifts for the young people."

She rummaged around in her bag and pulled out blue greeting-card-sized envelopes for Willa and Gemma and the little jewelry boxes for Jean and Rose.

Willa and Gemma tore open their envelopes and looked approvingly at the checks.

"Thank you, Grandma Bess," they both said, almost at the same time.

But everyone else was watching Jean and Rose.

They carefully pulled the ribbons off without damaging the bows. They pulled the covers off the boxes and stared inside for several seconds, unmoving. Jean's mouth fell open wide.

"Did you know?" Jean asked Bess.

"About the locket from your grandmother? Yes, Maggie told me."

Jean popped the catch on the locket and let it fall open.

"I wanted you to know we're your new family," Bess said. "But I wanted to say it in a way that honors your original family, so you know we're not asking you to forget them."

Jean immediately began to cry.

"Ah jeez," Willa said.

Maggie shot her a strongly discouraging look and she stared down at the table.

"Sorry," she muttered.

"I have to get a tissue," Jean said.

She jumped up from the table. But before she went off to get the tissue, she hurried to Grandma Bess and threw her arms around the older woman's neck. She said something close to Bess's ear. Maggie couldn't hear what it was, but it made her mother smile.

Then she hurried away.

Rose swiped quickly at her eyes.

"I'm not crying," she said.

"It wouldn't be a bad thing if you were," Bess said, glaring at Willa.

"Thank you, Grandma Bess. I mean, for saying that, but also for the really nice present. *Really* nice. It's nice to have a grandmother again. Well, actually . . . we sort of still have one grandmother. I think. But we're not sure where she is." She looked to Maggie, her eyes deep and lost. "At first they said they were still in their house but with nurses and a social worker. But it's been a while and I'm not sure if that's still true. You think there's any way to find out where she is now? We keep meaning to ask, but we weren't sure if we should."

"Sure, I could make some phone calls."

"That would be nice. Thanks."

Jean came back to the table, looking more composed, and they dug in to the food. Other than a few positive comments on the dinner, there was only silence for a long stretch of time.

Maggie began toying with whether this was a good moment to bring up the idea of the television appearance. It might be one of those things that ruined appetites. It was hard to know.

"Are you all right, dear?" Bess asked suddenly.

She seemed to be looking at Willa.

Maggie hadn't been paying much attention, but both Willa and Gemma seemed to be in an unusually dark mood.

"It's just that you gave them actual presents," Willa said. "Nice things. You know. That you picked out."

"I was thinking that, too," Gemma said.

"Well, I just can't win with you two, then, can I? I used to choose presents for you, and the older you got the more you told me you wanted different things. It was your idea that I give you money so you could choose your own."

"I know," Willa said. "That's true."

"Then the problem is . . . ?"

"Nothing. Never mind. Forget I ever brought it up. Can I be excused? I'm full."

"You've barely eaten at all," Maggie said.

"It's all I want. Can I go?"

A silence while Maggie considered the request. She could feel all eyes on her.

"I suppose."

Willa and Gemma both jumped up from the table and left the room, but Gemma took her plate with her.

"Now you see what I've been up against," Maggie said in the general direction of her mother.

"Oh, I never doubted what you were up against, dear. Teenagers are hard, and now you have four. But I'll give you my take on Willa and Gemma, if you care to hear it. They're being positively horrid.

Selfish and spoiled. But I don't think they know it. And I don't think they're *trying* to be horrid. I think they feel their pain is quite justified. I disagree, but I still think their pain is real. And I think it would be wrong to dismiss it. Whatever we think of their problems, they're still their problems."

"I agree with Grandma Bess," Jean said.

"Yeah," Maggie said. "I think I agree with her, too. And I think I failed them in that regard."

They ate in relative silence for the rest of the meal.

Chapter Twenty-One

Keep Your Sisters Closer

They sat out by the pool in the dark after dinner. Not all of them. Willa and Gemma still had not emerged from their rooms.

The only illumination was the spill of glow through the sliding glass doors and the lights in the pool itself. They cast a shimmering, wavy effect on the trees above them as Rose swam, or stopped and treaded water.

Maggie was full, and tired, and she found it hypnotic.

Sunny didn't bark, but he did follow Rose from one end of the pool to the other, stopping only when she stopped.

For a moment Rose grabbed the side of the pool and held perfectly still, staring across the water as it calmed. Maggie could see a distinct reflection of the moon on its surface, with a long stream of light beneath it.

"Look," Rose said. It was the first anyone had spoken for several minutes. "You can see a reflection of the moon."

"I was just looking at that," Maggie said. "Hey. Listen. There's something I want to run by you girls. I actually wanted to talk to all four of you at once, but that's turning out to be nearly impossible. Remember that piece we did for Eleanor Price and her Sunday-morning show?"

"No, I don't know who she is," Jean said. "A TV show?"

"I guess it aired before I met you. Yes, she did a segment on her TV show about Doctors on Wheels."

"First I've heard about it," Rose said.

"*I* remember it," Grandma Bess said. "They cut your interview down to one sentence."

"Be that as it may," Maggie continued, "she wants to do a follow-up story about our family. But I have no idea how my family will feel about that."

"You and Willa and Gemma?" Jean asked. The question sounded tentative. As though she didn't dare make assumptions.

"All of us. She's really interested in the follow-up—how I went to Louisiana to help out with Hurricane Mina and came back with two more daughters. But I'm not sure if you'd want that. Maybe you don't want to go on TV and talk about how awful that storm was for you."

In the pause that followed, Maggie could hear the gentle lapping of pool water as Rose let go of the side and began treading again. The wavy light show resumed on the bottom of the tree leaves and branches.

"I'm not sure," Jean said. "I guess it's okay. I mean, if you want us to do it."

"I'm definitely not pushing you. It's up to you."

"Would it help something? What's good about doing it?"

"It might help more people decide to foster and adopt," Maggie said.

"Or maybe she'll play up the conflicts," Grandma Bess interjected. "And then people might be *less* likely to do it."

"I think when people see how kind and polite these two are it'll be a net gain. But I have to tell you girls, even if you say yes to it, Willa and Gemma will probably say no. And it has to be unanimous."

Maggie glanced up to see Jean looking at her curiously in the wavering pool lights. She could just barely make out the girl's questioning expression.

"You think they'll say no?" Jean asked.

"I do, yeah. Why? Do you think they'll say yes?"

"I really do," Jean said. "Yes."

"I'm curious as to why you see it that way."

"Because they think they're right. They think they're hard done by, and they think you're wrong not to see it their way. I think they'd figure if they could make their case to millions of people then everybody would agree with them and call you wrong. And they'd get to say 'I told you so' and feel better about themselves."

"That's a very interesting theory," Maggie said.

She rose from her lawn chair and walked back into the house, down the hall, and stopped at Willa's door. She knocked twice.

"What?" Willa barked.

Maggie opened the door.

Both girls were inside, sitting on Willa's bed, their heads leaned close together.

"What is it?" Willa said.

"Remember that interview I did with Eleanor Price?"

"Yeah," Willa said.

"It didn't amount to much," Gemma added. "But Alex's part was good."

"If she wanted to do a segment like that about our family . . . about how hard it is to adjust to adding two new adopted girls to the family . . . would you consider that a good thing or a bad thing?"

The girls looked at each other for several seconds. They appeared to be communicating without a word spoken.

Willa broke the silence.

"So what you're saying is that we can pretty much tell everybody in the world our side of the story?"

"I doubt the whole world will catch the show, but definitely lots of people."

"And we can say why we mind this so much?"

"You can say whatever's true for you."

Another brief communication between the girls using eyes only. Then they both burst out with answers at the same time.

Willa said, "Hell yeah," and Gemma said, "This is great."

"Okay," Maggie said. "I'll give her a call in the morning."

She walked back outside, into the dim, quiet, and peaceful atmosphere of the family without her two biological daughters.

Only Rose had moved. She was sitting on the edge of the pool now, feet dangling into the water, Sunny licking her wet arms.

"You're a very smart girl," she said to Jean.

"I try to pay attention to them," Jean said.

"Because you're a good sister."

"Because she feels safer if she knows what they're thinking," Rose said.

———

Maggie was already in bed—but wide awake—when Alex got back from dropping Bess at her hotel for the night.

"Hey," he said on his way into the bathroom.

"Hey yourself," Maggie said.

She poked around on the news app of her phone until he came to bed. He had brushed his teeth and was wearing only boxers. He climbed under the covers.

Maggie set down her phone and they smiled at each other.

"Tell the truth," he said. "How do you feel about Bess moving here?"

"I think . . . good?"

"That's not exactly a ringing endorsement."

"In case you haven't noticed, she has a big personality. And I'm kind of feeling surrounded by big personalities right now. Plus she's kind of . . . uneven. Half the time she seems okay and the other half she's doing these things that are incomprehensible to me. But I could go back to work this way. And it sure would be nice to be able to get away now and then, just the two of us, and leave her here with the girls."

"Aaah," Alex said, drawing the word out long. "Now there's a lovely mental picture that I haven't even allowed myself to entertain."

"How do *you* feel about it?" she asked, tracing an index finger through the thick dark hair on his chest.

"I don't mind Bess."

"Do you mind *anything*? Oh, I'm sorry. That came out like a challenge or a criticism, and I didn't mean it that way at all. I meant it as a serious question. I feel like I should know after five years, but sometimes there are other layers to people. You're always so easygoing and uncomplicated. Which I love. But underneath all that, are there things you mind?"

He pulled a deep breath and sighed it out again as Maggie braced for his answer.

"I mind Willa and Gemma. I try not to say so, but I know you know. You've mentioned more than once that you're aware of how hard I try to hold my tongue and keep my thoughts about them to myself. I love them, but I find them hard to deal with. But anyway, they're nearly grown, and I want to be with you."

"Well that's an honest answer."

"Because you asked me straight out. You wanted an honest answer, right?"

"Absolutely."

"And where does that leave us?"

"Well. Nowhere different from where we were before. Of course it bothers me that there's friction between you and them. Then again, there's friction between me and them. I don't know that I have a reason to expect otherwise or that it's a problem with a simple solution. And it's not like I think you're wrong and they're totally easy to deal with. What about me adopting the two newer girls? Anything you're holding your tongue about there?"

"Nope. They're delightful. A real breath of fresh air. And I like Bess, big personality and all. And who knows? Maybe Willa and Gemma airing their opinions on national television will force some changes in the girls. Either way, I'm committed to you, no matter what they do or don't do."

Maggie opened her mouth to answer, but before she could speak a pair of tones signaled texts coming in on their phones at exactly the same time. They both grabbed their phones off the opposite bedside tables.

It was a text to both of them from Lacey.

"Not sure if you heard," it said. "Huge wildfire due east, halfway to the Arizona state line. Less than three hours from here. Growing to thousands of acres in no time flat. Zero percent contained. A couple of really small towns went up in flames and the only hospital in a hundred-forty-mile radius just burned to the ground. Medevac helicopters are working overtime and having trouble keeping up. I talked to the sheriff's department in San Bernardino County and they wouldn't say no to having us there if you're up for it."

She looked at Alex and he looked back.

"What do you think?" he asked. "I'm surprised Lacey's up for it, but I guess if she can do it so can we."

"She told me at the memorial that she was dying for a good disaster. I guess the house is just too quiet for her."

"Oh. Yeah. That actually makes a lot of sense."

"Text her and tell her we'll do it if my mom is willing to stay with whichever girls don't want to come, okay? And you could do me a favor and call Bess and see if she's willing to stay with the girls. I'm going to leave a message for Eleanor Price and tell her we're up for an interview whenever we can manage to get back home."

———

Maggie wandered back downstairs into the kitchen, her phone in her robe pocket, thinking she would pour herself a glass of milk and call

Eleanor Price from there. It didn't pay to have two people trying to talk on the phone at once in a small room.

She was surprised to find Willa sitting at the kitchen island, in the semidarkness, hovering over a hot drink.

"You're up," Maggie said.

"Obviously."

"What're you drinking there?"

"Coffee."

"I hope you're not thinking that'll help you sleep."

"It's, like, ten o'clock. I never get to sleep till at least one. I think I upset Grandma Bess."

"Over the presents, you mean?"

"Right, that."

"She's a big girl."

Maggie tried to brush Willa's hair back off her face as an affectionate gesture, but Willa jerked her head away. Maybe reflexively. Maggie wasn't sure.

"I didn't mean to seem ungrateful. She gave us a lot of money. It's just that what she got them was so nice. I feel like they're getting so much."

"Seriously?"

"Why would I kid about that?"

Maggie sat at the table and tried to look at her daughter, who averted her gaze.

"Honey, those two girls grew up lower-lower middle class at best. A hurricane brought part of a ceiling down on their parents, and they couldn't move it, and they had to listen to their own mother and father screaming for help as they drowned. They showed up in California just barely recovered from pneumonia with everything they owned in tiny little backpacks on their backs, and that was just what their social worker bought them. They got out of their house with the clothes on their backs and nothing else. Your grandmother and I could shower them with gifts at this rate until they're fifty and they still wouldn't be nearly caught up to you."

At first Willa didn't answer, and Maggie was beginning to think she wouldn't.

Then she said, "Yeah. I suppose. I see what you mean, I guess. It's not that I don't want them to have things. Just maybe from somebody else's mother and grandmother."

"Well, they're ours," Maggie said. "And tomorrow we're leaving to go to the scene of a big wildfire east of here. And I want to know if you want to come along."

"*They're* going?"

"Probably. If we're sure our position is safe enough. I haven't asked Jean and Rose yet because I figured they were asleep."

"What would we do there?"

"I would hope you'd be some help. Run errands. Keep the clinic and the RVs clean. It'll be smoky, so you won't want to spend much time outside. It might be really hot. I doubt we'll have power, so we'll have to run the generator to keep the AC going. I'll need somebody to drive one of the RVs to the closest open gas station with a safety can or two, so we can keep feeding it gas. But at least we won't have to listen to home-remodeling construction for ten hours a day."

"It doesn't sound like very much fun there."

"Oh, it won't be."

"Then why are you asking us to go?"

Maggie dropped her face into her hands and counted to three before answering. It would have been easier to bark back at her daughter in anger, but she chose to keep the urge in check.

"Because you got furious with me because I don't ask you. Remember? During your driving lesson?"

"Oh. Right. I think I was mad because you asked *them*. Not because you didn't ask *us*."

Maggie sighed deeply but quietly.

"Do you want to go? Yes or no."

"No."

"Think there's any point in asking Gemma?"

"No."

"Okay. Fine. That's what I figured."

She slipped her phone out of her pocket and called Eleanor Price. The call went to voicemail, as Maggie had assumed it would at that hour.

"Eleanor. Maggie Blount. Sorry to call so late, but we're leaving in the morning to go to that big fire in east San Bernardino County. I don't know how long we'll be gone. A few days. But when we get back, the answer to your question is yes. We'll do that interview. Amazingly, all four girls are on board."

She clicked off the call and looked up to see Willa staring at her in the dim light.

"Then we have to pack up and go to Dad's again?"

"No, I'm sure your Grandma Bess would be glad to stay here with you."

"Oh. Okay. Won't she be mad that you're going? She came all this way to see you."

"She came all this way to tell us she's moving here. And after she does, we'll see each other constantly."

"Oh. Right. That's true, I guess."

"We'll talk more in the morning."

Maggie turned and walked out of the room. Back toward bed. She realized she had forgotten the glass of milk, but it didn't feel worth turning around.

Then she was struck with a thought. The following day she had an appointment with the therapist. And it was too late to cancel without having to pay for the missed appointment.

She stuck her head back into the kitchen.

"Now what?" Willa said.

"I want you and Gemma to see that therapist tomorrow. Finally. You've been promising for ages, and this is your moment. I made an

213

appointment and it's too late to cancel. Just the two of you. You can complain to her until she says the time is up. It might be good for you."

"I don't even know where her office is."

"I'll make sure Grandma Bess knows."

Then Maggie walked back to her bedroom and climbed into bed. But sleep came very slowly. That is, what little sleep came at all.

Chapter Twenty-Two

Running with Pillows

Maggie drove the RV while Alex clicked around on his phone. Knowing him as she did, she figured he was probably accessing every available detail about the fire.

Now and then she glanced into the big, wide rearview mirror at Jean and Rose. They were sitting quietly on the RV's couch because it was equipped with seat belts for passengers. The dog was sprawled between them, on his back, paws flung wildly into the air. He was resting his head on Rose's lap, staring lovingly up into her face, and she was scratching his chest.

Maggie was thinking about the way life turns on a dime, usually impelled in some new direction by a tiny action that seemed unimportant at the time. It had started with a thought about how different Sunny's life would be if he'd picked any other object, any other structure, to hide under in the aftermath of the hurricane. Anyplace in the world that was not their RV.

Maggie's phone rang.

She had her phone sitting up in a holder in front of the dashboard so she could follow directions on its map app. Alex reached over and touched the button to pick up the call, putting it on speaker. It was an accepted safety measure when one of them was driving.

"Maggie?" a voice from her phone said, filling up the cab of the RV.

"Yes, this is Maggie."

"Eleanor Price."

"Oh, right. Good. You got my message."

"You're headed for the Rock Hollow Fire."

"We are."

"And it'll be your first trip since John Bishop passed away."

"You've been doing your homework."

"Maggie, I'm begging you. Tell me where you're stationed there. I'll send a camera crew. I promise they'll stay out of your way. They'll just be in the background, recording some of what you do when you're out in the field. They're used to disasters and they know to follow directions from any official on scene. I can interview the girls when I get home."

"Actually," Maggie said, "two of them came along with us."

"The two adopted girls?"

"Right."

"For the ride? To help out?"

"To help, yeah. They wanted to help."

"Is it safe for them there?"

"We made sure it was. The sheriff has assured us we'll be miles from the fire line and there are three separate ways to retreat. They said it would be safe for all of us, including minor girls."

"Oh my gosh. They'll be there! That is so much better. This is going to be amazing. This is such good television. Please tell me where they can find you. Maybe if it's safe I'll even drive out and interview you out there."

"But you have to get Willa and Gemma on video too. They're really looking forward to it and they'll be furious if they get cut out. And also, I really don't know where we'll be. We'll probably have to move as the fire moves, and we'll have to let the sheriff or Cal Fire tell us where to be stationed at any given time. It'll be someplace safe, as I said, or we wouldn't have ourselves and the girls there. But it won't be very . . . predictable."

"Do this for me," Eleanor said. "Please. Text me your coordinates. Latitude and longitude. You know how to get them, right?"

"I'm sure I can figure it out."

"They should read out at the bottom of the compass app on your phone. There's even a way to text me a map that shows your phone's location in real time, but I don't remember exactly how to do it and I'd have to check with one of my techier colleagues. But just your coordinates will do. And one more favor. Please consider this. I'd love to get this on the air while the Rock Hollow Fire is still in the news. I wouldn't normally, but I'm going to ask if I can interview your two daughters while you're away. They're at their father's?"

"No, they're at my house with my mother. Call my home landline and see if you can arrange it with my mom. If she's home and present with them during the interview that should be okay. She doesn't have to be on camera. Just there."

"You're an angel. I can't tell you how much I appreciate it. Don't forget to text me your coordinates when you get there, and if you have to move. I know all hell might break loose when you get there, but it just takes a second if you don't forget."

"I won't forget. Thanks."

"Thank *you*. Talk soon."

The call ended and the phone reverted to the map screen.

Maggie drove in silence for a mile or two.

Then she asked, "Was that a mistake?"

She directed the question half over to Alex in the passenger seat and half into the rearview mirror.

"Was what a mistake?" Alex asked.

"Sending her to the house to interview the girls while we're gone."

"Why would that be a mistake? They said they want to do it. And your mom will be there."

"But I was picturing us there to kind of . . . I don't know. Direct the . . . direction of the thing. They might be pretty uncensored without us. I think my mom knows enough to rein that in, but I'm not as positive as I would be with myself."

"In other words, you were going to try to make sure they come off fairly well."

"Is that what I meant?"

"Sounds like what you meant."

"I don't want this to be a complete disaster for them."

"But whatever it is for them, it should be based on their honest thoughts. Otherwise you're just running after them and putting down a pillow when you think they're about to fall. You're trying to get between them and their own consequences. Which I think is how we got into this situation in the first place."

Maggie could hear the irritation rising in his voice. She had asked him to say honestly what bothered him, he had confessed his dislike for her girls, and what she had unearthed was not about to be buried again.

"I agree with Alex," Jean said. "I mean, if you were asking us too. If I'm allowed to have an opinion. Like I said, they think their view of things is right, so let them—"

Alex's phone rang, ending the conversation.

"Oh, hey, Lacey," he said, picking up the call. A pause. Then: "Yeah, we absolutely do. They're in the fridge in our RV. I brought them from work, but I didn't have time to put them in the clinic bus. Two dozen doses, give or take." Another pause. "Got it. We're a little behind you. We're maybe twenty minutes out. But no need to evacuate him. We can handle it when we get there. Which will be soon enough." A final brief pause. Then: "Okay. See you soon."

He clicked off the call.

"Lacey and Brad just got there," he said to Maggie, "and they already have their first patient. A firefighter who stepped on a two-inch rusty nail going up and down the hills out there. Went right through his boot. She wanted to know if we had tetanus vaccines, so they don't have to waste a medevac copter or half a day of round-trip driving just getting somebody to a place where he can be given a shot."

"Going as fast as I can," Maggie said.

"Don't take chances. A few minutes here or there won't change his situation. And if we get pulled over or get into an accident, that might. So just . . . steady."

They drove on in silence and never attempted to pick up the conversation they'd abandoned. Because in that moment they were already out in the field, in an emergency, focusing on more important matters.

———

"Uh-oh," Jean said.

They had just come around a bend and over a rise, and they were suddenly able to see the fire. For most of the drive they had seen a frighteningly thick column of grayish-white smoke. But now they could actually see the fire burning all along a faraway ridge, its lines distorted by waves of heat.

A helicopter swept over that distant ridge, letting loose a long shower of orange flame retardant that settled on the hill as if in slow motion.

"A little scary, I know," Maggie said. "But the sheriff and the highway patrol and the fire people will keep us safe."

"Good," Rose said.

Maggie looked in the mirror to see Sunny sitting up, sniffing the air. "You girls okay?"

"Yeah, we'll be okay," Jean said. "If you went into the tail end of a hurricane for us we can go pretty near that fire for somebody else."

"We're not going to be very near it," Maggie said. "But I understand why it feels brave."

———

They stopped at a roadblock manned by a highway-patrol officer and his car.

Maggie powered the window down.

"You're gonna have to turn it around, ma'am," the officer said.

"We're Doctors on Wheels," Maggie said. "The sheriff's department is expecting us. If nothing else we have a tetanus vaccine for that injured firefighter."

"Let me phone that in," he said.

He stepped away from the RV and made a call on his radio that Maggie couldn't hear.

Then he moved the roadblock and appeared back at her window.

"Go slow and expect emergency vehicles to come flying around curves. Keep straight on this highway headed toward the fire. A sheriff's car will meet you on the road and guide you in. They've got a containment line now, and your friends are set up on the road so the line is between them and the fire. It's a good, safe location. But we told them this and we'll tell you the same. If anybody tells you to move, listen. There are several ways out and you'll have plenty of time, but you have to believe us and do it. If you have patients in your big clinic bus, move anyway. Take 'em with you. We'll sort out locations when everyone is safe. We're not going to let anything happen to you, but we need your cooperation to keep it that way."

———

"What can we do while you're gone?" Jean asked. Her voice sounded thin and a bit strained.

They had to speak up to be heard over the hum of the generator and the blasting air conditioner. Alex had already run to the clinic bus with the tetanus vaccines, and the girls seemed hesitant to be left alone.

Maggie finished texting their location to Eleanor before she answered.

"If you're nervous being here alone you can always come over to the clinic. You can sit up in the cab with Brad. But you can see the bus right out the window."

"But shouldn't we be helping?" Rose asked, sounding similarly cowed.

"And you will. But we just got here. I figured you'd be a big help cleaning up at the end of the day and maybe a little bit in between patients. And doing the dishes after meals. In the meantime there are tons of sandwich makings in the fridge and you can make lunch for everybody. Maybe have it ready around noon, but we might not have complete control over when we can take a break. But it's sandwiches. They can always stay in the fridge till we're ready."

"Okay," both girls said at once, seeming brighter and more settled to have something to do.

"And if we have too many patients at one time, and somebody has to wait outside, you can talk to them."

"Talk to them?" Jean asked. "About what?"

"Doesn't really matter. Anything positive. It calms people, and distracts them from the disaster of the thing. Helps them know they landed in a friendly place. You okay here for now?"

"Sure," Jean said. "We'll get started on lunch."

"You know where we are if you need us."

Maggie stepped out into the horrible, horrible midmorning.

The sky was thick and gray with drift smoke. The very air she tried to breathe was gray. The day had a heavy, dusky quality, because the sun could not get through. It was almost dark. The smell of smoke was overwhelming, and Maggie felt as though she were trying to breathe something nearly solid.

A sheriff's patrol car pulled onto the highway shoulder near the RV, and a young-looking, clean-cut officer jumped out and took a few hurried steps in Maggie's direction.

"You the doctor?"

"Yes. One of them," Maggie said. "I'm Dr. Blount."

"Got somebody for you."

But Maggie knew he did. Because she could already feel the shock of their pain.

He stepped toward the rear of his patrol car.

"What've we got?" she asked, moving with him.

"Burns. Twelve-year-old boy and his dog. I've got his parents here, but they're not hurt. Look, I know you aren't vets, but the kid is really upset about his dog. More than he is about himself. If there's anything at all you can do . . ."

"Sure, I'll take a look at him. Burns on a dog are not that different from burns on a person."

The deputy opened the back of his patrol car, and the parents spilled out.

"Give me Buster," the father said.

"No, I've got him," came a young voice from the back seat.

"But your hands."

"I've got him."

The boy struggled out of the patrol car and stood on the highway shoulder, looking at Maggie and hugging his dog tightly to his chest. The dog was short-haired and blond and looked like a cross between a golden Lab and a basset hound or dachshund. He must have weighed fifty pounds, but the boy showed no signs of setting him down. He was allowing the weight of the dog to rest on his wrists and forearms rather than his hands. He was wearing khaki shorts, and had obvious and angry-looking third-degree burns on his knees.

"Will you see to my dog?" he said to Maggie, clearly struggling not to cry. "He's whimpering. He never whimpers. That means it hurts. He needs help."

"I think you both do," Maggie said.

"You got this?" the deputy asked.

"Yeah. I'll take them into the clinic. We'll be fine. You go ahead." Maggie led the family to the bus.

"Tell me what happened," she said, ushering them up the stairs and inside.

It was the mom who answered.

"We were trying to evacuate, but Roddy couldn't find his dog. He wouldn't leave without Buster. We were going all over the property calling him, but I guess while we were out he'd snuck back into the house."

"Oh no. He was in a burning building? Here, have a seat on my examining table, Roddy. You can set Buster down right beside you."

"It wasn't burning," the father said. "It had already burned to the ground. One of the first to go yesterday. We'd just snuck back in to see what we'd lost and if we could save anything. We probably should've just stayed away. But anyway, I guess there was still a lot of smoldering wood and what have you. We tried to get Roddy not to go in after Buster, but no way he was leaving that dog. Fortunately he was wearing his good hiking boots. The soles got a little melty but he didn't burn his feet."

"But then I tripped," Roddy said.

Maggie looked around the clinic quickly. Alex and Lacey were nowhere to be seen, but the young firefighter was still sitting on Lacey's examining table, putting his boot back on.

"Just give me one minute," Maggie said.

She approached the young man, who looked up and smiled. He had an eager, open face smudged with soot. But under the smile he was in pain.

"You got your vaccine?" she asked him.

"Yes ma'am. That nice male nurse took care of it."

"You need someone to look at that foot?"

"No ma'am. The nice older lady doctor took good care of me. Cleaned me up and bandaged me and gave me some antibiotics so it won't get infected."

"And I'm sure she told you to stay off it for a few days."

"She tried, ma'am. But I'm going right back out there."

"You're kidding."

"No ma'am. I never kid about the work. We fight fires till we drop or till there's no more fire to fight. It's what we do."

Maggie looked up to see a man with a TV camera on his shoulder step into the clinic. He was closely followed by a young woman with a boom microphone.

"Okay to come in?"

"You couldn't possibly be Eleanor's crew."

"But we are."

"How did you get here so fast?"

"We were already here getting footage on the fire."

"You can only film in here with the permission of the patients."

"Understood."

"I don't mind," the firefighter said.

"Good," Maggie said. "Talk to this brave young man who just took a nail through his foot and is on his way right back out to fight the fire again. I have to figure out where my colleagues are and then I have to treat this young man and his dog."

"They're up front in the cab of the bus," the firefighter said, pointing to the curtain that separated the cab from the rest of the clinic. It was unusual for it to be drawn closed. "The lady doctor ran up there and that nice male nurse went in after her. Seemed like she was crying."

"Oh, okay. She lost her husband last year. He used to come out on the road with us."

"Sorry to hear that, ma'am. And here she is out in the field helping. Well, now maybe you'll all understand why I have to get back out there." He stood up, testing his weight on the injured foot. It hurt. Maggie knew from his face, and also she could feel it. He waved the camera crew toward the door with him. "Come on. We'll talk outside. Give the doctor a chance to do her work."

They stepped outside and Maggie glanced over at the curtain, then back at the waiting family. She chose the family. Lacey had Alex with her, and probably Brad, and Maggie had no medicine that would heal her anyway.

She stepped back up to the boy on her table. So much pain.

"Sorry for the delay. May I see your hands?"

Roddy did not immediately show her his hands.

"Can you look at Buster first? He's been crying."

Maggie looked to the boy's parents, one at a time.

"That's probably the best way to get where we're going," the mother said.

"Okay, Buster. Let me see those paw pads."

Roddy helped her turn the dog over on his side, and the boy gently calmed him out of trying to sit up again. The dog had vicious burns on the pads of all four paws. The pain of it hit Maggie like an electric shock starting in her throat and traveling down through her groin and into her thighs.

"Oh, poor baby," she crooned to the dog. "Here's what I'm going to do. I'm going to give him an injection to calm him down. It's mild, but it'll make him sleepy. Then I've got some pretty strong topical anesthetic, and I'm going to put it on those burns to ease the pain. And I'll put ointment on them and bandage him up. But he still needs to get to a vet. And you'll need to watch him every minute to make sure he doesn't chew off the bandages. A vet will have one of those cone collars, but I'm not a vet."

"We're going to my sister's in San Diego," the father said. "When we get out of this hell we'll follow up on everything."

Alex stuck his head around the curtain as Maggie applied the topical anesthetic to the dog's paws. He must have heard the dog, who had been crying each time she touched the burns. It was hard on everybody.

"I'm sorry," Alex said. "I didn't know we had another patient or I would have been out here helping."

"Maybe you could bandage this dog's paws while I see to his best friend here. Is Lacey okay?"

"She will be."

After that they stopped talking and set about their work. Lacey popped out, a little puffy-eyed but otherwise functional, and asked what she could do to help. And they went on with their workday.

Because that's what we do, Maggie thought.

———

When she was finished giving the parents final instructions, they stood awkwardly for a beat or two without speaking.

"Now we just have to ask the hard question," the father said.

"And that is . . . ?"

"How much do we owe you? Don't get me wrong. It was worth whatever you want for it. It's just hard, you know? Everything we had is gone. Or do you bill us? I can give you the address at my sister's."

"You don't owe us anything," Maggie said.

"Oh, I didn't mean it like that! I wasn't giving you a sob story to get out of paying. I'll pay."

"No," Maggie said. "We don't charge anyone. We don't ever charge. We just come out here to help. Most of the people we help are like you—just lost everything. The last thing people need at a time like that is an emergency medical bill."

The husband opened his mouth to answer, but his face twisted unexpectedly in an apparent attempt to hold back tears. It seemed to surprise him. Clearly he had been keeping the emotion of the day at bay and it was catching up to him hard.

The wife noticed, but bit her lip and said nothing.

"That's . . . I . . . I didn't think people were so kind anymore."

"People are still kind," Maggie said. "When they're not afraid to be."

Maggie looked through the clinic's window to see Roddy standing outside in the heat and the smoke, having a conversation with her girls. He was still clutching the heavy dog tightly to his chest, using his arms rather than his hands to support Buster. He looked heartbreakingly vulnerable and small in his khaki shorts and skinny, bandaged legs.

Roddy's parents turned around to see what she was looking at.

"What is it?" the father asked.

"Oh, it's just Roddy talking to those two teenage girls," his wife said.

"Can you blame him?" he said. "They're pretty."

"Your daughters?" she asked, turning back to Maggie.

Maggie opened her mouth to parse the answer. To say "My newly adopted daughters," or something similar. Something that would qualify and slightly dilute the situation. But she changed her mind.

"Yes," she said. "They're two of my four daughters."

Chapter Twenty-Three

The Brave Part

"You girls just did a wonderful job on these sandwiches," Lacey said. "Why, I swear I couldn't have done better myself."

They all six sat in a circle on their plastic chairs in the clinic bus, eating lunch. It was a little past two in the afternoon. The flow of patients seemed to have stopped, at least for the moment.

"Are you okay, Dr. Bishop?" Rose asked. "You look like you were crying."

Jean silently elbowed her sister in the ribs.

"Ouch. What'd you do that for? I just asked. What's wrong with asking if somebody is okay?"

"It's fine," Lacey said. "Yes and yes. Yes I was crying. Yes I'm okay."

"Maybe we shouldn't have encouraged you to go out again," Alex said.

"Oh nonsense," Lacey said, brushing his words away. "Granted, it did catch up with me pretty hard. Why I thought out on the road was gonna be better I'll never know. He was always with me out here too. But I break into tears at home, even after all this time, so that's nothing new. At least out here I have something to do to keep my mind occupied."

"A year is not that much time," Alex said. "Not for a thing like that."

"What happened to that camera crew?" Maggie asked, looking around outside as best she could through the bus windows.

"No idea," Alex said. "They were hanging around on the edges of things for a while, but I haven't seen them recently. They might've packed up and gone."

"Will you all excuse me?" Maggie said, wrapping the second half of her sandwich in the big paper napkin. "I want to call home and see if everything's okay."

She stepped out of the cool, air-conditioned bus and into the hellish afternoon.

It was so dim as to be nearly dark, and she had to strain to even locate a faint glow of sun as it attempted to shine through the smoke. Two helicopters swept over the ridges dropping orange flame retardant. Maggie was so used to the sound of their rotors that it barely registered as sound anymore. The highway— the whole area—was otherwise eerily quiet and deserted. The heat was nearly unbearable.

She called her home landline, and her mother picked up.

"Hey. It's me. Everything okay there?"

"Of course, dear. Why wouldn't it be?"

"Did the girls go to counseling?"

"They did. And then that TV lady came by and interviewed them on tape. I forget her name."

"Did it go okay?" Maggie asked, bracing against an inward wince.

"They said it did, but I didn't listen in."

"I thought you were supervising the thing."

"They told me they were fine."

"Mom. I was counting on you."

"Honestly, dear, I don't know what you're so upset about. They're big girls."

"They're minor children!"

"Oh nonsense. When I was Willa's age I worked a job and took the bus everywhere. You worry too much."

Maggie took a few seconds to clamp down on her words and try to bottle up her anger.

"Can I talk to them?"

"Willa is taking a bubble bath. You know how she loves her bubble baths."

"I do know that, but . . . at two in the afternoon?"

"What can I tell you? She loves her bubble baths. Gemma's right here though."

"Put her on, okay?"

Maggie stared at the sun while she waited. Or she tried to, anyway. It was still a challenge to locate that slightly brighter spot in the smoky sky.

"Hi Mom." Gemma's voice sounded uncharacteristically bright.

"Hey honey."

"What's it like there?"

"Kind of like we died and went to Hell. In other words, pretty much what we expected."

"I still don't understand why you want to do it," Gemma said.

Maggie opened her mouth to say *I still don't understand why you don't.* But she thought better of the idea and left it unsaid.

"What did you think of the therapist? How'd that go?"

"We like her."

"Really. That's pleasantly surprising."

"Yeah. She's good. We told her everything and she's on our side."

"What do you mean by 'on our side'?"

"She agrees with us."

"Define 'agrees.'"

"Well. We told her exactly how we feel. And she never told us we were wrong to feel that way like everybody else always does."

"Honey, that's not exactly how therapy works. A therapist helps you work through your feelings. It's really not their job to label things right or wrong."

"Well anyway. It was better than talking to everybody else."

"Good. I'm glad you like her. I think we'll be seeing her a lot more. What about Eleanor Price? Grandma Bess said she came and interviewed you. Was she on your side too?"

"Hard to tell," Gemma said. "She just kept saying 'Tell me more. Tell me more.' But we were pretty happy with how it went. When are you coming home?"

"Not sure yet. I'll let you know as soon as I know. Tell Willa I love her."

"What about *me*? You don't love *me*?"

"Of course I love you. I'm telling you right now."

"But you didn't *tell* me. You just told me to tell Willa."

"Let me start over," Maggie said. "I love you, and I love your sister. Tell her I said so when she gets out of the bath, okay?"

Maggie clicked off the phone and looked up to see the two-person camera crew approaching her from their van. They were not carrying any equipment.

"Eleanor wants to come out later today and interview you," the cameraman said. "If that's okay. Since you might be leaving tomorrow."

"Why would she think we're leaving tomorrow?"

"Because the sheriff said you can leave tomorrow."

"They didn't tell me that."

"They're on their way to tell you that."

As if they had been waiting in the wings and listening for their cue, a sheriff's patrol car pulled up, slowed, swung a U-turn, and parked in the empty traffic lane of the closed highway in front of where she stood.

Two deputies stepped out. Maggie had not seen either one before. A middle-aged man and a younger woman.

"Are you one of the doctors?" the man asked.

"I'm Dr. Blount, yes."

"We're pretty sure we've finished evacuating the area. We're doing a final sweep this afternoon. Probably in the morning you're good to head out. There can always be stragglers. I'm sure we'll get a few this afternoon, but of course I have no idea if they'll be injured. And a lot of the time we find people later who just refused to leave their homes, but we have two medevac copters on loan and they're both sitting idle, so I'm sure we can handle it. And anyway, there aren't really any homes left standing in there, so I'm not sure the rule applies. I'm sure you have families and jobs and such. There's a slight chance the fire could turn and take off in some other direction, like if the wind shifts, and then we'd have whole new towns to worry about. But there's not much wind in the forecast."

"We could always come back," Maggie said. "It's not a very long drive."

"Here's hoping that won't be necessary."

"Okay," Maggie said. "We'll stand by for stragglers and then leave in the morning."

The man tipped his uniform cap and headed toward his patrol car. The woman officer stayed a moment longer.

"And thank you for coming and helping out," she said.

The man stopped and turned back.

"Right," he said. "Sorry. I definitely meant to say that. Thank you for coming and helping out."

Maggie watched them drive away.

Then she texted Gemma's phone.

"Home tomorrow," her text said.

———

Eleanor Price arrived a little after six that evening, in the familiar van with the camera crew.

The girls had just finished washing up the dinner dishes and had gone to Lacey's RV to make up their own beds for the night in the loft sleeping area over the cab.

"We won't keep you long," Eleanor said as Maggie stepped out of the bus to greet her. "You have my word. The thing is, I do want you outside. I know it's beastly out here with the heat and the smoke, but we really want to get the fire line burning in the distance behind you. And at least it's not as hot as I'm hearing it was all day today. It was bad enough in LA, but with the fire here and the smoke trapping in the heat . . . anyway. We brought chairs. Like director's chairs. We'll set those up. Where are the girls?"

"They're in one of the RVs helping out. What about makeup? I'm wearing exactly none."

"Don't even worry about it. It's all natural lighting anyway. Just grab Alex and the girls and we'll get this done."

———

They sat in a line of director's chairs in front of that frightening and deadly backdrop. Sunny crouched submissively under Rose's chair. Eleanor turned her face into the camera and seemed to flip her own internal "on" switch.

"You may remember a segment we did during Hurricane Mina," she said to some amorphous viewer. "It was about a small nonprofit called Doctors on Wheels, and they were just on their way into that disaster area to help out those patients who overflowed the hospitals and who couldn't afford care after losing everything. Well, there's a very interesting follow-up to that story. Alex Anderson, RN, and Maggie Blount, MD, came home from that disaster with two more daughters."

"And a dog," Maggie said.

"Right! And a dog. We'll be editing this, so don't be afraid to just casually discuss anything you think might be relevant."

Like I just did with the dog, Maggie thought.

Oddly, she had forgotten until just that moment that her first interview with Eleanor Price had been mildly aggravating, like the scratchy tag inside the collar of a new shirt.

"Let's start by talking to the girls," Eleanor said. "Off the record for a minute . . . I know you lost both parents in the storm, and I know that must've been devastating, so don't feel like you need to say more about it than feels comfortable to you. My cameraman tells me he got some really lovely footage of you talking to one of the patients—a boy with a dog, both burn victims. He said you were very kind with him and it seemed to really help him."

Maggie wondered what they'd said to Roddy, but figured she could find out later. She found it curious that she had seen the girls talking to Roddy outside the window but hadn't seen the crew taping it. She remembered Eleanor saying they would be "in the background." Apparently they knew that role well.

Rose was the one to answer her.

"Maggie told us that when you talk to a person who's in a disaster like that, it lets them know they landed in a friendly place."

"That's nice," Eleanor said. "I like that a lot. That must have meant a lot to you girls right after the hurricane."

"Oh yeah," Jean said. "I don't know what we would've done otherwise. We were just . . . we were nowhere. We had no parents, no house. We were really sick. I just don't know how we could've made it through that without Maggie."

"Did you have any relatives at all?"

"We had two grandparents. A social worker came and got us and drove us to their house, but they were so old, and they were hardly able to take care of themselves, and she didn't want to leave us there. I think they might be in a nursing home now. I'm not sure. Maggie's going to find out for us."

Maggie realized she had been forgetting to make those promised calls. She wanted to put a reminder on her phone, but she figured she was still in the shot. Instead she repeated it over and over in her head. *Call Evie Moskowitz as soon as you get home. Call Evie Moskowitz as soon as you get home.* While she was trying to burn that into her brain the girls were saying lots of things she missed, or at least did not fully bring into focus. They seemed to have to do with why they had chosen to come along and help.

"And what about you, Alex?" Eleanor said, blasting Maggie back to the moment. "For those who don't know, Alex is Maggie's boyfriend of five years, and, if I'm allowed to say it, now her fiancé. Congratulations on that happy development, you two. Okay. Maggie. You just put your left hand in your pants pocket. Want to tell me what that's about?"

Maggie felt her face flush hot.

"It was kind of a sudden thing. The getting engaged, I mean. And we've been so busy. Then we put a bunch more money into the non-profit, and Alex got me kind of a placeholder ring. Until we can bounce back and get something permanent."

"I haven't gotten her a ring she wants to show off yet," Alex interjected. "That's what she's trying to say. Bad boyfriend, right? But it'll happen soon."

"Okay," Eleanor said with a laugh. "Got it. Busy medical professionals, finding your own charity work. You're forgiven for now. So. Alex. You're a young guy. Maybe about the age most guys want to start a family of their own. And instead you have four instant teenagers. How did you feel about the family growing so suddenly?"

"Oh, I love these two," he said. "No complaint *there*."

There was a subtext to those words that made Maggie wince. But she figured the viewers of the show wouldn't catch it. Willa and Gemma probably would, though.

"You didn't want kids of your own?" Eleanor asked him.

"Not really, no. I like kids well enough, but now that I've had a chance to see how much work they are, being empty nesters in just a few years sounds pretty appealing."

"I hear you," Eleanor said. "I think a lot of people will hear you. Now. The elephant in the room. All is not harmonious at home. The girls aren't getting along."

"I'm not sure that's a fair statement," Maggie said. "I wouldn't say they don't get along as much as I would say there's a struggle to adjust to some of this. I guess we all have a lot of stuff to work out about this new development. As a family."

"Indeed," Eleanor said. "They gave me quite an earful about it earlier today. And we'll be splicing their interview in right about here. We'll get that in their own words. But from you. Maggie. How do you solve a problem like this? How do you see this resolving?"

The question took Maggie a little off guard, but she wasn't sure why. She must have thought about it, she figured. Did she have a plan? Suddenly she wasn't sure. Was she so pessimistic about the situation that she simply *didn't* see it resolving?

Meanwhile Eleanor was waiting for her answer.

"People get used to things," Maggie said.

"Wait," Eleanor said, and raised one finger. A copter was flying overhead, on its way to dump flame retardant on the distant hills. Maggie waited for Eleanor's finger to drop. "Okay. Go on."

"It's this weird quirk of human nature, I think. Not that we get used to things, but that we're so sure we won't. We hate change and we dig in our heels and say 'I'll never accept this. I'll never get used to this.' And then life goes on, and the thing doesn't change except that it starts feeling less new. And then a year later that same person looks back and seems surprised that it was ever a big deal and says 'Oh, right. I guess I got used to it.' And yet somehow we never seem to carry it forward into the next thing. Each change we think will be different. *This* will be the one we can't ever accept.

"I guess when my girls were little, I wanted them to have everything they wanted. If they wanted something, I was going to at least try hard to get it for them. But I might have been doing them a disservice, because life is not a place where you almost always get what you want. It's just not that kind of party. Then they started identifying things they very distinctly *don't* want, like me going off to do Doctors on Wheels. But it's not that kind of party, either. I can't only do the things that somebody else finds comfortable. People's needs will always be in conflict. Sometimes you have to do what you have to do and other people have to be in charge of their own feelings about it. We have a good therapist, and all four girls like her, and I'm hoping that will help. Given time."

Eleanor nodded thoughtfully. Maybe a little more thoughtfully than necessary. Maybe an overly broad gesture for the camera.

"Back when you were fostering, you never considered sending Jean and Rose to another foster family? There are lots of good ones."

"Absolutely not. They were always family. They may have been newer family, but they were never lesser family. And they were never going anywhere."

"Which is a great intro into what it means to foster and adopt a child. So can we talk about that for a while?"

So that was what they talked about for the rest of the interview: What it means to foster a child. What it means to the child and what it can mean to the parent who reaches out.

———

They drove out the next morning in a caravan, with Alex behind the wheel of their RV.

"That fire was a little bit scary," Jean said when they had cleared the roadblock and were back on unrestricted highway. "Even though we could see it was pretty far away. Still scary."

"It *was* a little," Maggie said.

"Is it scary to go someplace right after a hurricane?"

"Some," Maggie said. "Less than what we just did, because once a hurricane has moved through it tends to keep going. They don't really reverse direction the way fires can. But we try to get there as soon after it's moved through as we can, and sometimes the wind is still blowing fifty or sixty miles per hour, and these are high-profile vehicles. They can be hard to handle in that much wind. It can feel like an adventure, yes."

"We're lucky you're brave," Jean said.

"I don't think I'm any braver than anybody else."

"I think you are."

"I just push myself a little harder than most people do."

"That's the brave part," Rose said.

Chapter Twenty-Four

Nobody Wants to be a Meme When They Grow Up

"Why are you staring at your laptops?" Maggie asked. "The show is about to start."

It was the following Sunday morning. The six of them were sitting in the living room in front of the big-screen TV. Willa and Gemma sat on the floor, cross-legged in pajamas. They actually weren't both staring at laptops. Gemma was staring at her phone.

"This is how we're watching it," Willa said.

"I don't get that," Maggie said. "There's a TV right in front of you."

Neither girl answered.

Rose got up from the recliner, where she had been sitting squeezed in with her sister. She walked to where Maggie sat on the couch next to Alex. She leaned in close and spoke quietly near Maggie's ear.

"If they watch the live stream on the network website they can see viewer comments in real time."

"Ah," Maggie said. "Okay. How do you know this?"

"I heard them talking about it."

Just at that moment the segment started, and Rose ran back to her seat.

"Oh, she's starting with the old interviews," Maggie said.

On the screen was Alex in her home office, describing the founding of Doctors on Wheels.

"It makes sense, though," he said. "Not everybody will've caught the first one. It's like a recap."

"Sure, I get it," Maggie said.

The scene on the TV screen cut to the line of family sitting on director's chairs in front of the Rock Hollow Fire.

"There's a very interesting follow-up to that story," TV Eleanor said. "Alex Anderson, RN, and Maggie Blount, MD, came home from that disaster with two more daughters."

"And a dog," TV Maggie said.

The cameraman zoomed in on Sunny, crouched cautiously under Rose's chair.

The scene cut to Jean and Rose talking to Roddy near the RV.

"Now the two new foster girls come along with Doctors on Wheels and help them out in the field," Eleanor said in a voice-over. "They make lunch and do dishes, and put other injured children at ease."

The voice-over ended and Maggie could hear the recorded conversation.

"I feel bad," Roddy said. "Kinda guilty, you know?"

"Why would you feel guilty?" Jean asked him.

"Because I went back in the burned house. I mean, I had to. I had to get Buster. But I still feel bad because now we have no house and everything in it got burned, and my dad can't really afford all this. You know. This medical stuff."

"But they don't charge for it," Jean said.

"Really? They don't? Nothing at all?"

"No, they see people for free."

"Wow. I didn't think anybody did that. But we still have to take Buster to a vet when we get to San Diego, and that costs money, and I know how a lot of people are about dogs. They say 'Oh it's just a dog.' But not to me he's not."

"Never let anybody tell you that," Rose said. "It's stupid. Only stupid people would say a thing like that. We have a dog, and I love him as much as any human. More than most of them, really."

"That dog?" Roddy asked with a flip of his chin.

Sunny was standing on the couch in the RV behind them, his paws up on the glass of the window.

"Yeah, that's Sunny. We love him."

"He's cute," Roddy said.

"He's a good boy, and he's as good as any person, and you should never let anybody make you feel bad. If you'd gone in after your little brother nobody would say bad things. Well, Buster is your little brother, and if they can't see that it's their problem, not yours."

"Thanks," Roddy said. "Yeah. I like that. Thanks."

The scene cut back to the family in chairs in front of the Rock Hollow Fire.

TV Rose said, "Maggie told us that when you talk to a person who's in a disaster like that, it lets them know they landed in a friendly place."

"That's nice," TV Eleanor said. "I like that a lot. That must have meant a lot to you girls right after the hurricane."

"Oh yeah," TV Jean said.

Maggie's mind wandered as Jean described the time right after the storm, and what it meant to her, as she had heard it before.

It snapped back sharply when Jean said, "I think they might be in a nursing home now. I'm not sure. Maggie's going to find out for us."

Damn, Maggie thought, and set a reminder on her phone.

She looked up again to see the replay of Alex talking about children, and the embarrassing announcement of the engagement with a placeholder ring. Maggie realized she was nervous—deeply nervous—to hear what Willa and Gemma had said.

"All is not harmonious at home," Eleanor said on the TV screen. "The girls aren't getting along."

"I'm not sure that's a fair statement," Maggie heard herself say. "I wouldn't say they don't get along as much as I would say there's a struggle to adjust to some of this. I guess we all have a lot of stuff to work out about this new development. As a family."

Willa gave Maggie a scathing look over her shoulder. Gemma kept staring at her small screen.

"Indeed," Eleanor said. "They gave me quite an earful about it earlier today."

And then there it was. The part Maggie had been dreading. Willa and Gemma on TV, being themselves.

"I mean . . . who goes out and gets two new kids?" TV Gemma said. "Think how that makes us feel. Like she just replaced us with new models."

"Well . . . not replaced you," Eleanor said. "That would suggest she got them and got rid of you. This is still your home too, right? And she still takes care of you."

"You don't get it," Willa said, barely containing her anger. "She never has time for us. She works all week, and she's on call most weekends. And then we have to go to Dad's when she goes out with Doctors on Wheels. And then she takes that tiny little bit of attention we're getting and says 'Okay, I'm going to cut it in half now. You only get half of it.'"

Maggie winced inwardly. It was a perfect example of a complaint from the girls that was neither unfounded nor wrong.

"But now you have new sisters," Eleanor said. "A bigger family. Isn't that more attention?"

"Wow," Willa said. "You really don't get it."

For a few beats, no one on the screen spoke. It was probably only two or three seconds, but it felt unbearable to Maggie. Like a painful amount of dead air. But maybe only because she was braced and nervous over what might come next.

TV Willa opened her mouth and spoke again.

"You know who the top donors are to Doctors on Wheels? I mean, Alex fundraises. Of course he does. But guess who the two biggest donors are? I'll tell you. Alex and my mom."

"But . . ." Eleanor began. She paused, seeming confused. "That's good, isn't it?"

"Good? How can you say that's good? I'm seventeen and I don't have a car. Every kid in my school got a car when they were sixteen. My mom said I had to earn money and buy my own car, but then she takes enough money for two or three cars and gives it to total strangers."

The scene cut back to the family at the fire zone.

Maggie glanced over at Alex and he glanced back. Very quickly, and without words, they shared a wince over what had just happened. Their eyes said *Ouch*. Or maybe, *That was even worse than I thought*. Or both.

"Maggie," TV Eleanor said. "How do you solve a problem like this? How do you see this resolving?"

"People get used to things," Maggie heard herself say.

But she was still utterly preoccupied with the sting of Willa and Gemma's interview. Only bits and pieces of her own came through.

"We hate change and we dig in our heels . . . And then life goes on, and the thing doesn't change except that it starts feeling less new . . . Each change we think will be different. *This* will be the one we can't ever accept."

Maggie glanced at Willa and Gemma but couldn't tell how much they were listening.

"I guess when my girls were little, I wanted them to have everything they wanted . . . But I might have been doing them a disservice, because life is not a place where you almost always get what you want . . . I can't only do the things that somebody else finds comfortable. People's needs will always be in conflict. Sometimes you have to do what you have to do and other people have to be in charge of their own feelings about it."

As she heard herself say it the second time, Maggie realized how much Willa and Gemma would hate it. How embarrassed they would be for their friends to hear that stark assessment of their troubles. And somehow that had not occurred to her at the time.

And then there was what she knew she'd said next, which was even worse, from their perspective.

"Back when you were fostering, you never considered sending Jean and Rose to another foster family? There are lots of good ones."

"Absolutely not. They were always family. They may have been newer family, but they were never lesser family. And they were never going anywhere."

The scene on the TV cut to Eleanor in the studio.

"We wish a lot of luck to this rather tumultuous blended family," she said, clearly signing off. "And if they're up for it, maybe we'll check back with them down the road and see how they're getting on. More *Sunday A.M.* after these messages."

Maggie reached over and muted the TV. And waited.

Willa and Gemma kept staring at their screens. They were faced mostly away, but based on their body language they seemed to have frozen like statues.

"Well?" Maggie asked, wishing someone would say something.

No one did.

"Willa? Gemma? Still happy with how that went?"

But she knew they weren't, because she could feel it. She had told Alex she picked up nothing around her daughters, but she was picking up something now. And it wasn't good.

A minute or two passed in silence.

Maggie got up and walked around in front of her daughters. She stood above them as they sat on the floor. Their eyes were glued to the screens in front of them. Both their faces seemed bloodless and drained.

She reached down and snapped her fingers in front of Willa's face.

"Say something," she said.

"Leave. Me. Alone!" Willa bellowed.

She scrambled to her feet, allowing the laptop to tumble to the floor, and ran for the safety of the bedrooms. A moment later Gemma stood, shot Maggie an angry glare, and threw her phone hard. It bounced off the wall and landed on the Persian rug, its screen cracked. Then she stomped off after her sister.

Alex picked up the laptop and brought it back to his seat on the couch.

Maggie sat next to him and said nothing. He read for what felt like several minutes, and Maggie did not ask him what he was reading. Probably because she mostly didn't want to know.

"This explains their mood," he said.

"The viewer comments?"

"Right."

"I take it they're not getting a lot of support."

Alex barked out a rueful, sarcastic laugh. "That would be wildly understating the case."

"Do I even want to see them?"

"Probably not," Alex said. "But you're human, so you'll probably be drawn to them at some point. They're kind of like that proverbial grisly car accident that you don't really want to see but you can't look away from it."

"All of them?"

"Everything I've read so far. Except one of them said it's not their fault, it's your fault for the way you raised them."

Maggie waited for that insult to land in her gut, but it only felt numb in there.

"That was inevitable," she said.

"Tons of praise for Jean and Rose. Helpful. Polite. Sincere. Good girls. Willa and Gemma: Entitled. Spoiled. Narcissistic. Terrible people. Insufferable brats."

"I didn't think it would be that bad," Jean said, her voice quiet. "Now I feel bad for them."

"You have nothing to feel bad about," Maggie said.

"I wanted them to do it."

"But they didn't do it because you wanted them to. They did it because they thought it would be a good thing for them."

Maggie's phone rang, and she saw her mother's name and number on the caller ID.

"Hey Mom," she said, picking up the call.

"That was really, really bad."

"It was."

"I mean, not all of it. You and Alex were fine, and Jean and Rose did very well. But that thing Willa said about how you should buy her a car instead of helping poor people whose houses just blew away? I just winced all over when I heard that. Do they have any idea how bad that sounded?"

"I think they're getting some feedback on that," Maggie said.

———

Maggie let them cool down for twenty minutes before knocking on Willa's bedroom door.

"What?" came the inevitable reply.

"It's Mom. Checking to see if you're okay."

Maggie pushed the door open. The girls were huddled together on Willa's bed, both staring at the one remaining unbroken phone. It was obvious that they had been, or maybe still were, crying.

"Maybe it's time to get off their website," she said. "I don't think reading the comments is such a good idea."

"We're not *on* their website," Willa shot back. "We're on Instagram. It's blowing up on Instagram. We're a *meme*! Somebody made us into a *meme*!"

"What kind of meme?"

"It's a picture of us from the show," Gemma said, "and somebody drew a thought bubble over us, and it says 'Why would you waste money on displaced poor people when you could buy us a car?'"

"Whoa," Maggie said. "That's harsh."

"You think?" Willa snapped. "My boyfriend just dumped me by text. I hope you're happy."

"Wait," Maggie said. "Wait, wait, wait. First of all, I didn't even know you *had* a boyfriend."

"I can't help what you don't know," Willa spit back.

"And I can't know what you don't tell me. Second, none of this was my idea, and of course I'm not happy. But I didn't say you had to do the show and I didn't put those words in your mouth. I realize you're going through something, and I'm not suggesting you're wrong to be upset, but I won't stand here and let you blame it on me or anybody else."

"But it *was* you!" Willa shrieked. "It was your fault! You brought them home!"

Maggie took a breath and resolved to remain calm.

"And you might take a minute to notice that you're not being criticized for having trouble accepting your new sisters. You're getting blowback for saying we should take money from Doctors on Wheels and buy you a car. That was where you stepped way, way over the line, hon."

She waited, but got no answer. The girls just scrolled and cried.

"It'll blow over," Maggie said.

"Oh my God!" Gemma shouted. "You know nothing about the internet! Things don't blow over on the internet. They blow up. And this is blowing up."

Maggie stood in the doorway in silence for a few beats.

Then Willa tore her eyes away from the screen of her phone and looked up at Maggie. Just in that moment she didn't look scornful or furious. Just lost and scared.

"What do we do?" she asked Maggie. "I don't know what to do."

"I'll schedule an appointment with the therapist."

"That's it?" Gemma said. "That's all you've got?"

"I don't have an 'off' switch for this, if that's what you mean. I really, really want to help you. I see you're in pain. But I can't make the internet stop. I can only offer to help you deal with what's happening. So I'm suggesting the therapy."

"Okay," Willa said. "Tell her it's important, okay?"

Just as Maggie was stepping back from the doorway, Gemma said, "Mom? Will you buy me a new phone?"

"I'm afraid not, hon. You know the rule. Break it accidentally, I fix it for you. Willfully break it, and you need to work out the solution for yourself. I understand why you were so angry in that moment, but my hope is that by requiring you to fix what you broke you'll learn better ways to express your anger. For your own happiness, if for no other reason."

She stepped out and closed the door behind her, then turned to find Alex standing in the hall.

"Good for you," he said.

"Too soon, Alex."

"Sorry." He held up Gemma's phone. "Still works," he said. "She'll just have to look at everything through a cracked screen."

"I have to go call the therapist," Maggie said.

———

They lay awake for a long time that night, not talking.

Finally Maggie said, "I've heard it's even hard for grownups when the whole internet starts piling on."

"Hard times are what change people," Alex said.

"I feel like you don't have any sympathy for them at all."

"And I feel like you want to mirror the world back to them in a way that's distorted, so it won't hurt their feelings. And if you never get your feelings hurt, why would you ever change?"

Maggie could feel their tension rising almost to the point of a fight. It was a rare feeling. They almost never fought, and when they did it tended to wrap up quickly.

"I think all parents want to do that for their children," she said, taking less of an adversarial tone.

"I'm sure that's true," he said, and his voice had softened in response. "And I have no children, so I have no right to judge. Let's try to get some sleep. It'll blow over."

"But first it'll blow up," Maggie said.

Chapter Twenty-Five

Everybody's Out of Step but Willa and Gemma

"I wish we could have had a private session with just the two of us," Willa said. "I mean, and you of course," she added in Scarlett Silverman's general direction.

Maggie sat in the office with the four girls, feeling very unsure of the direction the session might take. She had been looking around at the faces but hadn't offered much in the way of thoughts.

It was Monday morning. The therapist had come into the office early to see them on an emergency basis.

"If your mom agrees, we can schedule some future sessions with just you two girls."

"Fine with me," Maggie said.

"But right now," Scarlett said, "we're in *this* session, with all four of you and your mom. Let's just make of it what we can, okay?"

"I just think," Willa began, staring down at the soft brown carpeting, "that they'll get offended by what I want to say."

"Your new sisters?"

"Yeah."

Scarlett looked to Jean and Rose. "Your thoughts?"

"I can't really imagine how much worse it could be than what they've said in front of us all along," Jean said.

"Okay, fine," Willa said. "Here goes. I think it sucks that everybody likes them and everybody hates us. It's so unfair."

Maggie opened her mouth to speak—or to reflexively react might be more accurate—but the therapist held up a stop sign of a hand to quiet her.

"You'll get your turn, Maggie, I promise. But let me just address what Willa said."

"Fine," Willa said. "Tell me I'm wrong. I'm totally used to it."

"I acknowledge that it sucks," Scarlett said.

That seemed to surprise Willa, who opened her mouth but said nothing.

"It's definitely a painful situation. I see that and I have empathy for you because of it. It's a hard thing. It would be a hard thing for anybody, even an adult who had a good, well-established sense of identity and self-esteem. I can only imagine how hard it must be for teens in high school. But I disagree that it's unfair."

Willa opened her mouth again, this time seeming more ready to speak. But the therapist gave her the same stop-sign hand signal.

"Let me finish the thought," she said. "I hope you know that others are not obligated to hold you in high esteem. You can say 'I'm a human being so I deserve to be fed and to feel safe,' but I don't think you can accurately say the same thing about being liked. People will like you or not like you based on your likability. On how you treat them. It's not owed to you. You have to earn it."

"So you're saying we're not likable," Gemma chimed in.

"I'm saying a very large number of people heard you say something that they found troubling, and now they've decided not to like you based on that, because it's all they know about you. They have nothing else on which to base their feelings about you."

"And now our lives are ruined," Willa said. "Because it'll never go away."

"No, it will," the therapist said. "Just not nearly as soon as you'd like."

"Nothing ever goes away on the internet," Willa said. "Ever. Everything out there is out there forever."

"Let me give you an example. A client of mine tweeted a joke before she got on a plane. It was potentially questionable, but she meant it as a joke, and it was taken out of context. Like, literally misquoted. The misquote, not her actual tweet, started being passed around on Twitter, and by the time she landed it had gone viral. She lost her job. People doxed her on the internet. She got threats of violence from people who knew where she lived. This was three and a half years ago. Were you on Twitter three and a half years ago?"

"Of course we were," Willa said.

"What do you remember about it?"

"I don't know. People go viral for saying the wrong thing all the time."

"Thank you for making my point," Scarlett said.

They sat in silence for a minute or two. A flock of starlings was making a racket in the trees outside the office window, but it struck Maggie as a beautiful racket. Certainly preferable to the inside of the room.

Maggie had noticed a lot more silence in the house since the show had aired. Her daughters seemed more contemplative. Slower to throw their opinions out into the room. Then again, it had only been a day.

"Everybody's saying we're terrible people," Gemma said.

"Everybody?" Scarlett asked.

"Just about."

"Even your friends?"

"Even our friends," Willa said. "Even all my friends *with cars* think I shouldn't have said that. They're all texting me and saying, 'I wouldn't want it if it came right out of the pocket of a person whose house just blew away or whose parents just drowned. That was too far.'"

"One person told me she gets how we feel," Gemma said. "*One*. But then she also said if we were smart we would have kept those feelings to ourselves."

"Don't we have a right to feel the way we feel?" Willa asked the therapist.

"You do. But there might be a price to pay for it."

Another awkward silence.

Then Willa said, "Are we?"

"Are you what?"

"Terrible people."

"You girls are going to have to judge your own character yourselves. Ninety-nine percent of the world thinks you're wrong. You have to decide if you agree with them."

"We don't," Gemma said. "*They're* wrong."

"But it sounds like you're telling me that what you said—and what you feel—is normal. But normal is just what the average person would feel. I think if almost everyone disagrees with you, it's not normal."

"So we're wrong," Willa said.

Scarlett Silverman sighed. She had a sterling-silver pen in her right hand, and she clicked the point in and out as she spoke. Normally it would have aggravated Maggie, but in that moment it felt like a welcome distraction.

"There's an old story about a soldier marching with his regiment," Scarlett said. "He looks around and sees that everybody else is on the other foot from him, and he thinks, 'Everybody's out of step but me.' You see where I'm going with this?"

"I think I *see* it," Willa said, "but I don't think I *like* it."

"You're at a crossroads, and you need to decide who you want to be. If you want to be exactly who you are now, you can do that. You have that right. But then you're deciding to live in a world where almost nobody likes you. Or you can decide you want to be different. To be somebody who doesn't have to face so much criticism."

"How do we do that?" Willa asked, sounding surprisingly sincere. Actually, Maggie thought, more than sincere. She sounded desperate, as if asking somebody to throw her a lifeline. "How do you be somebody different?"

"It's not exactly becoming somebody different," Scarlett Silverman said. "It's more like you're still you but you function in a different way. The 'how' is called therapy, and it's what I do for a living. Now. Maggie. I cut you off before. Anything you want to add?"

"And I promise I'm going to do it right along with you," Maggie said to her girls. "Because I know I've made a lot of mistakes. I know you're angry and I know why. And I swear I can do better."

"Jean? Rose?"

"We don't think it's fair that they're being treated this way," Jean said. "Rose and I talked about it, and even if they said something they shouldn't have said, this is just wrong. Everybody's treating them like mean girls but then they're being just as mean. And I think we might say something about it."

"It probably wouldn't help," Willa said.

"But we'll probably do it anyway."

"Well . . ." Willa began. Then she seemed to stall. "Even if it doesn't help, thanks."

———

"Have you noticed that Willa and Gemma are being really quiet?" Alex asked.

They were in the kitchen, making dinner. Maggie was boiling pasta and Alex was putting together an elaborate salad.

Bess had Ubered over from her hotel for dinner and was setting the table.

"I did notice that."

"It's good," he said. Then, after a moment to think, he added, "And . . . I totally didn't mean that the way I just realized it sounded. I didn't mean it's good that I don't have to hear them talk. I mean it seems like they're thinking more than they're talking. I know it's too early to tell, but . . . it just seems good."

"I knew what you meant," Maggie said.

"Where *are* the girls, anyway?"

"In Willa's room."

"No, I meant all of them."

"Yes. All of them. In Willa's room."

"All four girls."

"Yes. All four of them are in Willa's room."

"Doing what? Do you even know?"

"I haven't even dared to ask," Maggie said.

———

"You girls are being awfully quiet," Bess said over dinner.

It seemed to take Willa and Gemma a minute to realize someone was talking to them.

Gemma was the first to look up from her food.

"Who, us?"

"Yes, you, dear. I haven't heard a word from you girls since I got here."

For what seemed like a long time, nobody spoke.

Then Willa said, "I guess I just started feeling like you really have to think about what you say before you say it."

"Always a good life lesson," Bess said.

———

Maggie arrived in the outer office of her practice at a little before eight the following morning. Two of the three receptionists seemed stunned to see her.

"Dr. Blount!" Terry said. "We thought you were going to be gone another month."

"That was the plan," Maggie said. "But my mom is here from Florida and she's looking for a house to buy here, so she's going to keep an eye on the girls during the day. Jacque knew I was coming back because she's the one who called all my patients and asked them if they wanted earlier appointments."

The young receptionist, Harper, punched Jacque on the upper arm. "You could've said something."

"Sorry," Jacque said. "Also, ouch. I figured when she walked in the door that would tell you everything you needed to know."

Maggie pushed through the door that read "Authorized Personnel Only" and joined them at the back of their reception desk, hanging her light jacket on a hook and changing into a scrubs top.

"Must be a lot of upset at home," Terry said.

"Oh, you have no idea."

"But those two girls . . . those two new girls you brought home from Louisiana . . . they are so wonderful. They are just the best. That video was just . . . I don't even have words."

"You mean the one of them talking to the boy and his dog?"

"Well, that too. But I meant the TikTok video."

Jacque jumped back into the conversation. "Oh, did you see it on TikTok? I saw it on Twitter."

"I didn't see it at all," Harper said, "but my mom told me it was all over her Facebook feed."

"Wait," Maggie said. "I'm missing something."

"You really don't know about the video?" Terry asked. "Everybody else in the world knows."

She pulled her phone out of her pants pocket and clicked around a bit, then handed it to Maggie. On its screen she saw Jean and Rose in Willa's room, with Willa and Gemma in the background. Somehow they had set up the phone to stand upright and record on its own.

Maggie pressed "play."

"I really think it's time to stop this," Jean said into the phone camera. "You're all being just awful to our sisters. Even if they said something wrong, you're all being just terrible. Like you never said anything and then wished you hadn't. Every single one of you. I'll tell you what.

Anybody out there who's never once said anything wrong, you get to keep picking on them. Everybody else needs to stop right now."

"Yeah," Rose said. "You're talking about them like they're these awful mean girls, but you're being even meaner. They didn't call anybody terrible names like you're doing. Then why are you acting like you're nicer than them? Because you're not."

"Just stop," Jean said. "They told us they're going to do better, so just leave them alone and let them try, okay?"

The images went still as the video ended.

Maggie looked up and handed back the phone. Then she wished she had scanned the comments first. But that would have taken time, and she had patients to see, beginning in a matter of minutes.

"Have you read the comments?" Maggie asked. "What's the consensus? How is this being received?"

"It's a mixed bag," Terry said. "Probably two out of three comments say Willa and Gemma are terrible but the adopted girls are just too nice to see it that way. But then some of them are like, 'If their own sisters want us to leave them alone, we should respect that. They're the ones who have to live with them.' That sort of thing."

"Thanks for showing me that," Maggie said.

She walked to an empty examining room at the back of the clinic and pulled her own phone out of her pocket. On it she found a message from Evie Moskowitz that had apparently been silenced while she was driving.

She played back the voicemail.

"Hi Maggie," it said. "Evie Moskowitz, returning your call. Hope the girls are really thriving. I feel bad not updating you before now. I shouldn't be making you ask. Of course the girls would be curious about their grandparents after so much time. We all know they couldn't stay in their home long term. They're in a shared room in an assisted-living facility in Mobile. I'm going to text you the address of the place in case they want to visit or call. Hope to talk to you in real time someday soon. Wish they were all like you. Bye for now."

Maggie called her home landline.

Grandma Bess picked up. Maggie could hear the familiar construction noise in the background.

"Hey Mom. Are Jean and Rose around?"

"We were just on our way out. Willa and Gemma are really into the idea of coming house hunting with me. I think they figure it's like clothes shopping but with more money on the line. I have a rental car and they're already in it. Rose is in the pool, of course, but Jean is right here."

"Put her on, okay?"

"Hello?" Jean's tentative voice said.

"It's me," Maggie said.

"Hi you. Not that I don't like to hear from you, but didn't you leave like . . . twenty minutes ago?"

"I know. That's true. I mostly just called to tell you I love you," Maggie said. "At least, I was just about to call you for no other reason than that when I got some other news."

A brief silence.

"You called to say you love all of us?" Jean asked, clearly afraid to make assumptions.

"I definitely *do* love all of you, but I called to say it to you and Rose."

"Did we do something special?"

"I think you know what you did," Maggie said. "Tell Rose I said so, okay?"

Maggie listened to a long pause on the line.

Then Jean said, "Thanks, Mom. What was the other news?"

"Oh. Right. Yes. I just heard back from that nice social worker who drove you to your grandparents in Mobile. I called her and left a message because Rose asked me to find out where they were. Your grandparents, that is. They're in a room together at an assisted-living place in Mobile. She's going to send me the address in case you want to write or go see them."

Maggie waited, but no words came back.

"*Do* you want to write or go see them?"

"Not really," Jean said. "We never liked them all that much if I'm being honest. But we still wanted them to be okay."

"And that," Maggie said, "is one of the many reasons why I love you. I have to go, though, hon. I have patients."

Maggie ended the call and got on with her first day back.

Chapter Twenty-Six

Only Ninety-Nine Miles to Go

It was about six weeks later. Summer was all but over.

The downstairs area for Jean and Rose was complete, and surprisingly nice, and the silence was an unfamiliar and very welcome thing. School was back in session, and Maggie now wore a simple but beautiful engagement ring on her left hand. It was still fairly new and she still caught herself admiring it regularly.

The flap on the internet had died down somewhat. Or at least Maggie thought it had. Willa and Gemma might have known more, but if so they weren't saying. Their private school had been back in session for three days and neither girl had come home crying at the end of the day, according to Jean and Rose, and Bess.

Maggie got home from her workday at six thirty to find Jean and Rose in the pool. The afternoon was warm, and the sun was on just enough of a slant to throw most of the yard into shade. Maggie moved into that dappled comfort and enjoyed the sense of arriving home to relative peace.

Their public-school year had just started that day, and Maggie was anxious to hear how it had gone.

She sat down on a chaise longue, and Sunny put his paws up on her lap and licked her ear. In fact, he tried to lick the inside of her ear, but Maggie laughed and redirected him slightly to her cheek, scratching under his jaw the way he liked.

The girls swam over to the edge of the pool, hooked their forearms over its concrete edge, and beamed up at Maggie. It might have been her imagination, she thought, but they looked even a little more happily excited than usual.

"I was just about to ask how your first day of the new school year went. But now I'm looking at your faces and sensing it went well."

"*Really* well," Rose said. "I mean, I thought it was good, but it was really, really, extra good for Jean. Tell her, Jean."

Jean blushed and turned her face away.

"No, stop it, Rose. You're being a pain."

"She met a *boy*," Rose said. She put a huge, awestruck emphasis on the word "boy," as if reporting that Jean had met a friendly space alien or a flying unicorn.

"Really," Maggie said. It did not come out as a question.

She found herself with mixed feelings about that. Willa and Gemma had certainly discovered boys, and Maggie's feelings about that situation were complicated enough. But somehow Jean and Rose felt more innocent and vulnerable to Maggie, and her urge to protect them felt even more unreasonably huge.

Then again, Jean was seventeen, and this had been bound to happen.

"It's nothing," Jean said. "I barely know him. I just met him. Rose is making it out to be a bigger deal than it is."

"But you like him," Maggie said. Also not a question.

Jean blushed even redder, if such a thing were possible.

"I guess."

"It's okay to like a boy."

"It is?"

"Of course it is. It's part of life."

"Does that mean I'm allowed to date?"

Maggie suppressed a wincing reaction to the word.

"Well. You're seventeen. So I guess the answer is a qualified yes. You'll have a curfew, of course. You don't get to stay out until one in the morning or anything. And I'll want to meet him."

"You'd like him," Jean said. "He's not a bad boy or anything. He gets good grades."

"It's the first day of school," Maggie said. "Who's gotten grades already?"

"No, not this year. He's a senior, and his grades are really good. He's going to get into a good college."

"Then he's older," Maggie said, suppressing another wince.

"Just a year. But he's a good boy. He's not a troublemaker."

"He's actually kind of a nerd," Rose interjected. "But he's sort of a cute nerd."

"Well, if it keeps working and he asks you out, you'll bring him around," Maggie said.

Rose answered for her sister.

"He already asked her out."

"Then bring him around," Maggie said. "Invite him over to dinner."

"Okay," Jean said quietly, her face still red.

"I hate to even ask, but where are Willa and Gemma?"

"Upstairs with their friends," Rose said. "Or at least Willa is. Gemma might be in her room by herself, but Willa brought two friends home."

Before Rose could even finish the last sentence, they heard shouting in the kitchen.

"Uh-oh," Maggie said. "I'd better go see what that's all about. At least I know they're not yelling at *you*."

Maggie jumped up and trotted to the house. She rolled back the sliding glass door into the kitchen to see Willa faced off with her friend Brittany.

She stepped inside just in time to hear Brittany shout, "Why would you even talk to me like that?"

"Because you didn't stand up for me!" Willa screamed back. "Everybody in the world was dumping on me and I never needed a friend more and you didn't defend me. Some friend! All you did was text me and say that thing about the car was over the line. You *have a car!*" Her voice rose to an absolute shriek. "You have a car and you had the nerve to tell me I was over the line to say I should have one. The only ones who stood up for me were *them*."

"Fine," Brittany said. "I'm leaving."

"Good! You should be leaving."

Brittany stomped out of the kitchen, and Maggie heard the front door slam. Seconds later Willa's friend Jen came down the stairs and stuck her head into the kitchen.

"I'd better go too," she said.

Willa paid her no attention. She only slumped onto a chair at the kitchen island as her friend let herself out. A moment later she looked up and noticed—seemingly for the first time—that Maggie was standing there.

"I didn't know you heard that," Willa said.

Maggie sat down beside her daughter and draped an arm around her shoulder. Surprisingly, Willa did not pull away.

"You want to talk about it?"

"Not really."

"I know I'm your mother and all that. But it really does help to talk about things sometimes."

"It's embarrassing. And besides, I know exactly what you'll say."

"Try me. I'll do my best not to be predictable."

For several seconds, nothing happened. Maggie was just about to accept that Willa was no more likely to cooperate than she had been for years.

Then the girl surprised her.

"They were making fun of Jean and Rose," she said quietly. "You know. The way they talk."

"Oh," Maggie said.

She wasn't sure if it was a good idea to telegraph her surprise or not. Until she could decide, she didn't.

"I know what you're going to say, so don't even say it. Just don't, okay?"

"What do you think I was going to say?"

"That I did the same thing, and not that long ago. Just don't."

"I actually wasn't going to say that. I know it happened, but I wasn't going to bring it up. I wasn't going to choose a moment when you did something good to pick on you for prior bad behavior. I was going to tell you I was proud of you for doing a good thing. Standing up for your new sisters."

"I don't need your praise," Willa said.

And for the first time, she ducked out from under her mother's arm.

"Wait," Maggie said. "I'm confused. You told me you *did* need my praise and that you were upset about not getting it. That you were watching Jean and Rose being praised and getting mad because you felt you weren't getting enough."

"Well, anyway, I don't need to be praised for *this*," Willa said.

She jumped up and stomped out of the room. Maggie could hear the sound of her heavy footsteps going up the stairs.

Before she could decide whether or not to follow, Gemma stuck her head into the kitchen.

"Did you know Jean has a *boyfriend*?" she asked Maggie. Her voice sounded almost . . . impressed.

Maggie looked over to see Jean standing behind Gemma, still dripping pool water from underneath a towel.

"He's not my boyfriend," Jean said. "I mean . . . I don't think he is. Not yet. I just met him. I didn't say I had a boyfriend. I just said I met a boy."

"Well, you have to do the first thing before you can do the second one," Gemma said.

They sat in Scarlett Silverman's office, the five of them. The four girls and Maggie. Willa and Gemma seemed to have dropped their request to see the therapist alone, though Maggie wasn't sure why.

"Your mother tells me you did something really nice this week," Scarlett said, directing her attention at Willa. "But also that you don't seem to want any credit for it. Do you want to talk to us about that?"

Willa squirmed slightly in her seat.

"Not really," she said.

"Will you anyway? Please?"

"I just . . ." Then she seemed to stall. "I don't know. I just don't want everyone telling me how good that was, because I'm not that good. They're only saying all that because they don't know what I'm thinking."

"Fine. Tell us what you're thinking."

"I just . . . I still mind," Willa said.

"Having two new sisters, you mean?"

"Right. That. I still mind it. I'm not saying everything about them is bad. Obviously not. I mean, they stood up for us. Nobody stood up for us, but they did. To everybody. Right out in the open like that. And when nobody else stands up for you, even your friends, a thing like that . . . well . . . you know . . . it's not something you're going to forget. But I don't want everybody treating me like I'm fine now, because I'm not fine."

"Nobody thought you were fine now," Scarlett said.

"Are you sure? People act like it's been long enough and we should just be over it."

"That's just not the way life works. Problems don't disappear in one big poof like that. It would be nice if they did, but they don't."

Willa looked around at her sisters, and at Maggie, scanning them one face at a time.

"Did you know that?" Willa asked them. "What she just said, did you know it?"

"I knew that," Maggie said. "I didn't think everything was all solved. I just wanted to praise you for doing a nice thing. I didn't think you were going to do nothing but nice things from now on and for the rest of your life."

"We knew problems don't go away that fast," Jean said.

"Yeah, we knew that," Rose added. "We talk to Scarlett all the time about our parents dying."

"I knew you weren't fine because *I'm* not fine," Gemma said.

"Let's say you had to walk a hundred miles," Scarlett said, "and you finally got over being daunted by that and you got up and walked a mile. And somebody praised you for getting started. For being willing to walk that first mile. It doesn't mean they thought you were done with the journey. It just means they think it's good that you walked the first mile. And you did. So take the praise. You earned it."

They sat in silence for an awkward length of time.

Then Willa shook her head hard. "I don't buy it. It just doesn't feel right."

"Can you be more specific?"

"You're telling me everybody understands. Everybody wants to give me credit for one thing I did right, even if I'm still doing lots of things wrong. But I live in the world, in case you didn't know. And that's just not how the world is."

"That's true," Scarlett said.

It seemed to surprise Willa, to hear the therapist say that. It took her a few seconds to close her mouth. She never answered.

"The world is not always a friendly place. It doesn't always feel safe. And the reason it doesn't always feel safe is because it's often not. People will judge you harshly and unfairly, like they're doing right now. People will bad-mouth you on the internet, like they've been doing. People get hardened by living in a world that doesn't feel safe, and you know what? I don't blame them for that. But we miss out on a lot of life when we allow ourselves to harden to the world. I'll just tell you these two things. One, this office is a safe place. You won't be judged or treated unfairly here. And two, that's why people have families. To get the kinds of breaks that are anything but guaranteed everywhere else."

———

Kirk, Jean's new almost-boyfriend, had been invited to arrive for dinner at six. And he arrived at . . . six. In fact, it was so straight-up six o'clock that he could only have been standing on the stoop staring at his watch.

The big grandfather clock in the living room began to strike its six chimes, and the knock fell on the second.

All four girls tried to descend on the door at once, but Maggie stopped them with one very commanding sentence.

"*I* . . . will get it."

Maggie opened the door.

The obviously nervous eighteen-year-old boy stood on her doorstep. He had a shock of curly black hair that reminded Maggie of Alex and made her like him immediately. He seemed to have trouble holding eye contact with her. His eyes seemed to be drawn down to the welcome mat. He held a small, colorful bouquet of flowers in each hand.

He was wearing a fairly new pair of jeans with a carefully ironed light-blue collared shirt and a blazer. Maggie pictured him struggling for hours in front of a mirror, not knowing how they expected a guest to dress for dinner and searching for that can't-miss look.

He didn't seem particularly nerdy to Maggie, but then again she wasn't a teenager.

"Mrs. Blount?"

"Dr. Blount, actually, but yes."

"Oh no. Oh, I'm so stupid. I knew that. I'm really sorry."

"You really don't have to be sorry. At all. It's really fine. And you still get to come in and have dinner."

He held his right hand and its bouquet in her direction. "This is for you," he said. "Because you're the hostess and her mom. The other one is for Jean."

"Oh my," Maggie said, accepting the flowers. "Did somebody raise you right, or what?"

She watched him try to stammer out an answer and suppress an embarrassed smile at the same time. Nothing intelligible emerged.

"Never mind," she said. "Just come in and meet the family."

———

"So. Kirk," Willa said over dinner. "What kind of name is Kirk?"

"What kind of . . . ?" He seemed unable to finish the thought.

"I mean, is it short for something?"

"Like what?"

"I don't know. Kirkus? Kirkland?"

"No, just Kirk," he said.

Maggie glanced over at Jean, who looked mortified.

"Can we please not give Kirk the third degree?" Maggie said, and Jean shot her a grateful glance.

"Tell us about school," Alex said. "In a nice positive way, I mean. Jean says you're confident about getting into a good college. Any career goals you care to share?"

"He's going to be an engineer!" Jean said. Then her face fell. "I'm sorry. I shouldn't have answered that. I should've let you answer that. You go ahead."

"I'm going to be an engineer," he said.

"Train?" Gemma asked.

"Civil," Kirk said.

For a minute or so the table fell silent again. Gemma nodded as though she knew exactly what that meant, but her facial expression said otherwise. She was also the one to break the silence.

"Anyway, Kirk. Have you dated a lot? Who was your last girlfriend? How much time in between? Was she your own age?"

Jean dropped her face into her hands.

"Gemma!" Maggie barked. "You're making this hard for him."

But unexpectedly, Kirk smiled.

"No, she's really not," he said in Maggie's direction. "They're just being good sisters. They're making sure I'm good enough for Jean. And that's nice. If they didn't care they wouldn't ask any questions, because they . . . you know . . . wouldn't care." He turned his attention directly on Willa and Gemma. "I hope it's okay to say this, but I've heard things. Who hasn't, right? But now I think they're not true, because you care about your sisters, even if it's not in that regular sort of outward, mushy kind of way. So I figure you just got a bad . . . you know . . . rap, or whatever. I figure you're okay."

That sat on the table in silence for a moment as Maggie waited to see how his thoughts would be received.

Willa spoke first. She looked right at Jean and said, "Good choice with him."

"Yeah," Gemma said. "He just got the Willa and Gemma seal of approval."

———

"He's nice, right?" Maggie asked Alex in the master bathroom later in the evening.

They were attempting to share the single sink to brush their teeth. The idea had been to replace it with a double sink, but neither one could bear the thought of any more construction, and anyway, they'd gotten pretty good at sharing.

"Yeah, he's great," Alex said, his mouth full of toothpaste. "Why? Do you have doubts about him?"

"No, not at all. And I almost wish I did. Except I don't really mean that. I'm happy for Jean. But I just feel so protective of those two." Maggie was surprised to feel how easily tears could come if she let them. She didn't let them. "He's this perfectly nice boy."

"And Willa and Gemma even like him, which is . . . I can't find the word."

"That word doesn't exist in the English language."

He smiled at her in the mirror, then spit and rinsed out his mouth.

"Then the problem is . . . ?"

"Hard to say."

"Must have something to do with being a mother of teenage girls."

"Yeah, I suspect a connection."

"And you have *four*."

"And I asked you before I ever took the other two if I was crazy."

"And I said you absolutely were, and that your version of crazy is one of your better qualities."

"Or words to that effect," Maggie said after spitting and rinsing. "I need to go to bed. It's exhausting being a mother of four. Whatever was I thinking?"

EPILOGUE

ONE YEAR LATER

Chapter Twenty-Seven

Something like Copernicus

"We fight," Willa said. "I don't want to be all phony or fakey and make it sound like we don't fight."

"Don't all sisters fight?" Eleanor Price asked.

They were sitting in Maggie and Alex's living room, the whole family of eight—including Kirk and Bess—taping the promised follow-up of Eleanor's first two stories. They all seemed to be doing their best to concentrate on the host and ignore the cameras.

"I know *Jean and I* fight sometimes," Rose said.

"And I fought with Willa lots when it was just us," Gemma added. "Still do sometimes."

"Too many times," Willa added. "But I meant as far as the two pairs of us working things out."

"Let me just interject something here," Eleanor said. "When I first spoke to you all on the subject, I got the impression that it wasn't really about you four girls getting along, exactly. I could be wrong, but it felt like Jean and Rose were bending over backward to get along with *you*, and it was more about you two girls being willing to accept *them*."

All eight family members laughed at the same time, as if on cue.

"Oh, that was the *old* Jean and Rose," Willa said. "Those were the good old days, huh? They weren't much on standing up for themselves back then, but they learned. They learned a little too well if you ask me."

"Just well enough," Maggie corrected.

"Whatever," Gemma said. "Agree to disagree."

"Okay, now, the elephant in the room," Eleanor said.

It struck Maggie that she had never done an interview with this TV host and not heard her use that expression. She wondered if Eleanor had ever tried conducting an interview without it.

"I know what you're going to ask," Willa said. "About the comments we got after the last interview, and how it went viral on social media."

"It can't have been easy for you girls."

"It was devastating," Gemma said. "It was so bad. I honestly think we had no idea life could be that bad."

"But you agreed to come on my show again, so I have to believe that you think people will see you differently this time. Tell us what's changed."

"Okay . . . ," Willa began, "well, we've been in therapy for a little over a year, after planting our feet and refusing to go for just about that long. And I guess . . . I'm not sure how to say it exactly. It's like some things change and some things don't. I'm not an entirely different person, but I do think I'm different in a lot of ways. I guess the best way to explain it is that I have these thoughts and feelings and they're not all that different from what they ever were, but now part of me stands outside them and thinks 'Yeah, sure, those are *your* thoughts and feelings but other people have *theirs*.' Or . . . if I want something, or think I have a problem, this voice in my head says 'Yeah, but other people have problems and want stuff too.' Does that make sense?"

"It does indeed," Eleanor said. "Sounds like our old friend the Copernicus Conversion. That's what I like to call it when we figure out we're not the center of the universe."

"Yeah, something like that," Willa said. "But I just . . . I want to say something but I'm not sure if I'll say it right. I'm not even sure if I've got it all sorted out in my head yet."

"Talk about it all you want," Eleanor said. "We'll be editing this, so it doesn't matter if it takes you a few tries to get it right."

"Okay. I'll try. Gemma's gonna kill me for this, though."

"Why?" Gemma asked, her voice guarded. "What are you about to say?"

"Just sort of . . . that I look back now and think maybe it wasn't entirely a bad thing that it happened."

"You've *got* to be kidding," Gemma said, her voice just at the edge of shrill. "That was the most entirely bad thing that ever happened to me."

"But it was *so bad* that it made me look at things a different way. Like . . . I felt like I had no choice. Everybody hated us."

"I didn't hate you," Maggie said.

"But you didn't like us," Willa said.

"Not a day went by in your entire lives that I didn't love you."

"But you didn't like us."

Maggie took a deep breath. Sighed it out.

"A lot of the time I did. But I'll be honest and say you didn't make it easy. But also I wasn't doing a very good job accepting you, and it was my job to. I hope I'm doing better now."

"You definitely are. And now you like us better, and our friends like us better. I think maybe even we like us better. And Alex even seems to like us now. But it never would have happened without all that awful stuff. I know it wouldn't have. I can feel it. It took something really bad. Like, something that completely shook us up. Right down to our . . . well, I want to say roots but I guess people don't have roots. But maybe you know what I mean. If everything had just gone along fine we wouldn't have changed anything. We never would've thought we needed to."

Eleanor nodded vigorously. In fact, Maggie had noticed her nodding through Willa's entire speech.

"I know exactly what you mean," she said. "And I've always believed in that, because I see it all the time. I wish I had a nickel for every time I've said 'People don't change when everything is going along fine. People change when the roof falls in.' Literally or figuratively. And now I realize I owe you an apology, Rose and Jean, because that's a painful metaphor for you, I'm sure, and I didn't make that connection until I heard myself say it. But I'll never forget this time . . . it was years ago when I was a junior reporter. I was covering this horrible freak tornado that just seemed to come out of nowhere. I walked up to this man who was standing in front of a massive pile of rubble that had been his house the previous day. Now it was like a huge load of scrap wood piled around a chimney. I stuck a microphone in his face, which I realize in retrospect was probably insensitive. Maybe I knew it at the time, but that's what a reporter has to do. You have to bring back that footage. Not just of ruined buildings, but of people. Its effect on people. The viewers at home want to know what that would feel like. Right or wrong, they want that. So I asked him to give me a reaction. And I'll never forget what he said to me. He said, 'I'm so lucky. My family is all okay.'

"I remember looking at that footage over and over and thinking, 'If I had asked that guy two days earlier, he would have told me his house was really important. But that day he knew it wasn't. It was a thing, and things can be replaced.' He might have mourned all those lost belongings later—in fact I'm sure he did. That's only human. But I'm betting he never forgot what he learned that morning: that only his family was irreplaceable. So, yeah. I get it. People don't make sweeping changes when everything is going along as usual. It takes a pretty deep shock to make someone rethink everything."

Alex spoke up for the first time since the cameras had been turned on.

"Maggie's mother—who by the way is sitting right over there on the end of the couch—always says, 'If nothing changes, nothing changes.' I think you can see where I'm going with this. Something changed, so something changed."

"What I really like," Eleanor said, "is how the girls can look back now and think maybe it was worth it."

A quick silence fell.

"Not sure *I* think it was worth it," Gemma said. "It was really bad."

"But we still would have been people nobody liked," Willa said. "Just . . . not as many people would've known about it."

"Can we talk about something else?" Gemma asked.

"Absolutely," Eleanor said. "Introduce me to the newest member of the family."

"Not exactly family," Kirk said, his gaze trained down to the carpet.

"Close enough to family," Maggie said.

"Family enough for us," Alex added.

"You're Kirk," Eleanor said. "Correct? And you're Jean's boyfriend."

"Actually I'm her . . ." His eyes darted up from the carpet and he caught Maggie's eyes. "Am I allowed to say it?"

"You're allowed to say whatever's true."

"I'm her fiancé. We're engaged."

"Well that's happy news," Eleanor said.

"*Is* it now?" Maggie chimed in. Maybe a little too loudly. "Don't get me wrong. We love him like a son, but he's nineteen and she's eighteen. We've been encouraging them to think in terms of the long game, but so far we're not making the sale."

"We wanted to get married now," Jean said. "But Maggie and Alex wouldn't give their blessing. And we feel like we need their blessing. We're legal adults, but we still want them to approve."

"They want you to wait until you're twenty-one?" Eleanor asked.

"We want them to wait until she's thirty," Maggie said. "But clearly that's not the way it's going to be."

"What about college?" Eleanor asked.

"Kirk got into a really good college," Jean said. "He's going to get an engineering degree. I'll go to college somewhere in the same city as him. And then he'll work as an engineer and support us while I go to medical school. I'm going to be a doctor like my new mom. After a few years I can go along when Doctors on Wheels goes out, and I can do more than just clean and make sandwiches. And when Maggie and Alex retire I can keep it going."

"Wow, you've thought about this," Eleanor said.

"We don't think about anything else," Kirk said.

"I'll be the one to go ahead and ask, then," Eleanor said. "Why the early engagement? Why not just be boyfriend and girlfriend for now?"

"That was mostly Jean," Kirk said, "so I'll let *her* answer."

For a few seconds, Jean seemed to struggle with her own thoughts. Then she said, "I just kept thinking about the day our parents died. They didn't wake up that morning thinking it was the day they were going to die. Same thing when Dr. Bishop died—the husband Dr. Bishop—which hit us kind of hard because we hadn't really worked through our feelings about our own parents. He didn't know it was about to be over and neither did the other Dr. Bishop—Lacey, his wife. I'm just not sure you should do much procrastinating when the world is so full of surprises."

Maggie exchanged a glance with Alex. They both silently noted with their eyes that it was almost exactly the reason *they* had gotten engaged. Which made it hard to dismiss.

"What about the rest of you girls?" Eleanor asked. "Boyfriends?"

"Ick," Rose said.

Gemma said, "Not at this exact moment, no."

"I *had* a boyfriend," Willa said. Something about her tone seemed to cast a pall on the room. "He broke up with me by text the night that interview aired. I really thought I loved him, but he couldn't have loved me because he didn't even ask me for my side of the thing. He just thought all that criticism would rub off on him or something. Since then I haven't had a boyfriend. I purposely haven't. And I'm not feeling sorry for myself, either, if that's what some people are thinking. I just decided the whole thing is tougher and more complicated than I thought. I think you have to go slower and really know what you've got in someone. Sorry if that was too much information."

"No," Eleanor said. "I like it. It's honest. While we're on the subject of love and marriage, last time you sat down with me, Maggie, you had your left hand in your pocket because Alex hadn't put the permanent ring on it yet."

"But we *were* engaged," Maggie said.

"Granted. And now your hand is out and on your lap and I see not only a lovely diamond engagement ring but a wedding band."

She held up her left hand, and Alex held up his and showed his matching gold band.

"And how did you girls feel about that?" Eleanor asked. "Were you all on board with it?"

"We were happy," Rose said. "We like Alex."

"We like Alex too," Gemma said. "But at first we weren't big on the idea because we were hoping our parents would get back together. But then our father got married again first anyway, so I guess why not?" She stopped talking for a moment, and her face changed to something less airy and more concerned. "Okay, got it. I just heard myself do that thing I'm not supposed to do. I was supposed to be thinking about Alex and my mom and wanting them to be happy but I was just thinking about me. But at least I *heard* it that time."

"I don't think anyone's going to fault you for wanting your parents to get back together," Eleanor said. "I think all kids want that. It's pretty universal."

"Oh. Okay," Gemma said. "I guess I just expect the worst at this point."

"Well, under the circumstances we're also not going to fault you for thinking everybody's going to fault you. I want to talk briefly to Bess about deciding to move here and help out with all these kids."

"Just what grandmothers do," Bess said. "We're actually well known for that sort of thing."

"That's it?" Eleanor asked after a pause.

"I think so. I wasn't there for the first two segments and nobody's wondering how I'm getting along a year later. I don't want to steal the show."

"Alex. You've been quiet."

"I live in a house with five women," he said. "It pays to choose your words carefully."

Eleanor laughed. "And how are you doing with that?"

"Oh, fine. I like women, fortunately. Though Kirk's testosterone is a welcome addition, I have to admit."

"Not feeling overwhelmed?"

"I didn't say *that*. But two of the girls will be in college soon. The other two aren't far behind."

"You're really looking forward to that empty nest, aren't you?"

"Yes and no," Alex said. "Mixed feelings. I like a big family. But yeah, time alone with Maggie . . . well, I can only imagine it at this point. It's not like something that ever actually happened to us before."

"Okay," Eleanor said. "Is that it? Feels like I'm missing something. Oh wait. Here's a question. Where's the dog? Tell me you still have the dog."

"Of course we still have him," Rose said. "He's out in the yard. I wanted him in but Mom said maybe you wouldn't want that. She said kids and dogs steal the show and we already had all these kids."

"Bring him in," Eleanor said. "I'm sure my viewers will want to see him. Who doesn't love seeing a formerly miserable rescue dog looking fat and happy?"

Rose jumped up and ran for the nearest sliding glass door. Seconds later Sunny came bounding into the room and leaped up onto the couch next to Jean, where he sat, a bit off-kilter and looking self-satisfied, his huge tongue hanging out in what looked for all the world like a grin.

"Oh my," Eleanor said. "Is it possible that he got *even bigger?*"

"Seventy-seven pounds," Maggie said, "but who's counting?"

"He turned into a very handsome dog."

"He really did," Gemma said.

Everyone turned and stared at Gemma, minus the TV people, who weren't surprised to hear it.

"What?" Gemma said defensively.

"You weren't his biggest fan," Maggie said. "You thought he was ugly."

"Not ugly, exactly. Just not really what I was expecting, I guess. But he's sweet. And he did turn into a nice-looking dog. Or maybe just when you love somebody they get prettier."

"And there's a thought for my viewers to take away," Eleanor said. "When you love somebody they get prettier. Is he allowed on the couch like that?"

Maggie sighed.

"Initially no."

"I thought the girls had him so well trained."

"Oh, they do. It's not that he started defying us. It was more of a gradual erosion of our rules."

"As long as you're okay with it," Eleanor said.

"Oh yeah. Who cares about couches, anyway? A couch is just a thing. Things can be replaced. The important thing is that my family is all okay."

———

Maggie changed into her one-piece bathing suit and joined Alex at the pool, where Jean and Rose were taking a swim. At least, she thought that was whom she was joining. But when she got there, all four girls were in the pool at the same time.

It was evening, and mostly dark, which made the rectangle of pool and its four young inhabitants the brightest thing in Maggie's world.

She stood with her bare toes at its concrete edge.

"You're in the pool," she said to Willa and Gemma.

"Duh," Gemma said.

"You never go in the pool."

"We're in the pool *right now*," Willa said. "Does that count, or what?"

Maggie turned and looked at Alex, who was stretched out on a chaise longue, fully dressed. They made eye contact as best they could in the dim light.

"You're not going in?"

"I just took a shower. I don't want to get all chlorine-y and have to shower again. Besides, it's crowded in there."

"And about to get more crowded," Maggie said.

She backed up, took a running start, and did a wild cannonball into the pool, forcing the girls to shriek and disperse to make room for her massive splash.

The shock of the cool water changed something about the way she felt, though she would have had trouble putting words to it at first. But it was a cleansing feeling, as if part of what had come before in her life was washing away and leaving her. A refreshing sensation.

When she popped back up again, she looked around at the faces of the girls. Three of them, anyway. Rose was swimming laps at one edge, but the rest of them treaded water and considered each other. The pool lights made it easy to see their wet faces.

"When does that thing we did today go on the air?" Willa asked, and Maggie could hear the stress in her voice. And she could feel it in the air between them.

"I don't know. She didn't say."

"The other ones aired fast, though," Gemma added.

"The other ones were tied in with a disaster that was big in the news cycle. She had incentive to get them on the air fast. This is more of a whenever thing."

Willa made a strangled sound in her throat.

"What?" Maggie said. "You're that anxious to see yourself on TV?"

Willa made that sound a second time and swam away.

"What?" Maggie said again, turning to Gemma.

"She's terrified," Gemma said. "We both are."

"You think people are going to jump all over you again?"

Gemma didn't answer. Then again, the answer was obvious.

Maggie caught Willa's attention as she swam by, tapping her on one wet shoulder. The girl's head popped up. A second later Rose appeared in the group, treading water and grinning.

"Are we having a family meeting or something?" she asked.

"Maybe," Maggie said. "Something like that. Willa and Gemma are worried about how that interview will be received." She tried to look right into Willa's eyes, but Willa wouldn't meet her gaze. "I can see how you'd be gun-shy after last time, but you know you did well. You can feel it, right? You were there. You heard yourself."

"Mo-om," Willa said. She drew the word out into two syllables, and it sounded exasperated.

"What? What am I missing?"

"We thought we did fine last time."

"Ah," Maggie said. "Right. Well. Let's go at it a different way, then. Last time everybody thought what you said was a problem except you. Alex and I looked at each other and winced. Grandma Bess called on the phone and said, 'That was really, really bad.' I'm not saying this to make you feel worse. I'm trying to assure you that the rest of us saw the reaction coming. Now. Jean and Rose, you weigh in, please. Honestly. How did they do this time?"

"Really good," Jean said.

"Yeah," Rose said. "Good. People'll notice the difference. They'll say 'Those girls changed a lot.'"

"Alex!" Maggie called out to him. "How did the girls do on this interview?"

Alex gave a thumbs-up. "Very good," he called back.

"I don't know if it was that good," Willa said. "I was complaining about my boyfriend dumping me and Gemma wasn't that nice about you marrying Alex and she wouldn't say it was maybe good what happened. I'm not sure we did very well."

"But that's what was good about it," Maggie said. "It was honest. You showed how much has changed and that not everything has. That's so important. If you'd sat there and acted like everything was perfect now it just would have come off sounding fake."

Willa looked around at her sisters' faces. Jean and Rose nodded vigorously.

"What she said," Rose added.

"Thanks, guys," Willa said.

Then, for the rest of their time in the pool, they didn't huddle or worry. They only swam.

———

Nobody actually watched the TV except Maggie. Everybody else watched the segment on their devices so they could see the comments as quickly as possible.

They were in the living room together, two Sunday mornings later.

Maggie sat on the couch with Alex, who sat cross-legged with his laptop balanced on his knees. All four girls sat on the floor. Jean and Rose had notebook computers now for school, and they stared intently at the network website as the program streamed live. Willa and Gemma watched on their phones. Gemma's screen was still cracked. More than a year later she had continued to choose to spend her allowance and birthday money on clothes and makeup and put up with the damaged phone.

Maggie watched the four girls on TV and was filled with an odd sense that there was something about them that was more . . . she struggled for the word in her head and landed on "cohesive." There was something more cohesive about them. They no longer seemed like they must have beamed here to Earth from two very different planets.

She leaned over and poked Alex gently in the ribs.

"Comments on the thread yet?" she whispered.

"Yeah. They're good."

"Oh thank goodness."

"The word 'progress' keeps coming up."

"Can I see?"

She leaned over him and scanned the long thread under the live video player.

"Those first two sure have changed a lot," one said.

"Gotta give 'em credit," another said. "They sound human."

"If that's real, it's a lot of progress, and it sounds real."

Maggie read until the program ended. Then she nudged Willa in the back, gently, with her bare foot.

"Told you they'd like you better," she said.

"Yeah, thanks. These are good. Really good, most of them. Even the ones that're a little nasty still give us credit for doing better."

A light bing sound announced a text on somebody's phone.

Willa picked up her phone and stared at it for a long time in silence.

"What is it?" Gemma asked.

"It's Eric."

"Who's Eric?" Maggie interjected.

"Her ex," Gemma said. "The one she thought was the love of her life."

Maggie leaned closer to Alex and whispered, "And all that time I didn't even know she had a boyfriend."

"In your defense," he whispered back, "they're teenagers, so 'all that time' might've been six weeks."

"What did he say?" Gemma asked loudly.

For a time, Willa didn't answer. She just stared at the screen. She seemed to be weighing whether or not this was a message she wanted to share.

Then she read the text out loud.

"Saw you on TV. You look great. You sound great. Let's get back together."

"Whoa," Gemma said. "Are you going to?"

"I thought he was with Krista McCullough."

"They broke up weeks ago," Gemma said.

"How do you *know* all this?"

"I go to that school. I have eyes. I listen. I keep my ear to the ground."

Willa seemed to unfreeze suddenly, and she typed a hurried message with both thumbs flying at once. Then she threw the phone down on the rug.

"I can't believe he thinks I'm that stupid," she said.

Gemma reached over and picked up Willa's phone.

"Whoa," she said again. "You really stomped him."

"How can he think I'd just get back together with him, just like that? After the way he treated me? I deserve better than that."

"You do, honey," Maggie said. "I'm proud of you."

Willa never answered.

A few seconds later her sisters moved in close to her, and Maggie saw by the heaving of her shoulders that Willa was crying.

Gemma set her head on her sister's lap and Jean and Rose leaned on her from either side, their arms draped around her shoulders. They seemed to be trying to compress her as a way of holding her together.

"You *do* deserve better," Jean said. "And you'll get it because you held out for it."

"What she said," Rose added.

Gemma only hugged her sister's legs in silence.

Maggie leaned over and kissed the top of Willa's head, then sank back on the couch next to Alex. She leaned in close to his side and he put an arm around her.

"And all that time I never even knew she had a boyfriend," Maggie said, even though she knew she'd said it before. "I want to do something supportive, but I'm not sure how to fit into that huddle," she said to him.

"You'll get your turn."

She laid her head down on his shoulder and they stared at the scrum-like embrace of teenage girls for several minutes without comment.

Then Alex said, "They look like a family right now. Don't they?"

"But tomorrow morning all hell will break loose and they'll be fighting again."

"Maybe so. But I don't think that's the point. I think the point is, they're doing it. That's how you know they can do it."

"I like it better your way," Maggie said. "I'll take it your way. Hey girls," she added, more loudly. She felt herself about to express an idea she hadn't seen coming. "What would you think about an RV trip? All of us. But not to any disasters. To someplace good, like a national park or something."

A silence.

Then Willa said, "Can we sleep all of us in that RV?"

"It'll be tight, but we'll manage."

"Where would we go?" Gemma asked.

"You girls decide. I just want to know if you're on board or not."

For several seconds the four girls exchanged glances. And not just with the sister they'd known all their lives, either. There was a lot of mixing and matching involved in the nonverbal conversation.

Slight nodding followed.

"Yeah, we'll go," Willa said.

"Great. Pick a place. Pack some stuff. In the morning we roll."

BOOK CLUB QUESTIONS

1. Maggie's two daughters, Willa and Gemma, have lived a very privileged life growing up. Maggie believed that giving them everything they could ever want would make them happy. But now she is struggling with her daughters' behaviors and expectations. Even though Maggie's intentions were good, why do you think she's so concerned with her daughters' attitudes at this time?

2. Considering the argument of "nature versus nurture," how much do you think Maggie's parenting style affected the way Willa and Gemma have grown up?

3. Maggie tells her girls early in the book that there are "always consequences for your decisions." At what point do you think Willa and Gemma begin to learn this lesson for themselves?

4. When Jean and Rose are brought into the family as foster children, the disparity in the behavior between both sets of girls is immediately apparent. Why do you think there is such a difference in the ways these girls view the world? In what ways might they help each other grow? Do you think Maggie made the right choice to bring foster children into her family?

5. After living with Maggie for a while, trying to find their place in the world, Rose says, "I thought people were more terrible than wonderful." Maggie replies, "People are like coins with two sides . . . People are capable of evil

to the same degree as they are of good." Do you believe this to be true or not? Why?

6. The characters in the book deal with a tremendous amount of loss, including the tragic death of the girls' parents and Dr. Bishop's unexpected passing. How do these heartbreaking events serve as a wake-up call in both Maggie's and Jean's decisions to get married?

7. In the age of social media, the myth of "the happy family" is widely promoted, which puts a lot of pressure and judgment on families dealing with real issues. What part does social media play in the book to highlight this dilemma even more?

8. After Willa and Gemma do their first TV interview, they're met by a backlash of cyberbullying. How do Jean and Rose turn this around and use social media to defend their new sisters?

9. In the final television taping of the family, Eleanor the TV host talks about an interview she'd done with a man who had lost all his belongings, much like Rose and Jean. Eleanor states, "[H]e never forgot what he learned that morning: that only his family was irreplaceable." What lessons do you think Maggie and her family took away from their own challenging experiences?

ABOUT THE AUTHOR

Photo © 2019 Douglas Sonders

Catherine Ryan Hyde is the *New York Times, Wall Street Journal,* and #1 Amazon Charts bestselling author of well over forty-five books and counting. An avid traveler, equestrian, and amateur photographer, she shares her astrophotography with readers on her website.

Her novel *Pay It Forward* was adapted into a major motion picture, chosen by the American Library Association (ALA) for its Best Books for Young Adults list, and translated into more than twenty-three languages for distribution in over thirty countries. Both *Becoming Chloe* and *Jumpstart the World* were included on the ALA's Rainbow Book List, and *Jumpstart the World* was a finalist for two Lambda Literary Awards. *Where We Belong* won two Rainbow Awards in 2013, and *The Language of Hoofbeats* won a Rainbow Award in 2015.

More than fifty of her short stories have been published in the *Antioch Review, Michigan Quarterly Review, Virginia Quarterly Review,*

Ploughshares, *Glimmer Train*, and many other journals; in the anthologies *Santa Barbara Stories* and *California Shorts*; and in the bestselling anthology *Dog Is My Co-Pilot*. Her stories have been honored by the Raymond Carver Short Story Contest and the Tobias Wolff Award and have been nominated for *The Best American Short Stories*, the O. Henry Award, and the Pushcart Prize. Three have been cited in the annual *Best American Short Stories* anthology.

As a professional public speaker, she has addressed the National Conference on Education, twice spoken at Cornell University, met with AmeriCorps members at the White House, and shared a dais with Bill Clinton.

For more information, please visit the author at catherineryanhyde.com.